It's Bliss

A Modern Old-fashioned Love Story

Alene Roberts

Published and Distributed by:

Granite Publishing and Distribution, L.L.C.
868 North 1430 West • Orem, UT 84057
(801) 229-9023 • Toll Free (800) 574-5779
FAX (801) 229-1924

Cover Artwork: Jennett Chandler
Cover Design: Tamara Ingram
Production by: SunRise Publishing, Orem, Utah

ISBN: 1-930980-09-4
Library of Congress Catalog Number: 00-110171

Other Best-selling Books
by
Alene Roberts

Fragrance of Lilacs: A Love Story

This is the story of Torry Anderson, a grieving, deeply religious LDS widow, whose husband leaves behind a heart-wrenching mystery.

Feeling compelled to leave her home in Denver, she relocates to a small rural community in Utah. There, Torry meets temporary resident David Mayer, a Jewish man from Dallas, Texas, when she enters his bank to apply for a business loan.

David is immediately drawn to this beautiful woman, who looks far too young to have two returned missionary sons in college.

Torry, who is in turn, feisty and confident, wary and vulnerable; and David, a wealthy and successful man of both principle and compassion, seem an unlikely match.

Alternately laughing and crying, women of all ages will find themselves drawn into the highly-charged drama of Torry and David: both hiding their own emotional wounds in a story that moves to a gripping climax.

A Rescued Heart: A Modern Old-fashioned Love Story

Delightful, humorous and romantic. Dilladora Dobson, the lonely, twenty-seven-year-old heroine, is convinced she will never find a man with the qualities of her beloved Uncle Obadiah who helped raise her. This strong-willed young woman, like a golden sunflower reaching for the sun, has planned an active, full life for herself, unencumbered by the complications of inferior members of the male sex.

Unfortunately, this same willfulness and tendency to act and speak her mind any time, any place for the cause of right, has landed her in several scrapes, including the scare of a threatened kidnapping.

A witty, clever, battle of the sexes, an up and down adventure which deftly inserts its message of "manners and morals" along with the laughs.

This novel should be read and enjoyed by both men and women—a page turner for both.

A Butterfly in Winter: A Love Story

Another once-in-a-generation love story by best-selling author, Alene Roberts. The unique and unpredictable plot of this gripping novel introduces us to two of her most unforgettable characters: Agnes McBride and Lucas Barnes.

A diminutive, legal package of dynamite, Aggie has earned the media description of "The Iron Butterfly." This beautiful, never married, thirty-one-year-old lawyer believes her view, that 'men are never to be trusted,' is the secret to her success both in and out of the courtroom. That is, until she confronts a legal problem of her own making.

Concluding that desperate measures are needed to bring her life back into focus, she makes a decision that takes her into a world where her past, present and future come together in a series of startling revelations.

The electricity generated between Aggie McBride and Lucas Barnes, two strong-willed people, ignites a relationship that will keep you, the reader, on the edge of your seat.

This powerful book is a must read for romantics of all ages—young and old. A soul-satisfying, uplifting story, that is filled with deep and eternal truths of life.

Acknowledgement

My love and thanks to my husband, Elliott, who didn't want any recognition for the use of his wonderful poem, *The Kiss*. And for all the continued help in reading, critiquing and revising of my work.

Dedication

To the memory of my father—a historian and great
teller of true stories—and my hero growing up.

Chapter One

It was the coldest January day on record for Claytonville, Illinois—and the gloomiest, one might add. It was on this bone chilling and dismal day that Miss Billie Bliss reached the absolute end of her rope.

Prior to this fateful day, Billie Bliss had bravely endured the many peccadillos and misguided attempts of her male coworkers to attract her interest. Several changes of employment had neither decreased the number, nor improved the quality of her would-be suitors, nor had it eased her occasional bouts of malaise brought on by vague feelings that her life was, somehow, out of control.

Today, one more sophomoric male had begun his conversational gambit with the words, "Hey, babe!" That was the final straw!

In this state of dire distress, an idea flashed into Billie's mind as brilliantly as fireworks on the fourth of July, and as swift and on the mark as an arrow hitting the bull's-eye.

"Of course!" The exclamation was muttered only to herself. "Why didn't I think of it sooner?" Yes! She could create her own environment. She could create a place where she could maintain a pleasant atmosphere in which to work—the very antithesis of the environment she was in now. *This* environment constantly sent her flying to the refrigerator for comfort, to the vending machine for solace or to the snacks in her drawer for distraction. She found herself constantly trying to nibble away her frustrations.

She let out a long tremulous sigh. Always she'd been a lean, trim five-foot-six until three years ago when she started gaining a few pounds here and there. Without dieting, the weight would come and go, depending on the situations in her life. Finally, it started staying on and even though it continued to go up and down, the 'downs' were not taking off all the weight the 'ups' were putting on. And now she was fourteen pounds overweight!

Billie knew it sounded much too simple to be true—but would it be possible that, by controlling her environment, she could control her weight problem? Today it seemed totally and absolutely possible!

~~~~~~~~~~

The professor, Dr. Sheldon Dodds Ackerman, shot forward in his chair, stunned.

"You can't be serious, Neal; what do I know about teaching an all-female class? You asked me to trudge across the campus in this biting January wind to…to inform me of this?"

The Dean of the School of Business, Neal Atwood, ignored the outburst. "Hear me out, Sheldon."

Sheldon Ackerman leaned back in the chair, the expression on his face challenging his colleague for a logical explanation.

Unperturbed, the dean began, "It will be Business Course 280 called *Women In Business*. It will be open, as we used to say, to both upper and lowerclassmen, or," he added with a wink, "to be politically correct, class 'women.' Which means of course, the 100 level as well as the 300 level students may take the class. Well…what do you think, Sheldon?" he asked, his self-satisfied smile matching the pompous, stodgy academic demeanor that always tended to make Ackerman question his own decision to teach.

"What…what do I think?" Ackerman jumped up from the leather wing-back chair, and paced back and forth in front of the mammoth ebony desk. Stopping suddenly, he leaned over the dean's desk and glared down at him. "As I said before, I know nothing about teaching an all-female class. And besides—it doesn't make sense."

"Sit down, Sheldon. I know you're busy," Neal Atwood said, placating the visibly shaken man before him, "but the class will start summer semester when you won't have a full teaching load."

Thoroughly annoyed that the dean wasn't taking him seriously, Sheldon paced about the office a few moments, then abruptly sat down and blurted out, "If you're determined to have this course, Neal, why not get Fred Collins to teach it?"

"But you don't understand, Sheldon. We decided on this class to enhance the image of the University. In the three years you've been part of the faculty, the two books you've written have brought some status to Fairfield University. It only makes sense that you be the one to teach it."

In the professor's mind, it was a useless program and he articulated this opinion with great irritation. "If young women decide upon a career in business, they should take the regular business courses."

Atwood, a short paunchy man in his fifties, taking himself and his position a little too seriously, meticulously catered to the politics of university life. "Now, Sheldon, you know we live in a different era. We need to give some heed to the social issues of today." Atwood nodded his head with such vigor, his brown-rimmed glasses slipped down to the tip of his nose. Shoving them up, he leaned back in his chair, placed his hands upon the roundness protruding above his belt, and pontificated further upon the benefits of this particular program.

In the end, Sheldon, against his better judgement, agreed to teach what was, in his mind—a totally unnecessary class.

Chapter Two

Billie Bliss studied herself in the mirror. Her face puckered in concern. Here it was the end of May, planted firmly in her *new environment,* and still she had gained five more pounds! Why? Or to be more specific, why was she still raiding the refrigerator?

Four months ago, she took, what she considered, life-changing steps in her career, and in her personal life. She quit her job and prepared to go into business for herself. To ready herself for this venture, she decided to take business courses spring and summer semesters at Fairfield University here in Claytonville where she'd graduated six years ago in accounting.

The steps she took in her personal life were more difficult and emotionally charged. She had always lived at home through college and through her various jobs, so the first logical step was to move into her own apartment. The second was the decision to totally give up dating.

Billie knew that even with the steps taken to improve her life, there was still, what she had come to call, in her own mind, THE PROBLEM. She had no control over *that*—but she hoped fervently that the changes she'd made would insulate herself from it. The result of all this changing, she believed, would automatically take care of her weight problem.

She now lived in the self-made environment of her own apartment, and in the protective cocoon of academia, away from the stress of real life—the stress of the market place. Yet—she had gained! Mentally, she carefully went back over everything.

When she enrolled spring semester, she found that all the classes taught by the new and acclaimed Dr. Sheldon Ackerman were filled, so she audited one. She found his lectures brilliant and interesting. Having learned a lot from him, she planned to enroll early in order to get into his new summer semester class, called *Women In Business.* The first six weeks of the spring semester in this pleasant and stimulating environment, she returned to her normal self—having no desire to snack excessively. However, as the semester progressed, for some reason she started going down hill.

She frowned and shook her head as she thought about it. The only thing disconcerting in her life at the moment was how she was beginning to react to Dr. Ackerman. His lectures were so interesting, she hadn't noticed at first, but something about him bothered her. What? Why? She couldn't figure out the 'what,' so, of course, she didn't know the 'why.'

"Oh well..." she said to her reflection in the mirror, "everything will turn out as I planned, I'm sure. It will just take a little time."

Chapter Three

It was Monday, the first of June and the first day of summer semester. It was also the day Dr. Sheldon Dodds Ackerman would begin his new class—the dreaded all-female class! He asked himself, not the first time, why he'd let the Dean foist this upon him? In mounting agitation, he glanced at his watch, noting that it was almost 10:00 AM and time for the class to start. Quickly scanning his notes, he dropped them back onto the desk, and stepped out of his office toward the classroom—which was only next door—a convenience he'd requested when he joined the faculty.

Like a man going to his own execution, he nervously entered the room. Totally unaware of the collective buzz and furtive glances at each other by the class members, he began his self introduction as he moved toward the podium. There, with no preliminaries, he promptly launched into his lecture. First, explaining the purpose and goals of the class and what was expected of them, he then recounted his experience with successful women in the business world. Upon ending the lecture, he refrained from bolting, but exited as quickly as dignity would allow, closeting himself inside his office.

Dr. Ackerman was also unaware of the flurry of excitement that erupted the moment he left the room.

"Did you notice he didn't have a wedding band on?" a class member asked.

"Yes, I did notice, and I also noticed how handsome he is," answered someone.

"I couldn't take my eyes off those blue, blue eyes!" exclaimed a young woman in a breathy voice.

One of the older members of the class, seated on the front row, had noted immediately, as the professor strode into class, his classic Roman profile—a nicely shaped, but prominent nose and a strong jaw to match. Finding the front view just as distinctive, she was hardly able to keep her mind on his lecture. In addition, he seemed totally unaware of his good looks, something she found very attractive in a man. Standing up to leave, she turned to the class and stated emphatically, "An artist ought to paint that face!"

"Oh, yes!" exclaimed a young girl beside her. "Isn't he gorgeous with that gray hair and those dark brows?"

Billie Bliss had also noted the professor's striking good looks when she first walked into his class spring semester, but her decision to give up men—in combination with her vague and barely acknowledged annoyance with him—nullified any curiosity about him personally.

"I wonder how old he is," murmured someone.

"I was wondering that, too," stated another.

Josie, probably the youngest in the class said, "I'm sure he's at least fifty."

One a little older than Josie, disagreed, "He's no more than forty."

An older girl announced, "He's only in his late thirties."

The following Wednesday, the whole class, in a quandary over his age, wound up making bets with each other, everyone, that is, except Billie Bliss. She listened from the sidelines, amused. She wasn't the least bit curious about his age; however, she was puzzled over the contradictory nature of the man. His dress and mein were that of a sharp, well-to-do business man, but his personality was that of an eccentric and somewhat stuffy professor.

~~~~~~~~~~~

Two weeks later, sitting in Dr. Ackerman's class, a dismayed Billie Bliss ruminated on the fact that the carefully planned changes she'd made were not working after all! Her mind wandered back to last spring semester when she audited a class from Dr. Ackerman, remembering, once more, how something about him had begun to disconcert her.

Carefully peeking above the shoulder of the girl seated in front of her, she studied him, realizing he was bothering her more than ever. In fact it was more than that; it had turned into bona fide irritation. As she continued to watch him, trying to analyze why she was feeling this way, she finally realized it had something to do with the way he looked at the class. There! He was doing it again!

Glowering at the class, Dr. Ackerman shook his head over what he considered a wretched and irritating assortment. Twenty were enrolled, and not once had they all managed to be on time. And, he calculated, at least seventy-five percent were overweight, careless and slovenly in their dress. Twenty-five percent had other problems. Several young women, who dressed neatly and seemed capable, weren't dedicated students by any set of standards, especially his.

What irritated Sheldon the most was—he felt sorry for these ignorant, misguided young women, and he intensely disliked feeling this way! This sentiment had grown each time he'd faced their collective apathy these short two weeks. He seriously wondered if anyone in the class would succeed in the way she hoped or had a burning desire to—if indeed, he agonized, any one of them had a burning desire.

Deciding he needed some feedback, he'd asked the class to write down why they were taking this course and what their goals were in the business world. He watched from his desk as they struggled to fulfill this simple request.

His dark brows creased, wondering how many of these young women felt good about themselves. How many felt their lives were out of control? He shook his head, marveling over how difficult it would be to manage a business or a career in business if one could not manage himself...herself.

It was at this moment, an *idea* struck him. It couldn't have affected him more if it had been a bolt of lightning. He jumped up from his seat as if he'd been hit by it. Pacing back and forth behind his desk, he contemplated the idea, unaware that he'd startled the class with his sudden movement. All heads swiveling silently side to side, watching their eccentric professor and his unusual behavior, saw his tall, angular, albeit well-built body, with head bobbing up and down as though agreeing vigorously with his own thoughts. The concerted ping-pong movement finally made its way into his consciousness. He stopped abruptly, catching these assembled heads almost, as it were, in mid-movement. Realizing that it was he who had disrupted them, he promptly sat down, and stared at them sternly until they bowed their heads and returned to their work.

And he returned to his, deliberating on not a new, but a most amazing and extraordinary concept. He needed an idea for another book. If this worked, it would be just what these poor fledglings needed, and...at the same time, please the dean, which in reality, he could care less about. Nevertheless...leaning back in his chair, he stretched out his long legs under the desk and pondered on the idea, feeling quite pleased with himself.

Billie tried to analyze this puzzling performance. First—he was frowning at the class through black rimmed glasses as though inspecting some inferior species; now—glued to his face was a peculiar smile, the tips of all ten fingers tapping...tapping together.

Yes! She finally understood why he irritated her; it was his pompous and demeaning attitude! It was only two weeks into the semester, and she realized that Dr. Ackerman's attitude was annoying her more each day. Her effort to gain control over her environment so she could manage her weight was not turning out well at all. To begin with, she had been fourteen pounds overweight. She had gained five pounds while auditing Dr. Ackerman's class last semester and three in only two weeks of this one. It was happening again! Twenty-two pounds overweight—more than she'd ever weighed!

She went over every aspect of her life since returning to the university, mentally listing each change she'd made. She'd improved her situation in a number of ways: by quitting her last job, by moving into her own apartment and by preparing to go into business for herself. Suddenly, she realized something—the only common denominator to her problem—was Dr. Ackerman!

She gazed at the blank piece of paper on which she intended to write what he'd requested. Feeling more irked by the minute, she impulsively printed in big block letters:

IT'S YOUR FAULT, DR. ACKERMAN!
then signed her name and immediately felt better.

Josie, a blonde, with an attractive wind-blown hair style, noticing Dr. Ackerman was preoccupied, leaned over and whispered in Billie's ear, "I really buttered up ol' Dodds this time," she said, using his middle name. "I told him my goal was to become president of this University. What did you put down for your goals, Billie?"

"Absolutely nothing. I mean, I put something down, but not what he asked for."

"Oh-oh. You'll be called into his office and that's no fun, believe you me. He called me in a week ago and did I get a lecture."

Billie smiled at Josie, wondering why she was in this class or in college at all. She had managed to become a sophomore, yet still had the typical high school mentality of fun and boys.

Dr. Ackerman's low drawl boomed out. "Class is over. Please place your papers on my desk as you leave."

While the girls got their things together and did as he asked, his mind returned to a more stimulating venue—his idea. Leaning back in his chair, he gazed into space, thinking, while the fingers of his right hand drummed upon the desk to the rhythm of his thoughts.

Billie, on the verge of changing her mind about handing in such a stunning accusation, hesitated a moment, that is, until she studied her professor. She noticed how he ignored each girl, totally absorbed in his own world. Standing by the desk, she stared at him intently, daring him to look in her direction. Finally, frowning at his total unawareness, she shoved her paper under the pile that was already there, and breezed out of the room, a satisfied smile upon her face.

As the last student placed her paper on the desk and filed out, Dr. Ackerman pulled his long legs out from under the desk, stood up and stretched. Gathering the papers, he smiled, glad that it was Friday for more reasons than one. Friday night was the night the "DeePees," as they called themselves, met. He could hardly wait to pass his fascinating idea by them.

Chapter Four

"Well, Sheldon, all through dinner, you've acted like the cat who swallowed a textbook," Dr. Hal Ozog said, smiling. "What's up?"

The five had just enjoyed a delicious meal in the dining room of the Maple Woods Country Club. They were now settling themselves into the comfortable chairs and sofas of the small private lounge where they held their after-dinner discussions.

As usual, the waiter entered, carrying a tray of after-dinner coffee, transferring the cups carefully onto the glass topped coffee table in the center.

Most of the time they were joined by their spouses, in which case Sheldon Ackerman was the odd man out, the only single one of the group…and the youngest…though, Doc' Bittle, the resident psychologist of the group, said, only half in jest: "Shel's thirty-eight-years-of-age belies his fifty-eight-year-old persona."

Sheldon smiled at Hal's question, thinking as always, what an odd group they were. They had known each other for three years. Belonging to the country club of this small college town, they soon became acquainted and were intellectually drawn together. Stimulated by each other's thinking as they agreed and disagreed on many diverse subjects, they fell into the comfortable habit of meeting every Friday night for dinner at the club.

For brevity, they decided to call themselves the "Deepees." Classy and trim fifty-five year old Nettie Newman, with lovely tinted-blonde hair, and her husband, Don, owners of the Diet center, were the 'D' of the DeePees. Don, also a walking advertisement for fitness, was good looking, blonde and well built. On the quiet side, Don sat back most of the time, his eyes twinkling with amusement as he listened to the group discuss the issues of the day—unless the subject of discussion was either football or politics.

Dr. Robert Bittle, one of the 'P's of the DeePees, was fifty, and a practicing psychologist. He had more patients than a sane person should have, but also had a sense of humor to keep him that way. He was short, stocky with thinning light brown hair and had a pleasant open face which invited confidence.

Dr. Hal Ozog, a family practice physician, was the second 'P.' At sixty-five, unlike Bittle, he was tall and had a full head of dark hair, peppered with silver. Newly retired, he now enjoyed his wife and fifteen grandchildren full-time.

Sheldon Ackerman, a professor, was the last of the 'P's. He had successfully foiled all attempts of the other three, who were happily married with children, to match him up with a once-in-a-while or permanent partner. They now reluctantly accepted him as a hopeless bachelor.

"Yes, tell us what's on your mind, Shel," Nettie said, smiling, the crows feet at the corner of her lovely blue eyes becoming pronounced.

Sheldon, grinning, his own intense blue eyes alight with excitement, blurted out, "How would you all like to help me play *Pygmalion?*"

Immediately, the four were on the edge of their seats, intrigued. This was definitely something out of character for Sheldon Ackerman.

"You mean," Nettie began, "like *Professor Higgins* in the musical *My Fair Lady?*"

A smile tugged at Sheldon's lips as he contemplated her question. "Well…maybe."

Nettie chuckled. "Oh sure," she said in a skeptical tone. "Where's the *Eliza Doolittle* you want to make over?"

"I have a whole class full of them," he said, grinning.

"Come on, Sheldon, be serious," Robert countered.

"Okay…okay so I was exaggerating. Let me tell it like it is." Sheldon told them about his all-female class and of his frustrations concerning it, especially what he felt were the student's personal handicaps to success in the world of business.

"The idea came to me this afternoon. Now, mind you, it's just an idea. If all of you find that it sounds improbable or foolhardy…" he grinned, "I know you'll tell me. As I explained, most of them are overweight and careless in dress with the loss of confidence and self esteem these bring, and since they are the majority, I would like to work with *them*. What if…" he began as he placed his palms together, tapping his chin with the fingers, then lowering them, "what if we have the class fill out a questionnaire, one that all of us design—one that asks pertinent and telling questions. Then we, after studying the questionnaires and discussing the candidates, will choose four. This is where I will need the expertise in your different fields. I'm sure that the financial benefactor, who has helped me out with other projects, will be interested in this one.

"As I've heard you say, Nettie, losing weight is difficult and complicated, and I might add, has become a national pastime for women. So…what if we offer our four candidates a reward of a compelling amount of money toward their education at the end of a specified time—if they're successful. Then they will also receive another amount at the end of a year…*if* they still are successful and self disciplined in their weight, dress and studies." He paused and searched each of their still surprised faces, "Well, what do you all think?"

Robert Bittle responded first with a chuckle and then with a question, "Do we believe this folks?" he asked, looking at the other three, who laughed and shook their heads. "Well Sheldon, I see that you're serious, so the first thing I would like to say is—it probably won't work."

"Why?" Sheldon asked, unruffled by their reactions.

"Because, in some cases there are psychological reasons behind the problems you mentioned."

"Oh, I forgot to explain," Sheldon said, "If it turns out that the candidates we work with happen to be overweight, I feel they should not be more than thirty pounds overweight."

"That's wise, Shel," Nettie said. "Since this is an experiment, that would be easier to work with."

"I agree," Hal Ozog, added. "But, sometimes there are medical reasons for people gaining weight, so if we were to take on this preposterous idea, they would have to have a thorough medical exam first."

"Good idea, Hal, good idea," replied Sheldon. "I think that is a must since it would be a special study. I would have to first get the approval and support of the dean, Neal Atwood, and then if this experiment turns out to be successful, and after several more such experiments I would write a book about it. I'm hoping it will help young women everywhere who want to be successful in the business world, but who are totally naive and ignorant of the principles of success. In my mind, the first principle is: a person must learn to manage him-self...herself," he corrected.

Nettie bristled. "Shel, you are sounding a little callus, insensitive and ignorant when you say overweight young women are not good managers of themselves. I know quite a few women, young and old, who are efficient in every way, successful in the business world—and yet they are overweight—in spite of their unsuccessful efforts to lose."

"I agree with Nettie," Hal said.

Robert and Don nodded their agreement and all four pair of eyes bore into him unmercifully. Sheldon shifted uncomfortably. "Okay...okay, so we don't quite see eye to eye. It's just that we don't know if these girls would be successful if left to their own devices. I simply believe that we can greatly enhance the odds that they will be. Now, tell me what you think of the idea? Can I count on your help and support?" he asked, looking at each.

"Hey, leave me outa this, Shel," Don stated firmly. "In our diet center, my expertise is in male fitness. Nettie handles the female part. I'll just go along with whatever she says on this."

"All right, Don."

Robert answered next. "I'll have to think this over carefully, for at least a week, and discuss it with my wife."

Then Nettie and Hal agreed they also needed a week to think about taking on such a daunting task. Hal wanted to talk it over with his wife, also.

"And while you're thinking about it," Sheldon added, "I need you to think about doing me another big favor. Would you each consider being a support for one of them, myself included, and meeting with them on a regular basis, say once a week, to see how they are doing and to encourage them?"

"If we decide to do this," Robert said, "meeting with them on a reg-ular basis will be important...but I suggest that in addition to that, reg-ular group meetings should be held once a week, for a while, as an added support to the girls."

"I agree with Robert about adding the group meeting," Nettie said. "In spite of your attitude, Shel, this promises to be a very unusual and interesting experiment. I may be able to learn something valuable for our Diet Center if we go ahead with it."

"Nettie will be valuable in helping the girls learn how to eat right," added Hal.

"But," interjected Robert, "the big question is...can we find four out of that class of yours who have a strong enough *desire* to improve themselves?"

Sheldon frowned. "Hmm...that's a good question, Robert. I'm wondering about that myself."

"And" continued Robert, "bribery may work and it may not. I think you'll need to check up on each of them at the end of two years to see if it really worked."

Sheldon mulled this over. "I think you're right again. In order to make it a solid experiment, that should be done." He heaved a sigh. "Maybe it won't work...it's just that I've seen successful business women and I've noticed the qualities that got them there, and I would like my class to..." his voice trailed off.

Nettie came to his rescue. "I think it's wonderful that you want to try this, Shel. We'll give it some serious thought and meet next Friday."

"Thank you, Nettie. You are one of those successful business women I was talking about. My class could learn from you."

~~~~~~~~~~

Saturday night after toasting several frozen waffles and heating some precooked ham slices, Dr. Sheldon Ackerman sat down at the kitchen table to eat and go over the assignment his 280 class handed in Friday. Discouragement set in as he read their goals. It was obvious that some were quickly thought up statements just because it was a request from their professor. They were unrealistic and absurd. So far, only a couple seemed to be thought out in advance. He sighed as he lifted the page to read the next one. He was stunned. Instead of written goals, there was a one line message to him! He read the cryptic sentence over several times trying to internalize it.

IT'S YOUR FAULT DR. ACKERMAN!

"What is my fault?" he asked the signature which accompanied the accusation—Billie Bliss. He knew the name, but only the name. He remembered it because it was unusual and because of the two brief tests he'd given thus far, her scores were the highest in the class. He tried to think of her face, but knew it was useless. Females were an enigma to him. He only looked at them as a group, not individually. Of those few he had noticed specifically, he still wouldn't be able to recognize them from the others if his life depended on it. Remembering female faces had never been his long suit.

"What is my fault?" he demanded of the absent and elusive Miss Bliss. His ire was up. "Why that impudent young woman!" He was definitely going to have a serious talk with her Monday after class.

Chapter Five

Monday at 10:00 AM, Dr. Ackerman, his dark brows arching majestically above his glasses, studied each young woman who entered the 280 class. Soon, his brows knit together in irritated concentration as he tried to decide which one was the impertinent Miss Bliss or to be more correct, he supposed it should be Ms Bliss. Maybe, he thought, it's the flippant looking blonde who flounced in. Or maybe…maybe it's that carelessly dressed girl with the stringy hair and sour expression…yes, she must be the one. His eyes followed her as she shuffled to a seat near the front. Studying her while she rummaged through the backpack, he saw her pull out a book…a paperback romance! The audacity of the girl. Of course—she was probably the one who completely flunked the last test and was now blaming it on him! No. He forgot. Billie Bliss got the highest score on the last exam. That girl couldn't possibly be her. The bell rang, startling him, signaling it was time for class to start.

Just as he stood up to begin his lecture, two girls straggled in late, giggling and whispering. After one dropped a book and the other one stumbled over it, causing more giggles, they finally settled down, both looking up innocently, expectantly.

He glared at them, then cleared his throat to begin. There was no text for the class, only his hard-earned years of knowledge gained in the business world. The class was expected to take notes from his lectures and read assignments from the books on business and money making that his unknown benefactor had donated to the Fairfield University library.

"The lecture today," he began, "is on reasons for small, new businesses not succeeding. We will learn the whys, and what can be done to insure success instead of failure." He stopped as he noticed the girl still reading the paperback. All heads followed his gaze.

"You know, class, you are expected to take notes. You will be tested on my lectures and not" his voice rose, "on romance novels." The girl jerked her head up from the book and stared at him blankly. The class tittered. He repeated the admonition, certain that she hadn't heard it all. The girl gave him an 'I could care less' look and took her time closing the book and putting it away. More impudence! he thought. Frustrated at the minutes wasted, he continued the lecture.

Eight minutes before the end of class, he concluded by saying, "I have read your goals and I would like to interview each of you concerning these goals. Here is a paper on my desk with the schedule of my free time. I want you to sign up for a time as you leave. The interviews will vary from ten to thirty minutes. Now, will a Ms Billie Bliss raise her hand?" Mid-way down the middle row a hand rose reluctantly, but he couldn't see her very well. "Will you please stay for a few minutes after class, Ms Bliss?"

He sat down and began studying a book while pandemonium took place. Finally, the last class member finished and walked out. Sensing someone standing in front of the desk, he looked up to face Billie Bliss. The first thing he noticed was...of course, she looked a little overweight. But—she did hide it nicely under the navy blue blazer over the white shirt and jeans.

"I'm Billie Bliss, Dr. Ackerman."

"I would assume so, yes," he said.

"You want to see me about what I put on my paper," she stated matter-of-factly. "Here are my goals as you requested." She handed him a paper.

He glared at her. "Handing your assignment in late, does not explain what you meant by that accusation."

"I know," she said undefensively.

"That is an impudence I won't tolerate in my class, Ms Bliss."

"*Miss* Bliss," she corrected. "I didn't intend to be impudent, Dr. Ackerman. Truly I didn't."

He eyed her skeptically. "Then what did you mean by that statement?"

"I merely stated a fact," she said simply.

"A fact?" He raised his voice. "A FACT?!"

"Well, it is *your fault,* Dr. Ackerman. But I assure you, you aren't to *blame.*"

"You speak in riddles, Miss Bliss."

"Nevertheless, that's the way it is."

Miss Bliss' forthright and undefensive manner disarmed him, robbed him of his righteous anger and left him thoroughly puzzled. In his experience, limited though it was, he found the opposite sex totally illogical. And again Miss Bliss had validated his conclusion that this was hopelessly their nature. He heaved a sigh. An illogical nature that, he supposed, all married men had to put up with.

Grateful that that excluded him, he asked. "Do you have a class right now, Miss Bliss?"

"No, I don't. I have two hours before the next one."

"Could you step into my office for a few moments, please?"

"Yes."

He stood up, gathered up the papers, then led her out the door to his office. "Please have a seat, Miss Bliss."

"Thank you." She pulled up one of the small padded office chairs and looked around the large room. On the right stood an old oak bookcase full of books. An overflow of books was placed in neat piles on a credenza which sat under a window behind his desk. What a brain, she thought. On the left was a computer, printer and a fax machine. His desk, a severe old-styled mahogany, was full of organized clutter and several open books.

Dr. Ackerman walked behind his desk and sat down facing her. "Now," he said, putting his elbows on the desk and tapping his fingers together, "what is my fault, that I'm not to be blamed for?"

"I assure you, Dr. Ackerman, you don't want to hear it."

His eyes bored into her. "Then why did you write it down and hand it in if you knew I wouldn't want to hear it?"

"I was feeling quite exasperated with you right then...so at that time I wanted you to hear it." She shrugged her shoulders and gave him a small apologetic smile.

Dr. Sheldon Ackerman struggled to keep his mental balance. "Oh, is that right? May I ask again, what is my fault, that I'm not to be blamed for?"

"But, Dr. Ackerman, after you hear the *what,* you will want to know the *why*."

"Try me and see," His lips parted in what he intended as a smile. His eyes said otherwise.

"All right," she sighed. "It's your fault that I've gained eight more pounds."

Sheldon Ackerman gaped at her. Myriad thoughts darted through his mind. Could she have guessed about his observance of her weight? Why would she say this outrageous thing just...just as he was planning the project with the DeePees? Could someone have overheard them? He shook his head trying to reject these thoughts.

He repeated slowly, "It...is *my* fault that you gained eight more pounds," he repeated, still trying to believe she'd said such a thing. "Now, Miss Bliss, I'm not asking you why it is my fault, I'm asking you why you are saying it right at *this time*?"

Billie Bliss looked puzzled. "Because...it's true at this time as it was true that I gained five of the eight last semester when I audited your 302 Business course...and now it's true that after only two weeks into this semester I've already gained three more." Suddenly, a distressed expression appeared on her face. "Just think how big I'll be by the time the semester ends!"

Dr. Ackerman was speechless. His mind—muddled with unformulated questions—tried to make sense out of what she had just said. Unable to, he jumped up. Placing his hands on the desk, he leaned over and glared at her. "Miss Bliss, people who blame their weaknesses on others need help."

Billie also stood up. Folding her arms tightly across her midsection, she gazed directly into his face, "But, I'm not blaming you, Dr. Ackerman," she reiterated in exasperation.

"Fault, blame...what's the difference?"

"There...is...a difference, Dr. Ackerman." she said, emphasizing each word.

"All right then," he said, straightening up, trying to regain his composure, "tell me why it's my fault?"

"I told you the *why* would come next."

"So you did, Miss Bliss, so you did. Now, let's both sit down and be calm."

They both sat down and he, as patiently and calmly as he could manage, asked once more, "Why is it my fault?"

"How many days and weeks do you have, Dr. Ackerman? It's hard to put it into words. I don't know how to explain it or at least in a way you'll understand. I have a problem—and you would have to see it in action. If you did, maybe you could tell *me* how to explain it."

Ackerman's mind felt muddled again. "Uh...uh take a wild stab at it. What *is* your problem?"

"In trying to explain it to several past boy friends, they stated what they thought my problem was."

"Oh? And what did they come up with?"

"That I was allergic to men."

Fearing to tread on personal ground, he asked somewhat hesitantly, "Uh...is that true?"

"No, it isn't."

He leaned back in his swivel chair and scrutinized her. "Have you ever thought of seeing a psychiatrist, Miss Bliss?"

"Oh yes, several times. I finally went to see one, and he didn't understand me."

Dr. Ackerman nodded. "Somehow I can understand that."

"But" she continued, "I *can* tell you what brought me to the point of putting it on paper."

"Please do," he stated in a condescending tone.

"Your pompous and demeaning attitude toward the class. I didn't see this attitude last semester toward the boys in the 302 class, just the girls, so it must be women you feel this way about."

Sheldon Ackerman was shocked. "Pompous, demeaning? Why..." his voice trailed off, realizing that his impatience over what he perceived as their inept self-management might be construed as such.

"Then, Miss Bliss," he began slowly, his words deliberate, "my so-called pompous and demeaning attitude toward all the young women in the 302 class and the 280 class did cause and is causing you to gain weight. Is that correct?"

"Yes...and...no. Well...at least not for the reason you may think. You see, it's symptomatic."

He threw up his hands. "I give up, Miss Bliss. I would suggest if you are planning to get married someday, that you figure yourself out first."

"I assure you, Dr. Ackerman, I *have* figured myself out and that is why I'm not going to get married."

He stared at her still trying to understand. "Well," he said finally, "that's…probably for the best."

Tears sprang to her eyes. He noted that they were beautiful brown eyes. Instantly he felt contrite, "I'm sorry…what I said, did it…"

"Oh no, it's just me," she said, blinking back the tears and immediately smiling. "Could I ask you a question, Dr. Ackerman?"

His heart softened, he answered, "You may."

"Your eyebrows are almost black and your hair is gray. Why is that?"

Chapter Six

The 280 business course was a three credit-hour class, meeting Monday, Wednesday and Friday, so Wednesday morning, Dr. Ackerman began a two-part lecture. The first part would occupy Wednesday and Friday. The subject matter was: 'managing yourself versus managing a business, or a career in business.' The following week he would carry on the second part of the subject, using the question and discussion method, all this in preparation for the possible 'project.'

He proceeded with care, not wanting to come over to the class as pompous or demeaning. He most certainly did not want Miss Bliss to gain one more pound! If, indeed, he was the cause of such.

Billie Bliss could immediately see the difference in Dr. Ackerman's attitude and was pleased. Somehow, she thought, trying to explain her actions Monday must have actually done some good. Chalk one up to 'ol' Dodds,' she commended silently. Because of this change, she could tell that the class was responding with greater interest in what he had to say.

The subject of the lecture, self-management, was of great interest to Billie. And, in her mind, it reflected Dr. Ackerman's own lifestyle. He was a professor who was always organized and well prepared. In fact, she mused, he even managed himself well in the aspect of grooming. His white shirts were always crisply ironed, sporting what looked like designer ties, which, in turn, set off his expensive looking suits and sport coats.

Today, his finely fitted charcoal-gray sport coat hung nicely over his broad shoulders, tapering down to gray slacks and well shined shoes. It was an ensemble which enhanced both his dark brows and thick, slightly wavy gray hair, which, he had explained to her Monday, had begun turning prematurely gray at the age of twenty-five. He had further informed her, that his brows had not yet caught up. After this disclosure, she almost followed the urge to satisfy the curiosity of the class, but changed her mind, deciding that to divulge his confidence, might not be respectful.

"Miss Bliss!" the voice of Dr. Ackerman boomed, jerking Billie out of her reverie.

"Uh…yes, Dr. Ackerman?"

"I see that you are not taking notes. May I remind you again, I expect all of you to take notes. Other than the texts in the library which I may ask you to read now and then, there is no text for this class—just my lectures, and you will be severely tested on those. Do I make myself clear, Miss Bliss?"

"Yes, Dr. Ackerman. I'm sorry. It's just that my mind was wandering off on the subject of your lecture."

"Oh?" he questioned, skeptical. "Would you mind telling the class what your mind wandered off to since it was, supposedly, on the subject?" He watched her contemplate what to tell him, noting a small ghost of a smile come and go.

"I was reflecting upon what an excellent example you were of self-management."

Caught off guard, he blinked a couple of times, then scrutinized Miss Bliss—while the class scrutinized him, waiting for his reaction. Inwardly, he was pleased.

"Thank you, Miss Bliss. But I assure you, flattery will not get you an A in this class."

The class erupted with laughter. He waited, his face one of unflinching sternness. When it died down, he said, "Now…may we resume the lecture?"

~~~~~~~~~~

Billie walked quickly toward her small studio apartment just off campus, smiling and thinking of Dr. Ackerman's class. She soon arrived at the old brick home with its tall maples and lush landscaping front and back. When looking for a place to live, she immediately fell in love with this old place and the studio apartment in the back part of the house. The apartment consisted of one large room—a combination front room, bedroom and kitchen, and one small bath.

Unlocking the door, she stepped into the neat and cheery room which she had furnished herself. A flowered chintz, pull-out couch doubled for a bed. A chair, upholstered in leaf green and white stripes, matched the green in the couch. Throw pillows of plain leaf green on each end of the couch tied in both pieces of furniture. To Billie, the room was inviting, attractive and comfortable. She had also purchased a small white desk and bookcase. Bringing pictures and plants from home had added nice touches to the decor. The landlady had carpeted the room in light beige and had provided white mini blinds for the large window

Her family had been in a state of bewilderment, unable to understand why she would want to move away from home since they lived only three blocks from the campus. The environment in her parent's home was pleasant and lovely, but since four of the five members of the family were feeling more and more concern over her 'marriageless' state, it exacerbated her weight problem.

Her mother and father, Aunt Tilly, Grandpa Bliss and Uncle Henry, all independently confronted her with the ludicrousness of the move and repeated the same logical arguments for living at home.

Aunt Tilly, her mother's sister who had never married, was the most vociferous in her objections. "Now, Billie, it would make sense if you moved out because you were getting married. But you don't really want to be alone do you? Look at me, so alone that I moved in with your mother and father. Look at Grandpa Bliss and Uncle Henry, both widowers, neither wanted to live alone. It will get awfully lonely...unless," she looked hopeful, "you change your mind and decide you want to get married."

Billie assured Aunt Tilly and the others that all their arguments certainly did have merit. "But," she had reminded them, "I'll be twenty-eight years old soon. It's about time I moved out on my own." Then she promised to visit often and reminded them that they could visit her.

She had moved out just before the spring semester and now two and a half weeks into the summer semester, her family was finally adjusting to her living alone, three blocks away.

She took off her linen blazer, which was really too warm to wear during the summer, but since it covered up her figure she wore it anyway.

Suddenly, she realized she hadn't gone to the cupboard or refrigerator to munch. This was the first day after attending a class of Dr. Ackerman's, that she didn't have the 'munchies.'

Humming a song, she stuck a potato in the microwave and began preparing a salad.

Chapter Seven

After a nice dinner Friday evening, the DeePees were settled in the small lounge of the country club contentedly sipping their coffee—all except Sheldon. He was so anxious to learn each of their decisions, he could no longer contain his restlessness.

"Well?" he asked, looking at each of them in turn.

Hal Ozog smiled at him in a fatherly manner. "You've been acting like a kid who can hardly wait to try out his new bike."

Sheldon smiled, his deep, blue eyes sparkling with excitement. "To tell the truth, Hal, that's exactly how I feel, but I want all of you to know that I will understand if you feel this project isn't feasible or if you feel that your lives are too busy to participate in it. I can get someone else to help me, but as you well know, I would rather have you four."

Don Newman held a palm outward and grimaced. "Hey, Shel, as I said before, don't count me in on this. I'm just a friendly bystander, but one who'll be cheering you on—whatever all of you decide."

"Okay, Don. I'll at least appreciate you cheering us on." His expression turning apprehensive, he looked at the other three. "So—how about the rest of you?"

Robert Bittle smiled. "Well, Shel, we three have conferred with each other by phone this week and the consensus is—we'll take it on."

"Wonderful!" Sheldon exclaimed, beaming from ear to ear.

"But," Robert continued, "*if* any complications arise that concern anyone of us, we've agreed to abandon the project."

"Oh." Sheldon's dark brows furrowed. "That presents a problem. How will I broach this possibility to the participants?"

"Be frank with them right in the beginning, Shel," Nettie Newman suggested. "You might inform them that this is only an experiment and that you may have to abandon the project if complications arise and present a problem that would reflect badly upon Fairfield University."

Sheldon considered this, his long fingers tapping together methodically. He nodded. "I think you are all wise in this decision. I suppose complications certainly can come about, considering that we will be working with women. They tend to become emotional at times."

Nettie smiled. "Well, yes, Sheldon, but physical complications could arise with any one of them."

Sheldon, silent a moment, responded, "I'll have to confer with my benefactor and see if he'll be willing to remunerate these young women even if we have to abandon the project."

"Good," Robert said. "Now with that out of the way, I would like to read to you what I've come up with in the way of a questionnaire for the class in order to choose which four would be good candidates."

Sheldon Ackerman was more than pleased, he was happy. His friends had come through. "Read on, Robert."

When he was through, Nettie exclaimed. "That is excellent, Robert. I would add only one question—one that will inform us of their major. I'm sure that not all in the class will have chosen business as their field of study, Shel. What if one or more of the four we choose hasn't chosen a business career. Will the dean and your benefactor go along with that?"

Sheldon raised his brows and nodded. "I don't know why I didn't think of that. I feel that at least two of the four should be in the field of business. However, I'm sure that the dean and the benefactor would be amenable to the other two young women succeeding in whatever field they choose to go into."

Hal had two additions and the three of them vetoed Sheldon's one, suggesting that he didn't know women very well, which—he conceded, was true.

After naming the upcoming experiment, "Project Success," they parted company, each having an assignment. Sheldon was to confer with the dean and his benefactor. Nettie was to prepare a contract for each participant and later, after visiting with them individually, a uniquely designed nutrition program for each. Hal offered to prepare a medical form that the participants could take to a medical doctor to fill out after the mandatory physical examination. Robert was to revise the questionnaire and have his secretary type it up.

They shook hands and promised to meet again next Friday night as usual.

Sheldon Ackerman loved challenges and *Project Success* promised to be a satisfying one. It would help the young women, he was sure. And it certainly would make teaching the 280 class more interesting. He leaned back in his large leather chair, his feet up on the ottoman, relaxing and thinking. His masculinely decorated condominium was a comfortable place for him to think and plan, with its forest greens, beige and browns. His condo was on the top floor of this ten story condominium complex that he had designed and built. No one in the community knew he was the owner and builder—and he intended they remain ignorant of it indefinitely. The 'benefactor' with whom he would confer this week was none other than himself.

A brilliant teenager, Sheldon had entered college at sixteen. At twenty-two years of age, he graduated from Harvard with an MBA and a doctorate in behavioral science. He ventured out into the world with a small inheritance from his grandfather. From the start, he seemed to have the Midas touch. He bought property and the value went up. He bought stocks just before they split. He seemed to have a sixth sense about what to buy and when to sell. Soon he began investing in property on a regular basis and constructing office buildings, commercial buildings and shopping centers. And now he had amassed considerable wealth but had no one to spend it on except his well-chosen and well-planned charities.

He was the only child of Sheldon Dean Ackerman and Elaine Dodds Ackerman. Born late in their lives, it was destined that he was not to enjoy their company for long. His mother, frail in health, was not able to conceive until she was forty-three years old.

Elaine Ackerman, a loving and devoted mother, taught her son strong moral values from the Bible. His father, Sheldon Ackerman, from whom he felt great love, was a shy enigmatic man who taught his son, by example, the value of hard work and dependability. Both had passed on now, and he was alone.

Like his father, Sheldon was shy and didn't pursue the company of young ladies as he would have liked. At twenty-seven years of age, he fell head over heels in love with a lovely young woman and promptly got his heart broken. From then on Sheldon replaced his need for love with long hours of hard work and the heady experience of making money, and basking in the power that attends wealth.

The total focus on making money, however, began to pale about two months before his thirty-fifth birthday, so he turned his attention to what he always had a yen to do—teach business on the university level in a small college town. Placing his business interests into the hands of trusted managers through a holding company, he applied for and received a teaching position at Fairfield University soon after he turned thirty-five. During the three years he'd been teaching, he'd written two books on business, and built the high rise condominium complex. Now, he was working on an idea for a third book and feeling quite satisfied with his life here in Claytonville.

He smiled as he thought about how well his 280 class had been going of late. The young women seemed to be responding in a way they hadn't before. Could it be that he was beginning to watch his manner of speaking and tone of voice so as not to come over as Miss Bliss had accused him—pompous and demeaning? If so, he would have to give Miss Bliss her due.

When Sheldon conferred with Dean Atwood, on Monday the start of week four, telling him of his idea for a project and suggesting that it and others following would be good material for another book, Dean Atwood fell all over himself with approval. After all, Dr. Ackerman had an "in" with a wealthy benefactor who often chose to donate funds to Fairfield. And, the good professor had already made the college more illustrious and well known by the success of his two previous books, which were presently being used in several other universities as well as in Fairfield.

It was now Thursday evening and Sheldon could hardly wait until tomorrow night when he'd be meeting again with the DeePees. He wasn't the most patient man, he knew, and with the go-ahead from the dean, he knew they could get started on the project right away.

The first part of the meeting, Friday night, turned out well; each was pleased with the other's contributions and thus, pleased with the whole package.

They agreed that after Sheldon had his class fill out the questionnaire on the following Monday, they would meet Wednesday night at 7:00 in Sheldon's condominium, go over the responses, and choose four candidates. Sheldon, they decided, would then meet individually with the four students to see if they would like to participate and report back to the DeePees Friday night.

"Now," Robert began, "I would like to nip a problem in the bud. None of you have been in my office, but I have french doors with opaque glass in them between my office and the reception office. You can't see through them but you can see people moving around. The glass is double pane to block out sound so that my counseling is totally private. Do any of you know why?"

Hal spoke up. "Of course. As a physician I also had to be careful."

Nettie frowned, thinking, then nodded. "Oh. I know."

Sheldon looked blank.

Robert continued. "I'm a married man, and I want everything to be free of complications and have the appearance of total moral correctness."

The two agreed wholeheartedly, but Sheldon still looked blank.

"Sheldon," Nettie began, "would you want the young woman you work with to tell people that you had come-on to her?"

Sheldon looked horrified. "Good grief, no!"

"Well, then," finished Robert, "when we're in a room with them alone, we need to be in view of others or have others near or leave the door open or whatever we have to do to protect our reputations and that of Fairfield."

"I...uh...never thought of that. I do have a window in the door of my office with a mini blind. I will definitely keep it open," Sheldon said, still looking concerned.

"And I'll invite the young woman to my home and leave my office door open, with my wife near by or have my wife there with me," Hal said.

"Good," Robert said. "Now let's decide on our criteria for choosing the four and I'll write it down."

"I hope it's possible that we can choose four who are overweight," Sheldon stated, "because I see *that* as the biggest self-management problem in my class."

Nettie looked askance at Sheldon, but Robert wrote it down.

"Remember," Hal added, "we decided that if any of the girls we choose are overweight it can't be by more than thirty pounds." Everyone nodded in agreement.

Nettie said, "I think in order for it to be a good experiment, she has to have struggled over her weight or other problems for at least three years."

"You are the expert on the weight, Nettie," Hal said.

"She has to admit she has problems, weight or otherwise," Robert said, "and have the desire to overcome the problems." The three agreed.

"After starting the program, she will have to have lost a significant amount by the end of three months based on her particular circumstance," Nettie said, "in order for us to give our time to her."

"Yes," they all said.

"How often we meet with the young women individually, should be what we think is best, but as I said before, I feel, for a while anyway, that we should meet every week as a group," stated Robert emphatically.

"Should we review the experiment in three months?" Hal asked.

"Yes," Robert said. "And, actually, if they are really serious about improving themselves, we shouldn't have to hold their hands much longer than six months, just give them support and encouragement now and then."

"They will have to agree to a sound nutrition program and moderate exercise," Nettie said, "regardless of what the problems are. And later we'll need to get into the other area which is important for their future success—good grooming."

"They also need to get decent grades and be able to manage all areas of their lives in order to succeed in business," stated Sheldon dogmatically.

Hal smiled. "Shel, I'll have to admit, you manage your life well."

Sheldon glowed with satisfaction. "Thank you."

"In fact," Hal Continued, "you manage your life better than all three of us. But...you see, in addition to our professions, we have a spouse, children and, like me, grandchildren who are all added to the equation, and they really can't be *managed,* so to speak. It seems, Shel, there is one area of *your* life, which is empty, lacking, so you can't judge other's managing skills by your own. Your life is not complete."

Sheldon Ackerman's mouth dropped open. Hal Ozog had never been so blunt. Sheldon's gaze traveled around to the other three, including Don, and found them nodding their heads in serious agreement.

Feeling a little uncomfortable, Sheldon grinned and quickly asked, "Uh...how would you all like uh...how about a game of Monopoly?"

Chapter Eight

Billie's small suitcase was packed. She had just picked it up, slung a book pack over her shoulder and stepped to the front door of her small apartment when the phone rang. Stepping over to the kitchen counter, she picked up the phone. "Hello?"…Oh yes, I remember you. We met in the computer class. How are you?…A movie?…Thank you, but I'm going home this weekend."

She was out the door about to lock it, when it rang again. Leaving everything on the porch, she walked back in.

"Hello?…Oh hello Jordan, how are you?…I can't, I'm going home this weekend…No you can't come over to my home…Because, I am planning to visit with my family…Jordan, I have to go, I was just walking out the door when you called…goodbye…no…goodbye, Jordan." She hung up.

As she walked to her small, white Honda, she frowned in consternation. Maybe, she thought, I should just be blunt and say, I don't want to date you. Or even better, I'm not going to get married *so I don't date anymore*, not *anyone*! Yes, that's what I should say, she told herself as she opened the trunk and placed her things inside. Sliding behind the wheel, she started the car, backed out of the driveway, turned left and drove down the hill toward home. But, she knew she couldn't say that because—way down deep, her natural optimism kept popping up, bringing with it a tiny glimmer of hope. "I guess I'll just have to live with that tiny bit of hope till I'm dead and gone," she said aloud, feeling very annoyed with herself that she couldn't say no in every sense of the word. Her heart kept contradicting her mind!

Billie drove through the portico of her parents home, parked behind the three car garage, walked up the steps of the back porch and went into the kitchen. Her mother was standing at the stove, stirring something.

"Hello, Mother."

Her mother turned around and threw her hands up in the air. "Oh my! My girl is home."

"Yes, Mother," Billie said, smiling as she hugged her mother affectionately. "Just like I was two weeks ago."

"But it seems much longer than that, Billie. Now if you weren't alone, the time wouldn't..."

"Mother dearest, what smells so good?"

"Oh, just some corn chowder. If I had known you were coming, I would have..."

"You know I love corn chowder. Where's Papa?"

"He's still at work, but he's due home shortly."

"Well, bless my soul! Our girl is home!" cried Aunt Tilly as she came through the door trotting over to her niece.

Billie gave her aunt a hug and a smile. "How's my favorite aunt?"

"Very well now that you're here, Billie," her aunt said, beaming.

"Billie, go on upstairs," directed her mother, "and put your things away, and relax. Dinner is almost ready."

"What can I do to help?"

"Oh run along, Billie, I'm helping your mother."

"Yes, go on dear. There is just fruit to cut up for a salad and Tilly will do that."

Billie paused at the door and smiled as she watched the two sisters who were so unlike each other. Her mother, a trim and stately five foot seven with gray strands running through her short dark, nicely styled hair. Her hazel eyes, full of depth and warmth, reflected the care and love she had given to many during her life, especially to her own and extended family.

Aunt Tilly, eight years older than her sister, was shorter and slightly plump with short, curly hair that had been dyed red. Billie wasn't sure what color her hair was naturally, but thought she remembered it being light brown. Her eyes were also hazel but had an intense quality—especially when she was fussing over and giving important advice to a family member. Though not as attractive as her mother, Aunt Tilly was sweet and pretty.

She turned and walked into the utility room and up the back stairs to her bedroom, which looked big to her now. She could fit almost two studio apartments into this bedroom. And the decor was much more expensive and tasteful. Lovely sea green rugs covered the rich, polished oak floor. And the honey maple four poster bed with its peach and green bedspread and ruffled pillows piled high, was much more comfortable than her pull-out sofa bed.

Plopping her things on the bed, she opened the suitcase and pulled out a pair of white knee length shorts and a blue T shirt. Pulling off the cotton, empire-waist dress, she put on the more casual clothes.

It was the end of the third week in July and very warm, so going into the bathroom, she brushed her long, thick auburn hair and twisted it into a french braid. She studied her face in the mirror. The two pounds she'd lost didn't reflect in her face. To her it still looked plump! She sighed, knowing that if she stayed home more than two days, she'd gain it right back. Aunt Tilly's fussing over her turning down dates, Uncle Henry's caustic remarks about her becoming an 'old maid' and Mother's and Father's unspoken concerns over her single state, would invariably bring on the 'munchies.' And it didn't help that all the family were in denial over her weight gain.

She dashed down the front stairs to find Grandpa Bliss, the only neutral one in the family, the only one whose twinkling brown eyes found humor in the family's concern over her 'marriageless' state.

She found him in the library playing a game of chess with Uncle Henry. He looked up when she walked in.

"Snooks! You're home!" he exclaimed, smiling. "And what brings my lovely granddaughter home to see her poor lonely folks?"

"Because, they're poor and lonely, Grandpa," she said, smiling affectionately, walking over and giving his wrinkled, grinning face a kiss.

"Humph! what brings you home on a *Friday* night?" grumbled Uncle Henry. "Most young people are out on dates."

"And hello to you, too, Uncle Henry," she said, leaning down and pecking him on the cheek. "So who's winning?"

"I am of course!" replied Uncle Henry.

"I let him win now and then so he won't be so ornery," stated Grandpa.

Billie pulled up a chair to watch the game. Instead she watched them. Grandpa had lived with them for over sixteen years. She was eleven years old at the time he came, and she was sure he'd come just to be her friend and confidant. His height of six feet had shrunk some, but he still had a full head of gray hair and lots of energy. He did the yard work in the summer, shoveled snow in the winter, fixed faucets, washers, toasters, hung wallpaper, painted, in fact did anything that needed doing.

Uncle Henry, with his short stature, brown hair and paunchy middle, looked more like his sister Matilda than his sister Margaret, her mother. He was between them in age. Uncle Henry's distinctive down-turned nose and mouth betrayed his cynical outlook on life. But, like grandpa, he too earned his board and keep by taking on the vegetable garden in the summer, helping Grandpa with his repair jobs and doing the dinner dishes. Sometimes he annoyed Minnie, the housekeeper, with his help when she came once a week to clean house. When Uncle Henry's wife died ten years ago, her mother and father invited him to come live with them. He accepted the invitation, to the relief, Billie was sure, of his three grown sons and their wives. When his sons came to visit, bringing with them their children, the five extra bedrooms soon filled up.

Billie contemplated this household with its strong-willed occupants, each with such different personalities. She had often wondered how everyone got along so well. A few problems would crop up now and then, but they were short-lived and often with apologies afterward, though Uncle Henry's apologies were peculiar to him. Not until Billie was older did she understand how her family was able to live together in such harmony. It was her grandpa Bliss' tradition. One he'd started in his own home—which his son now carried on in his. Every morning early, all the family gathered around the kitchen table and read the Bible together, always ending in prayer. Billie sorely missed this part of living with her family—but carried it on by herself in her own little apartment.

She, Grandpa and her parents had bedrooms on the second floor. Aunt Tilly and Uncle Henry's were on the third. Papa, looking to the future, had an elevator installed.

"Billie girl!"

All heads turned toward the library door. "Papa!" exclaimed Billie, getting up and running to him. Throwing her arms around his chest, she gave him a squeeze.

He grunted, put his briefcase down and returned her hug. "How's my girl?"

"How's my papa?"

"Are we both fine?" he asked, studying her as she pulled away.

"It looks like it," she said, smiling at him. "You look as handsome as ever." And he was. Tall and broad shouldered, he was always dressed in a superb suit and tie with white shirts that were starched and ironed by Aunt Tilly. His thick auburn hair graying at the temples, complemented his warm brown eyes framed by wire rimmed glasses. Her father owned two hardware stores and a feed store. At one time, he rolled up his sleeves and worked with the help, but now, William Bliss was the true executive, delegating and managing.

"Come, come!" Aunt Tilly's voice floated across the foyer before she appeared at the library door. "William, go wash up, you don't want the chowder to get cold."

"No, I certainly don't, Matilda," the lines around his eyes crinkled as he grinned. "I'll rush right on up and wash my hands." He ran upstairs, and Billie disappeared into the dining room.

Tilly trotted over to the two playing chess. "Stop that game of chess right this minute, dinner is ready."

"We heard you, Tilly, we heard you," growled Henry.

"He's just mad because I'm about to beat him," Bill Bliss explained, grinning at Tilly as he stood up.

Tilly led the procession as the three marched quickstep into the dining room.

Chapter Nine

Sheldon Ackerman, his eyes alight with excitement, studied each girl as she sauntered into class Monday morning. Most of them noticed and smiled and said, "good morning, Dr. Ackerman." He just nodded at each, a pleasant look on his face, totally unaware of the blush on a couple of faces. No one was late today. But by the time they had all settled in, and it did seem to take young women an inordinate amount of time to settle in—stopping to comb their hair, adjusting their clothing, searching through their backpacks for an interminable length of time to find a notebook and pencil, putting on lipstick, etc.—his patience was wearing thin. He'd wanted to start the class right on time today, if not a few minutes early.

When everyone was through fidgeting, he stood up and walked around the desk and began.

"Good morning, class. This morning, I'm not going to give the usual lecture. Something important has come up." He noted their surprise and curiosity. "There is a wealthy benefactor who has been donating to Fairfield College and now he has offered something new. He's very interested in women succeeding in the business world, so he has asked me to hand out a questionnaire to this class. He, along with a select committee, are going to review the questionnaires that you fill out, discuss them and choose eight of them, then out of the eight, they will carefully choose four. The committee will meet with these four and inform them that they're going to get some special help and instruction to further their goals in the business field or in any other field they wish to choose. If these four choose to do it and fulfill all the requirements, they will receive a generous sum of money to help with their education. The benefactor regrets not being able to choose more than four participants, so to compensate for this, he will pay each one of you for filling out the questionnaire. But it has to be filled out with careful consideration and thought, and with total honesty. One of the committee is a seasoned psychologist. He will review them, and he'll be able to tell if the answers are not sincere.

"Please be sure to put your phone number in the space allotted. I will be calling four of you this week. Are there any questions or is there anyone unwilling to fill out the questionnaire?" He stopped, waited, giving the class members time to respond. Not one hand went up; they only stared at him in wide-eyed surprise. He continued, "It is not mandatory for this class, and your grade will not reflect it either way." Again he waited. Silence followed as the girls tried to digest the information. No one objected, but the young woman with the stringy hair and sour expression raised her hand.

"How much will he pay us to fill it out?" she asked in a skeptical tone.

"Two hundred dollars each, Miss Lemmon," he answered, pleased that he'd remembered her name.

The girls all gasped, staring at him in shock while Lora Lemmon mumbled, "Uh...thank you."

Unknown to Dr. Ackerman, Billie Bliss' pensive face revealed concern. She was almost certain that she would not want to be one of the four, even though she could certainly use the money. But, she thought, she would just have to wait and see.

By the end of the period, all questionnaires were placed on Dr. Ackerman's desk. When the last one left, he gathered up the papers and went next door to his office to go through them.

~~~~~~~~~~

Wednesday evening, shortly after 7:00, the DeePees, now called 'the committee,' were sitting comfortably in Sheldon's condominium reading through the questionnaires. Each was through picking out eight candidates by 8:30.

Robert shook his head. "It's clear from reading these, that the majority are just taking the class to fill credit hours."

Hal and Nettie agreed and Sheldon added, sounding quite intolerant, "I'm no psychologist, but it's very plain to me that most of these girls are not serious about a career in business."

Nettie, a successful business woman herself, spoke up. "Or even a career, period. But—there's nothing wrong with that, Shel. After all, there are so many men out there who are not willing to commit themselves to marriage, many young women are forced into a career whether they want it or not."

Sheldon thought about this a moment, and thoroughly missing the point made to him, said, "I didn't realize that, Nettie, but it doesn't make for a very stimulating group to teach."

The four looked at each other, and slightly shook their heads over his failure to get the punch line, then dismissing him, looked through the papers. They each narrowed the eight to four and compared notes. It wasn't surprising that they totally agreed on three. They had each chosen a different one for the fourth.

Hal looked at the one he chose and smiled. "This girl seems very well adjusted, but her answers contradict themselves. Her answers to the questionnaire were quite confusing, but I'm going to choose her for the fourth, anyway."

"I remember that one," Robert said. "She didn't fit into any one category.

"I remember one like that," Nettie said. "She had an unusual name I believe."

Sheldon smiled knowingly. "I'll tell you her name. Billie Bliss."

Surprised that he would know who they were talking about, they all smiled and nodded, then Nettie asked, "Do you know her or have you had an opportunity to visit with her, Shel?"

"I've had an opportunity to visit with her, but I certainly can't say I know her."

"Why don't you tell us about the visit," Nettie suggested.

Sheldon hesitated, then smiled, "I don't know whether or not to incriminate myself."

"Incriminate yourself?" Nettie asked, her eyes wide with curiosity. "Please do," she cajoled, smiling eagerly. Don's eyes twinkled in amusement.

"Well...uh...Miss Bliss thinks that it is...uh *my* fault that..." he cleared his throat uncomfortably, "that she gained five pounds in my class spring semester and already three pounds in the first two weeks of this one."

Eyes blinked, eyebrows raised—then all four laughed. Sheldon tolerated their amusement. When they were through, he said, "I'm glad that gave you some fun."

"Do tell us more, Shel," Nettie said, tickled beyond words.

"If you think her answers to the questionnaire were confusing, you should have heard the interview I had with her."

"Oh?" queried Hal. "Tell us about it."

"I couldn't relate my questions and her answers if you tied me to the rack. I've never been so confused in my life."

The three were intrigued. They had never known Sheldon Ackerman to be confused.

"Come on, give it a try, Sheldon," Robert insisted.

"Well…" Sheldon began, grimacing, "I asked the class to write their career goals down and turn them in. When I came to Miss Bliss' paper, she…"

"Go on," Nettie said.

"She had something on the paper, but—not her goals." He stopped, glanced at each of them, wondering why he was divulging this.

"Shel!" Nettie exclaimed in exasperation. "Do we have to pull this out of you inch by inch?"

Sheldon smiled and shook his head. "I know how you three will react if I tell you any more—but here goes. She had only one sentence on the paper which said, 'It's your fault Dr. Ackerman.'"

They were silent for a moment as it sunk in and then they roared with laughter. Sheldon smiled indulgently and waited.

At last Robert said, "Well, what happened next?"

"Needless to say, I asked her to come into my office. I asked her what she meant by that statement but the more she talked or answered questions, the more confused I got. Listen to this, see if you can make sense of it. She said, and I quote: "It's your fault Dr. Ackerman, but I assure you, you're not to blame."

The men looked at each other, puzzled and Nettie laughed. Sheldon turned to her. "You understand that?"

She laughed again. "Yes."

"It's a female thing," Bittle said.

Nettie ignored the statement and asked, "What kind of a student is she, Shel?"

"She got the highest scores on the two short exams I've given so far and," he added, "she keeps herself nicely groomed."

"I vote for Miss Billie Bliss as the fourth participant," Hal stated firmly.

"I second it," Robert and Nettie said at the same time.

Sheldon raised his brows. "All right, but I'm warning you."

"And—I vote that Sheldon works with Miss Bliss," Nettie said, holding back a smile.

"I second it," Hal and Robert added consecutively.

"You can't mean it!" Sheldon exclaimed, panicking at the thought.

"We do," Robert said and the other two nodded their agreement. All four grinned, enjoying Sheldon's discomfort.

"This isn't fair, you three are ganging up on me." Sheldon half laughed, half groaned.

"Oh no, Shel, we just feel that you are the one that can help this young lady," Nettie said with exaggerated fervor.

"She may need help, but, I assure you, I'll need more if I take her on."

We're all here to help, Sheldon," Robert said, "We'll all have lots of good advice for you." Then the four laughed again.

"All right, all right, you've had your fun. Which ones are you going to work with?"

"We don't know them, so it's just a toss of a coin. Just hand us a questionnaire of one of the other three we agreed upon," Hal suggested.

Sheldon looked at the other questionnaires and handed one to each of them. "I might point out," he said feeling very pleased, "these four all have chosen business as their major."

Deciding he'd better close the meeting before they came up with any more unwanted suggestions for him, Sheldon said, "Now, if I can pull it together for Friday night, where shall we meet? I have asked the dean if we could use one of those nice lounges in the Franklin building. What do you think?"

"That sounds good, Sheldon," Robert said. "It's on school grounds and yet it's more comfortable than a class room—and more friendly, so to speak."

"Good, now we need to decide how we're going to introduce them to the program, how we're going to proceed with them individually and as a group," Sheldon said, "then...how about a bowl of ice cream?"

Chapter Ten

Thursday evening at 7:00, Billie's phone rang. So deep in thought, while writing a paper, it had to ring again before she became conscious of it. Reaching for it, she answered distractedly, "Hello?"

"Hello, Miss Bliss, this is Dr. Ackerman."

"Dr. Ackerman?" Billie asked, startled—suddenly alert.

"I'm calling in regard to the questionnaire you filled out Monday."

"Yes?"

"The committee has chosen you to be one of the four participants for the program. I've spoken to the other three that have been chosen, and they were all delighted to accept. How do you feel about being chosen?"

"I don't know."

Sheldon had prepared himself before he called her, so he wasn't too surprised at her response.

"I know this is late notice, Miss Bliss, but the group is meeting tomorrow night. Uh...when do you suppose you will know?"

"I don't know."

"Can you explain why you don't know?"

"Dr. Ackerman, did you notice on the paper I handed you that I only put down one goal, which is owning a business of my own?"

"Let me see, I have it right here. Oh yes, I see that."

"Did you also notice that I stated that that goal was plan B?"

"Yes, I see that," he said, wondering why there wasn't a plan A.

"That's why I wonder if it would be fair of me to accept."

Sheldon could feel things getting sticky. "Miss Bliss, I think we could understand one another better if we were to discuss this in person. Is that all right with you?"

"Yes, Dr. Ackerman."

"Is there somewhere we could meet?"

"You are welcome to come over here to my little apartment."

"Uh…no. The school would not approve of that," he said, feeling grateful for Robert's advice about this very thing. "Would it be possible for you to come up to my office right now?"

Billie looked at her unfinished paper and sighed. "All right. I'll drive up. I only live a block from the campus so I'll be there soon."

"Thank you, Miss Bliss. I wouldn't ask you come up tonight, but it's important that the project gets started right away."

"I understand. I'll see you in a few minutes. Oh, Dr. Ackerman, may I come just as I am—very casual?"

"That will be fine, Miss Bliss."

Sheldon, relieved to have this part out of the way, smiled as he hung up the phone. Immediately, he got up from his desk and went to the mini blinds on the window of the door and opened them.

Seventeen minutes later, professor and student were facing each other across the professor's desk. Sheldon noted that Miss Bliss was dressed casually, as she said, in knee length shorts with a man's shirt over them.

Miss Bliss noticing his examination of the shirt, said, "This was my father's shirt. You see he has auburn hair also." Her professor looked puzzled, so she explained further. "Hunter green is my favorite color and also my father's. It enhances our hair, Papa says. I coveted this shirt, so he gave it to me."

Sheldon, now looking at her hair, discovered, that indeed, it was auburn. He hadn't noticed before. She had it pulled up off her neck with some kind of a clip, the underside ballooning, making it look like an old fashioned style with tendrils of hair escaping here and there. Quite an enchanting hair-do, he decided. Suddenly realizing that he'd been staring at her hair for some time, quickly stated the obvious, "Uh…yes, I see that your hair is…uh auburn. Now…Miss Bliss, let's try the best we can to understand one another. You said on the phone it wouldn't be fair for you to accept participation in the program. Would you please tell me why?"

"Because my goal to own a business is only plan B."

"So what is plan A?"

"It's *was,* not *is,* Dr. Ackerman."

"All right…what *was* plan A?"

"I really hesitate to say."

Sheldon Ackerman, feeling edgy, said, "Miss Bliss, you must have wanted to tell me, or you wouldn't have brought up plan A in the first place."

"No, I don't want to tell you," she said matter-of-factly. "It only explains why I don't think it's fair for me…"

"Tell me Miss Bliss," he ordered. She looked at him, shocked. "I'm sorry," he apologized, "please tell me."

"Plan A was…getting married and having children."

Sheldon wondered why he hadn't guessed, but still puzzled, he asked, "Then why don't you do plan A? Apparently you want to do that more than plan B."

"Yes, I did—but now it's out of the question."

"I'm sure you'll get an opportunity to get married, Miss Bliss, if you are patient."

Ignoring his patronizing tone she answered calmly, "I've already had several opportunities, Dr. Ackerman, but it's out of the question."

"Why?"

"As I asked once before, how many weeks do you have?"

"Why can't you just come right out and say it?" he blurted out in frustration.

"I can, Dr. Ackerman," she stated wide eyed, "but you wouldn't understand any more than my family does."

"Can we…uh…circumvent this, and you tell me in another way why it would be unfair to accept the program?"

Billie thought a minute. "I won't be as dedicated a student of the program as you would like me to be, because owning a business is not my number one desire."

"But…you've made the decision to go with plan B haven't you?"

"Yes."

Sheldon sighed with relief. "Well, Miss Bliss, that is dedicated enough to participate."

"It is?"

"Yes," he assured her eagerly.

"All right, I'll be a participant."

Sheldon Ackerman's deep sense of relief, though silent, was no less profound.

Chapter Eleven

The Franklin lounge was for faculty use only. The soft, muted colors of blue and rose in the upholstered chairs and couches at one end, a small conference table at the other end, encircled by blue padded chairs, made the room pleasant and comfortable. The only disharmony in the room was Sheldon Ackerman, who was feverishly pacing its perimeter. Nervousness had set in. He was now wondering if taking on this program was utter foolishness. In his experience, lacking as it was, he'd found women complicated and unpredictable—especially the one he was assigned to work with! Anything could go wrong.

"Shel, you're here already," Nettie said, entering the room.

"Nettie, it's good to see you," he said, relief written all over his face. "Where's Don?"

"He's chosen not to attend our *Project Success* meetings," she replied, tipping her head to one side, and studying Sheldon's face. "What's the matter, Dr. Ackerman, getting cold feet?"

"I'm afraid so, Nettie. In fact, I'm sure they're both frost bitten. Working with the opposite sex isn't my area of expertise, I'm afraid."

Just then, the rest of the committee walked in, adding more support to the beleaguered professor. After greeting each other, they sat down and quickly went over the agenda.

"Excuse me," came a sweet, dulcet voice from the open doorway, "Dr. Ackerman?"

They all turned to see the first arrival of the four participants—a strikingly beautiful young woman, Nettie, Robert and Hal noted.

Sheldon stood up and walked to the doorway. "Do come in, Miss Bliss." He looked at his watch and saw that it was 7:00 o'clock on the nose. "You're right on time."

At the mention of Billie's name, the other three looked quickly at one another conveying a message that clearly said, 'So this is the girl who has Sheldon all twisted up!'

He led her over to the group. They all stood up as Sheldon made the introductions. "Miss Bliss, this is Mrs. Nettie Newman. She and her husband Don, own the Diet Center, Dr. Robert Bittle, a prominent psychologist, and Dr. Hal Ozog, one of Claytonville's most outstanding family practice physicians, newly retired. And this is Miss Billie Bliss who has accepted the opportunity to participate in *Project Success*."

Billie was impressed. They each smiled warmly and shook her hand and commented on how happy he or she was to have her in the group.

Sheldon noticed, with satisfaction, that Miss Bliss was tastefully dressed in an emerald green dress with an ivory jacket over it. Her hair was pulled up into the same charming style as last night.

The three other girls soon arrived, all dressed in pants. Vickie Blume, Jane Bentley and Sandra Potter were introduced and the four girls greeted each other.

It was decided that they would all assemble around the table. Dr. Ackerman began the meeting by welcoming the girls and explaining that the committee was a group of successful community minded people, who were presently donating their time and expertise to help young women who want to succeed in their chosen field or in the business world. He then explained that they would be working as a group and that they would also be individually guided and supported by one of the committee.

As planned, Nettie then explained the first goal of the project. "As a woman in, what is now, a successful business, I have learned some valuable rules of success. Most of these things I've learned by trial and error. One of the first things I learned, was that we women seem to feel better about ourselves when we are pleased with our appearance. Do you all agree?" The girls all nodded. "Appearance is many faceted, a few of the facets are good grooming, the glow of good health from eating right, getting the proper rest and exercise, and inner happiness and so on. Is there one thing at the moment that is most pressing to you concerning your appearance?"

Nettie asked each girl to write it down on a piece of paper, and hand it to her, which they did. Nettie read each one silently then told them that they unanimously agreed that their weight was their first concern.

After Nettie encouraged the girls to ask any question that might be on their minds, Sheldon asked Hal and Robert to say a few words to the them. When they had done this, Nettie informed the girls that the first thing on the agenda, since weight control was their main concern, was to get a medical examination, then go to her diet center and confer with her concerning a nutrition and exercise program. Nettie explained that it all could be done tomorrow, Saturday, if they had time, because Dr. Ozog had arranged with a physician friend in advance to do the examinations.

Sheldon then explained to the four young women that when they felt that their appearance was what they wanted it to be, the next thing on the agenda was personal help and guidance with their career goals. Until then, he told them, they would be meeting with their counselor as often as they mutually agree upon and would meet as a group every Friday night at 7:00 here in the lounge.

"Is this all right with each of you?" They all nodded.

"Now," he continued, "Vickie Blume, you will be working with Nettie Newman, Jane Bentley, you will be working with Dr. Robert Bittle, Sandra Potter, you will be working with Dr. Hal Ozog and, Billie Bliss, you will be working with me. The meeting is over, but before you leave, get your medical form from Dr. Ozog and meet with Nettie for a few minutes to arrange a time for your medical exam and for a diet and exercise consultation with her. After that, meet with your counselor for a few minutes and make an appointment for your first get-together. Thank you all for accepting the program and for arriving so promptly tonight."

The group separated. The girls picked up their medical forms, gathered around Nettie, and made appointments with her, after which they found a place to sit next to their assigned partner. Sheldon and Billie Bliss sat at the table.

"Well, Miss Bliss, when shall we meet? I would like to meet Monday night, if you can get your medical exam and conference with Nettie both done tomorrow."

Billie thought a moment, then said, "I've made appointments for both of them tomorrow. Monday night will be fine."

"Good. I've been trying to think where we can meet on a regular basis. We can meet at my office and uh...leave the blind open. Do you...uh...have any other suggestions?"

Billie smiled inwardly at his obvious discomfort. "Your office is fine, and maybe we can meet at my parent's home at times."

"Your parents are in Claytonville?"

"Yes. They live only three blocks from the school at 303 Maple Ave. We have a library with glass french doors since you want privacy but want things to look proper."

"Would your parents mind?"

"Definitely not. In fact," she said, thinking of their very positive reaction to any man she might bring home, "they would be more than happy to offer their home. Shall we meet there on Monday night?"

Sheldon couldn't have been more pleased. Maybe, he thought, I can understand her better when I meet her parents. "Thank you, I think that will work well for us. Is 7:00 a good time for you?"

"Yes, but, Dr. Ackerman, I'm certainly surprised to be working with you."

"You are? Why is that?"

"I think it's rather obvious isn't it? I believe I've frustrated you each time we've talked, haven't I?"

He looked at her quizzically, then smiled. "As a matter of fact you have, but I think we can work things out, don't you?"

"I...don't know, Dr. Ackerman," she said, wide eyed, shaking her head. "I—don't know."

Chapter Twelve

Sheldon was sitting at the kitchen table, reading a book and enjoying a donut with a glass of milk, when the phone rang. He looked at his watch.

"Who could be calling at 8:00 o'clock Saturday night?" he asked out loud as he reached out and grabbed the phone off the kitchen counter.

"Hello?"

"Hello, Shel, this is Nettie."

"Oh, Hello, Nettie. What's up? Did everything go all right with the girls today?"

"It went very well. All four came and I worked with each one—but I thought I'd warn you before you met with Miss Bliss."

"Warn me? Uh-oh…go ahead."

"First of all, Shel, Billie Bliss is quite a girl. As you can see, we don't have to worry about her grooming or dressing for success. Nor do we need to worry about her nutrition. She already eats right and—in fact feels strongly about eating nutritiously. She does need to exercise more but…." Nettie paused, trying to think how to phrase it.

"Go on, Nettie, or you'll cause me to get frost bite again."

"Well, Sheldon, she doesn't fit the mold of many of us who struggle with a weight problem. Neither parent is overweight. She seems to feel good about herself except for her weight. I asked her if she knew what caused it." Nettie paused, smiling at the thought of him taking on Billie Bliss.

Sheldon was holding his breath, waiting. "Get on with it, Nettie."

"She just looked at me in surprise and said, 'I'm overweight because I get the munchies.' So I asked her why she got the mun…"

"And what did she say?" he interrupted.

"She said that I probably wouldn't understand, because her family didn't."

"Is that all?" he asked disappointed.

"Yes. The other three are good candidates for the project, but Billie Bliss may not be."

"That's what she said to me in a round-about way."

"Oh?"

"Nevertheless, Nettie, we'll proceed as if she were a good one and maybe it will turn out that way."

Nettie smiled as she hung up the phone. What Sheldon didn't know was that this girl would turn twenty-eight in a few days. The other three girls were younger. Vickie Blume was twenty-three, Sandy Potter twenty-two and Jane Bentley twenty-one.

When she learned of Billie's age, the matchmaker in her reared its eager head. However, she couldn't imagine how it could possibly happen, Sheldon was so set in his ways, so oblivious! He probably hadn't even noticed how beautiful she was. When Billie wasn't even smiling, the upturned corner's of her full, exquisite lips gave her face a cheerful countenance. Nettie's interview with the young woman also indicated a cheerful and happy nature—a perfect compliment to Shel's intense and serious one.

Nettie sighed, knowing it was best to squelch the idea. Walking over to the couch where Don was sitting and watching television, she sat down beside him. Linking her arm in his, she took his hand and gave it a squeeze. He smiled at her, responding with his own affectionate squeeze.

On the whole, Sheldon had managed to stay calm and confident until Monday evening when he pulled out of his underground parking space and headed toward the Bliss home.

When the idea of this project first came to him, the theory had sounded lofty and philanthropic. He hadn't even considered his basic shyness with the opposite sex because he'd learned to interact with women in business and in a teaching capacity here at the university. And he certainly hadn't envisioned taking on a young woman like Billie Bliss! The here and now reality of counseling with her one-on-one tonight left him feeling like a sailor must feel when walking a short plank over very deep water. He tried unsuccessfully to focus on the worthy goals of the project, the good that it might do these four girls, but his lack of skill in the area of women left him feeling totally inept. By the time he drove into the driveway of 303 Maple Avenue, he just knew he was going to act like a bumbling idiot.

The large home in front of him grabbed his immediate attention. It appeared to be a three story 1920's Prairie House with the typical wide veranda covering the whole of the front and with the distinctive portico on the right leading to the garages behind. The whole house, including the massive square pillars, whose only purpose was to support the porch roof, was made of a light brick. The contrasting wood trim, between the floors and around the two dormer windows protruding loftily from the hip roof, was painted a delicate cream color, giving the whole structure a look of simple elegance. It was apparent that the house had been meticulously cared for and kept up.

The rolling, two-level lawn, divided by a walk and steps up to the front porch, was lushly green and neatly trimmed against the walk. It was also neatly trimmed around the large oak trees and around the beds of blooming chrysanthemums, gladiolus and rose bushes.

He got out of the car, straightened his shoulders, automatically buttoning his light blue Christian Dior suit. Feeling his heart hammering against his chest, he took a deep breath and moved toward the porch on the rock-laid path that led from the driveway. Pausing on the top step, he inspected the impressive cream colored door with its two eighteen inch, rectangular windows encased in the upper half. Flanking the door were two matching rectangular windows accented by low concrete pedestal urns filled with delicate flowering plants.

The door opened almost as he touched the bell. An elderly gentleman with twinkling brown eyes smiled warmly.

"Come on in here, Dr. Ackerman," he said, as though greeting an old friend he hadn't seen in years.

Sheldon, surprised by the greeting, stepped inside.

"I'm William Bliss senior, Billie's grandfather. Most people call me Bill." He held out his hand and shook the professor's hand firmly, affectionately. "Billie will be right down."

"Thank you," Sheldon smiled, feeling himself relax to a considerable degree. The large expanse of the foyer had been updated with a lowered ceiling, inset lighting and a large attractive lighting fixture.

The rich oak floor was covered in the center with a light gray-blue, low-cut pile carpet. Plants in large, attractive ceramic pots and paintings of flowers, decorating walls between the doors leading to other parts of the house, made this space warm and inviting.

"Come and I'll show you where the library is," Bill said, "that's where you're holding your meeting."

Sheldon followed his host past the front room on the left, which had been, he was sure, the old parlor, and on to the adjoining french doors where they entered the library. Book shelves filled the whole wall on the right end of the room, except for a fireplace in the center with its lovely wood-carved mantle above which was a large floral painting. Sheldon noticed that the gray-blue color of the entryway carpet was repeated in both the front room and the library. Navy blue leather couches and chairs spaciously encircled the fireplace. Several bowls of colorful fresh flowers were placed here and there, indicating the touch of a woman's hand. No doubt by Miss Bliss' mother, who, he decided, appeared to be an excellent homemaker.

"Find yourself a seat, young man."

"Thank you." He was about to sit down, when Billie entered, all smiles.

"Good evening, Dr. Ackerman. Did you meet my grandfather?"

"I did, thank you."

"Well, I'll leave you to your meeting," Bill Bliss said. "Shall I close the doors on my way out, Billie?"

"Please, Grandpa."

No sooner had they seated themselves than Aunt Tilly knocked on one of the french doors. Billie motioned for her to come in, and Sheldon stood up as she entered.

Tilly scurried over to them and stood transfixed before Sheldon. Billie waited, and when nothing happened, gently prompted her aunt.

"Yes, Aunt Tilly, was there something?"

"Oh...uh...yes. I just wanted to see if you and your guest would like some cookies and lemonade." During this speech, Tillie's eyes had not strayed from Sheldon's face.

"Would you like some, Dr. Ackerman?" Billie asked, suppressing a smile.

"If you would like some, Miss Bliss, feel free, but I would not care for anything."

"We wouldn't care for anything, Aunt Tilly, thank you. But I would like you to meet my Professor of Business Administration, Dr. Ackermen. Dr. Ackerman, this is my aunt Matilda."

Sheldon nodded and smiled. "It's nice to meet you, Matilda."

Aunt Tilly smiled, clasping her hands together. "It's very nice to meet you, Dr. Ackerman," she said in a breathless voice. "Billie has told us how brilliant you are and how much she has learned from you."

The compliment was so unexpected, Sheldon felt tongue-tied for a moment. "I...didn't know that. Thank you for informing me." He smiled at her. "It's certainly nice for a teacher to get positive feedback now and then."

"Aunt Tilly, would you do me a favor?"

"Why, yes of course, dear."

"Go find Uncle Henry, Mother and Father and tell them that I would like them to come to the library and meet Dr. Ackerman?"

"I would be delighted." She hurried out.

"I'm sorry for the interruption, Dr. Ackerman, but my family is so curious, they would all manage to find a reason to come in here to meet you during our meeting, so we might as well get it over with all at once. Do you mind?"

His amusement was apparent. "I don't suppose it would do me any good if I did?"

Billie laughed. "No, I'm afraid not."

"Are your aunt and grandfather visiting?"

"No, they live with us and so does Aunt Tilly's brother, Henry, who lost his wife ten years ago. Both are my mother's siblings. They have all lived with us for years, for which I'm grateful because I'm an only child."

A beaming Aunt Tilly led the group through the library doors, and Billie introduced everyone. Billie's father shook the professor's hand. "As Billie said, my name is William Bliss, like my father, but people call me Will."

"People call me Sheldon. Glad to meet you, sir."

Henry was next. "Glad to meet you, Sheldon," he said, his eyes scrutinizing him.

Billie's mother, the gracious Margaret Bliss smiled. "Dr. Ackerman, we're grateful that you're helping our daughter with her goals of a business career."

"Well, Mrs. Bliss, Billie is the top student in the class."

"Oh? How nice to hear."

In the void which followed, there was an expectant expression on each of the smiling faces.

Will Bliss broke the silence. "We'll all leave you to your meeting now, Sheldon. Come again. You're welcome to meet here as often as you need to," he added, shepherding the group toward the door.

"Thank you, sir, I might just take you up on that."

After they had all left and teacher and student— 'Pygmalion and student'—sat across from each other, Billie said, "I didn't know I was the top student in the class."

"You received the highest grade on both exams and according to Nettie Newman, you deserve accolades on your grooming, dress and diet. All in all you are the most promising student of the four."

He noted that she didn't seem as pleased over this as he thought she should be. "What kind of a business would you like to own, Miss Bliss?"

"I don't know. As of yet, one hasn't come to mind that fits my personality and needs."

"Well, we can work on that in the future. The committee has chosen to work on first things first, take one step at a time. The first step is self-management in the area that seems to concern the four of you— weight."

Billie's eyes probed his. "Have you chosen us four because we're fat?"

"Uh...fat? I don't consider you fat, just...Miss Bliss, we chose you four for many reasons. It just so happens you four have expressed concern about your weight. And after all, isn't attaining an appearance you would like, a significant part of self-management?"

"Yes and no."

"What do you mean by yes and no?"

"Yes for the other three, no for me."

"Why no for you?" Sheldon asked, starting to feel concern.

"Because my overweight condition for the most part is not caused by lack of discipline, rather, it's arranging the conditions of my environment and the people I associate with. However, if the conditions aren't right for me, then I don't have self discipline—or I choose not to in order to ease my frustration."

"Miss Bliss, you are confusing me."

"I know. I confuse everyone."

"Were the conditions of my class that you attended last semester wrong?"

"No."

"This semester's class?"

"No."

"Then why would you tell me you gained weight in both classes?"

"Because I did. But—I've thought about this after we visited in your office, and I think my gaining weight in your classes does not fit the usual pattern."

A small sigh escaped him. He said hurriedly, "All right, all right, may we by-pass this for now?"

"Of course."

He began again—this time proceeding carefully, slowly. "You all agreed with Nettie Newman that if a woman does not feel good about her appearance, it's hard on her self esteem, right?"

"Right."

"Then the four of you all said that your weight was your greatest concern, right?"

"Right."

"Then," he took a deep breath, "may we work together on this as the first step?"

"Yes...but I hate to see you waste your valuable time, Dr. Ackerman, because it won't do any good."

"Why?"

"I can't *tell* you why, I would have to *show* you why."

"Then you must show me."

"You won't want to do what it will take to show you, I promise you."

Sheldon was feeling warm and his tie was choking him. He loosened it and got up and began pacing around.

"Dr. Ackerman?"

He stopped and frowned at her. "What?"

"Please take off your tie and coat. In July, the air conditioning in this big old home just isn't adequate at times."

"I don't feel that would be quite proper."

"I think it would be very proper. You're not in the classroom. And I also think we both should dress casually during our meetings. If we're both comfortable, we'll be able to understand each other better."

He studied her, then chuckled.

"Why are you amused? It only makes good sense."

"It does at that, Miss Bliss, it does at that."

He smiled as he took off his coat and tie and sat down again. "That feels much better, thank you. I'm amused, as you say, because I feel like I'm on a merry-go-round, and I'm wondering if I ought to close my eyes so I won't get dizzy."

Billie giggled, but not knowing how to respond to this she got right down to business. "Now what would you like to ask me?"

"I have no idea."

"Shall I coach you?"

"Coach me?"

"Yes. Shall I tell you what questions to ask me?"

He gaped at her, a look of incredulity on his face. Then he smiled, the smile turning into a chuckle, the chuckle into a laugh.

Billie smiled, glad to see her stiff and proper professor unbending a little.

When he got his amusement under control, Sheldon felt a little chagrined. This was not going as he'd planned. He cleared his throat, trying to resume the tenuous dignity a professor should have when working with a student. "Now, Miss Bliss, why would you have to *show* me? Why can't *telling* me suffice?"

She sighed in frustration. "It would not suffice. As I've said several times now, you would not understand."

Sheldon ran his hand through his hair in frustration. "Have you ever *shown* anyone…this mysterious…uh…thing?"

"After I tried to tell every young man that I dated, I tried to show several."

"Young men? What do they have to do with it?"

"Everything."

"Uh…never mind," he said for fear of getting off on another confusing side road. "You say you tried to show them? Either you show or you don't show," he said, agitation in his voice.

"I showed them, but they didn't understand."

Sheldon was rapidly becoming more frustrated. "Miss Bliss, how then can I understand when you show me?"

She looked at him as she considered his question. "Well, you probably won't be able to, but I thought maybe because you are so brilliant…you just might…but…" she frowned as her voice trailed off. Abruptly she stood up and walked to the mantle and rested her folded arms on it, her chin resting on her arms, her back to him. He noticed that her hair was shiny and loose down her back except for a curl resting on her right shoulder.

Sheldon waited while she thought about it—holding his breath almost.

Her back still to him she said, "I guess being brilliant in the dynamics of business wouldn't necessarily help you understand this…oh dear."

Sheldon was feeling the first stirring of panic. "Miss Bliss…I…"

"Dr. Ackerman," she interrupted, turning to face him, "are you married?"

"No."

"Uh…have you ever been married?"

"No!"

"Oh dear." She walked back to the couch and sat down. "Do you enjoy the company of women or that is…would someone your age call it dating?"

"Miss Bliss!" he exclaimed, standing up and stepping a few feet away, then pivoting around to face her. "It seems we are far afield here. What does my personal life have to do with all this?"

"It does, Dr. Ackerman, believe me. Please answer my questions."

"No! I'm not married, I have never been married, and I haven't dated in years."

"Oh," she frowned, her face full of concern. "Then I don't know if this is going to work, Dr. Ackerman. And—I *am* sorry you've led such a lonely life."

"Sorry? I didn't ask you for...for sympathy concerning my personal life." His voice had edged a decibel higher. "I just want to know uh..." He looked blank. "What do I want to know?"

"You want to know why you would understand when I show you when others I showed...didn't."

"Thank you, yes."

"I don't know that you won't understand, but it's likely you won't."

Sheldon sat down again, baffled and worn out. "Tell me again," he said slowly, "why you have to show me anything?"

"Because you want to help me manage my life, starting with my weight problem...and I told you that it would be a waste of your time because..."

"Stop! Don't say another word. I can't handle another explanation, if one could call it that. Just show me and we'll see if I can understand."

"How much time do you have, Dr. Ackerman?"

His patience was at the breaking point. "Enough to get this solved!"

"Are you willing to do what it takes?"

"What do you mean?" he asked warily.

"I'm wondering..." she bit her lip, thinking, "well, it might not look proper."

"I'm getting dizzy on this merry-go-round. Everytime you open your mouth, I get dizzier."

"May I qualify something?"

Sheldon exhaled. "If you can, Miss Bliss—without complicating it."

"I think I can arrange it so it will look proper."

"Good! Now how long do you think it will take?"

"It may take two weeks, a month, two, who knows. Depends on your time and your ability to grasp or comprehend my problem. Then you'll want to find a solution and then you'll find that..."

"Hold it!" he exclaimed, holding both palms outward. "What if after a month, we find that I can't even fathom your problem, what then?"

Billie looked down at the floor, pulled her hair up off her neck thinking, then leaned back on the couch. Her arms still holding up her hair, she stared at the ceiling.

It seemed like an interminably long time she was frozen in her odd thinking position. He waited her out.

Finally dropping her hair, she sat up straight and looked him directly in the eye. "I'll have to drop out of the program."

"But, Miss Bliss…"

"Dr. Ackerman, I thought we four would be working with Mrs. Newman on this. I didn't understand that you and I would start by working on my overweight condition."

"The other three girls are also working on this with their individual counselors."

"Why is that necessary?"

"Because…" he began, shaking his head ever so slightly, "This way you'll get more personal attention and help. I want you four young women to succeed in the business world. And won't…uh feeling good about your appearance give you more confidence that you can succeed?"

Billie studied her professor's intense and concerned blue eyes. She leaned toward him. "I never would have guessed it, Dr. Ackerman— but you really are—a kind and caring man."

~~~~~~~~~~

The family, who had gathered out on the back porch, were in the midst of speculating on Dr. Ackerman's age, when Billie joined them.

"He's no more fifty, than Billie is," exclaimed Matilda.

"No, he's at least fifty-five, Tilly, Uncle Henry countered.

"He's probably a very young looking fifty," suggested Margaret.

Will Bliss, relaxing on a reclining lounge chair, smiled as he listened to the debate.

"You are all a little daft," stated the patriarch of the family, Bill Bliss, "that young man is no more than thirty-eight or forty."

Noticing Billie standing there smiling, her mother asked, "Oh, Billie, is your meeting over?"

"Yes, Dr. Ackerman just left."

"Do you know how old he is, Billie?" asked Aunt Tilly.

"No, just like all of you, the class is in a dilemma over it and have made bets on it."

"How often are you going to have these meetings with Dr. Ackerman?" her father asked.

"It depends. It was first planned that we meet with our individual counselors as needed and every week with the group. In fact we've arranged to meet again tomorrow night...but I...uh need to tell you something. When we four candidates for the project met with the committee, we all agreed that our first need was to lose weight."

Will Bliss frowned. "Is that necessary? I thought this was a project to help you girls learn how to succeed in business."

"It is, Papa, but the committee feels that in order to have confidence in our own ability to manage a business, we have to learn how to manage ourselves."

"That makes sense," he conceded.

"So Dr. Ackerman is supposed to support and counsel me as I need. But," she stopped, hesitating, knowing how her family would react, "I need to show him first *why* I have a weight problem."

Mother and Aunt Tilly gasped, "Oh Billie," her mother began, "is that wise? Besides, dear, you really don't have a weight problem."

"If you do show him, Miss Billie," snorted Uncle Henry, "he'll be out the door so fast, he'll leave his long, skinny shadow behind."

Will Bliss and his father Bill exchanged glances and chuckled knowing that the respectable and stately Dr. Ackerman was in for the ride of his life.

Chapter Thirteen

After showering and changing into his robe, Sheldon felt better. Relaxing in his favorite chair he sipped a cup of cold herb tea and wondered how soon he would be calling on Nettie's knowledge of femininity, Robert's knowledge of psychology and Hal's fatherly wisdom. He wanted to call each of them right now, but felt they had already committed all the time they could give. Besides, what could he ask? He as yet didn't know enough to even ask an intelligent question.

Not knowing how much time it would take to solve the mystery of Miss Bliss' problem, he was glad that it was summer. His class load was not as heavy. In addition to his 280 class, he only had one other class this semester.

Sheldon loved a challenge—but the kind of challenge Miss Bliss presented was more than he'd bargained for. Nevertheless, it was a challenge. He sat there mentally preparing himself for what he knew was coming: more confusion, more frustration and hopefully in the end, a successful conclusion.

He found himself actually looking forward to their next meeting tomorrow night. Not only was he feeling challenged, but his curiosity had been aroused to a fever pitch. The next get-together was to be held again at the Bliss home where he felt comfortable. The family was warm and gracious in their hospitality, and he also found them to be interesting people.

~~~~~~~~~~

Tuesday, after her last class, Billie went to the video store and rented a couple of videos in preparation for tonight's meeting with Dr. Ackerman.

Today was her birthday and her family was having the usual birthday dinner. It was not a happy occasion. She was twenty-eight years old and what did she have to show for it? Most of her friends were married and had children, and the rest had careers. She had neither.

Dr. Ackerman would be at the house at 7:00 and she felt far from sanguine about trying to help him understand her problem. What she was going to do tonight would only bring the problem to her mind again and then it would happen—as it usually did. She sighed, deciding that she must find something positive about this evening other than being with her family.

~~~~~~~~~~~~~

At 7:00 PM, Sheldon rang the doorbell of the Bliss home. This time it was Billie who opened the door. Her brown eyes twinkled as she looked at his casual shirt and pants.

"Why, I was expecting Dr. Ackerman. Your name, Sir?"

He tipped his head to one side, studying her as a smile played around his lips. "And who might this audacious Miss be? Miss Bliss knows her professor well."

"Why, Dr. Ackerman, where have you been hiding this sense of humor?"

"Are you going to invite me in, Miss Bliss?" he asked in a mock seriousness, "or must I stand on the porch all evening?"

She grinned. "Do come in."

Aunt Tilly came trotting over to them. "Good evening, Dr. Ackerman."

"Good evening, Matilda," he returned, smiling.

"We are about to cut Billie's birthday cake, would you like to join us for a piece?"

A look of consternation came across his face. "Am I intruding upon your birthday, Miss Bliss?"

"No. We've already had my birthday dinner with all its trimmings. Would you like a piece of cake?"

"It's very good, made from scratch, Dr. Ackerman," coaxed Matilda.

Sheldon was tempted. "I think I would, thank you, but later after we're through with our meeting."

Billie led him down the hall, past the library to a room whose generous windows faced the large back porch. Under the windows stood two white, three-legged wicker planters and a rectangular one. All three were overflowing with green plants, giving the room the feel of a solarium. On one wall was an entertainment center holding a large television. Facing the television was an old and slightly worn, oversized sectional couch and one large upholstered chair. The other two walls were covered with maps and family photos. Sheldon found the room comfortable and inviting.

"I like this room," he said.

"We're meeting here for a reason, Dr. Ackerman."

"Oh? Fine."

"I'm glad that you dressed more comfortably."

"Thank you." He noticed she, too, was dressed more comfortably in a gold cotton shirt over gold pants. He noted that the color looked very nice with her auburn hair, which hung long, loose and was slightly curled. "You also look...uh comfortable," he said.

"I am, thank you."

She sat down on one side of the curved couch leaving him the center section facing the television.

He smiled. "So it's your birthday. And how old are you today, Miss Bliss?"

An expression of sadness came across her face so suddenly, he was alarmed. "Oh! I'm sorry. You don't have to tell me."

"I don't mind telling you, Dr. Ackerman. It's just that I mind the age that I am. I turned twenty-eight."

He stared at her, open-mouthed, "Twenty-eight, did you say?"

"Yes," she said in a small plaintive voice.

"Why...uh I thought you were only in your early twenties."

Now it was Sheldon who looked concerned. He had just turned thirty-eight. She was only ten years younger! This was still quite a few years, he realized, but nevertheless, it made him feel slightly uncomfortable.

"What is it, Dr. Ackerman? Is something wrong?"

"Oh no...no. It's that I...uh now can't feel quite so 'fatherly' toward you knowing your age."

"Why? How old are you, Dr. Ackerman? Almost all the class are making bets on it."

Sheldon was shocked. It never occurred to him that his students would be interested in his age. "I'm rather surprised at this, but you can relieve their minds. I just turned thirty-eight."

She grinned. "Grandpa Bliss was right."

"Your grandfather?" he asked astonished.

"Oh, yes, my family was arguing over your age last night."

"And you, Miss Bliss, did you bet with the rest of your class-mates?" he asked, suddenly interested.

She smiled, "No, I just found it amusing, but I was curious about something."

"Oh? What may I ask?"

"No, you may not," she stated, chuckling to herself.

"Well, I too, am curious about something, Miss Bliss. May I ask you why you are still in school at your age?"

A pained look crept over her face. "Because I need to get on with a business of my own." The appearance of concern, then confusion on Dr. Ackerman's face propelled her to explain further. "I graduated from college in accounting when I was twenty-two and went to work with an accounting firm here in Claytonville. The situation there began to cre-ate the problem I have now. I began to gain weight, so I quit and imme-diately lost it. I then took some classes in computer science, and eventually went to work for some attorneys. The situation was much worse there, exacerbating my problem even more. I quit and immedi-ately returned to my usual weight. I went to work for a group of lawyers. Several weren't married and my problem got worse. I quit and this time I didn't lose as quickly." Seeing more confusion on his face, she asked, "Shall I go on?"

"No! I'm thoroughly lost, Miss Bliss. Please explain what the com-mon denominator is in all these jobs that caused you to gain weight?"

"Why...men, of course."

"Men? Miss Bliss?"

"They asked me out."

"Were they married?" he asked with concern.

"Oh, some married ones asked me out, too. But, of course I didn't go out with them. I don't count them, that is, they don't figure in all this—just the single ones."

Sheldon was grappling with this totally unexpected revelation and was asking himself why he'd gotten into this. "Miss Bliss, did you go out with the single ones?"

"After I got to know them, yes."

"Did this problem only begin when you dated men at work?"

"No, it began in college."

Suddenly, Sheldon Ackerman paled. Did he dare ask her what happened on these dates to cause her such distress?

Billie noticed his expression. "Dr. Ackerman what's wrong?"

"I'm afraid I don't dare ask you what happened on those dates,...I..." he couldn't go on. He knew his face must be red as a beet.

"Oh no, Dr. Ackerman, nothing like that. I'm sorry, I do need to be more plain."

Sheldon couldn't have agreed more.

"You see..." she began hesitantly, because the moment she'd been putting off—was here, leaving her feeling nervous and anxious, "my problem is...I'm...I'm a hapless...hopeless romantic!"

Sheldon didn't know what he'd expected, but it certainly wasn't this. His breath came out in a rush, breath he hadn't realized he'd been holding. Relief replaced anxiety. "A romantic?" Not quite believing the problem could be so—innocuous, he blurted out, "Is that all?"

"Is that all?...All?!" she exclaimed, totally distraught.

"I mean...is that uh...all your problem?" he hedged, realizing all of a sudden he was on slippery ground.

"Yes...because...because..." pausing, her face a picture of anguish, she hesitated.

Sheldon had never seen a face like hers, one that could go from pleasantness to pain so quickly. He helplessly watched as she became more and more distraught. She stood up and walked a few feet away, standing with her back to him.

Though wondering what could be so serious with being a romantic, her excessive emotion caused him to again hold his breath in anticipation of something worse. "Go on, Miss Bliss," he hesitantly encouraged, "because of what?"

She whirled around. "Because...ROMANCE IS DEAD!"

Sheldon thought he could almost hear a funeral dirge as he gazed upon her grief stricken face. His first impulse was to say 'I'm sorry,' but he didn't know what he was sorry for—only that she was upset. Questions were swirling around in his mind, but he knew instinctively that he'd better not ask again his previous question, 'Is that all?' So he asked, "Are you sure?"

"Positive! And I can prove it to you."

"Please sit down, Miss Bliss," he coaxed, his voice gentle. "Help me understand, will you?"

She nodded and sat down looking very close to tears.

"Please be patient with my obtuse male understanding, but what do dates with the young men at college and work have to do with romance being dead?"

"Men are most of the problem! That's why I can never marry."

Nettie Newman, where are you when I need you! he thought. I don't understand feminine thinking. He felt the water closing over his head—he knew he was too far from shore. A little desperately, he asked, "Why are men most of the problem?"

"Because they don't understand what romance is or don't care. They are mainly responsible for society's destruction of romance and think nothing of it."

"What about women? As you know, I don't have much experience with them. Do all women think romance is dead?"

She blinked back tears. "That is the saddest part of all. Most of them just stand by and let it happen—some even become pawns to it, until they don't know what real romance is. They just hurt and don't know why."

"Forgive my lack of understanding, Miss Bliss, but what is romance, exactly?"

"It's…uh…it's…oh! I can't put it into words. That's why no one understands. That's why I have to show you what it is and I have to show you what it isn't."

His mind felt muddled. His patience running out, his first impulse was to reprimand her. Instead, he calmly asked, "Can you show me, now?"

"May I ask you some questions?"

"Miss Bliss, I'm not a patient man."

"I know, but I need to ask you some questions first."

"All right! But get on with it."

Nervously she curled her legs up on the couch. "Have you read the book *Jane Eyre*?"

He was so surprised by the question, he couldn't think for a moment. "Uh....I believe I have...yes."

"Did you like it?"

"Yes."

"I read it when I was a young girl. It was the very first love story I had ever read, and I loved it. You see, Dr. Ackerman, romance is the precursor to love, and it's the spark that keeps a marriage special. Without romance, you can't have true love. And, in my mind, *Jane Eyre* is the epitome of both. Don't you think so?"

"Well...uh, I haven't really thought about it, Miss Bliss. Refresh my memory. What made it uh...romantic?"

Her face became wistful, her eyes distant, faraway. "You know, the romantic way they met out on the moor—how she frightened his horse. Then their conversations—oh, their many conversations. Mr. Rochester got to know Jane and she got to know him and their love began to grow though they had hardly touched each other. Isn't that wonderful?"

He blinked his eyes, his lips moved wordlessly as he tried to answer her, but no sound came. Finally, he muttered, "Why yes, that was nice...yes."

"It is more than *nice,* Dr. Ackerman," she said with a touch of reproach. "It's very *unusual* in *today's* world."

"Oh? I don't understand. There are many love stories written today. I see them in the book stores."

"Have you read any of them?"

"Well...no."

"Then you don't know!"

"Know what?"

"That the majority of those books have *killed* romance." The pain appeared on her face again. "And the movies! Oh!" she put both hands over her mouth and closed her eyes.

Sheldon fought the urge to smile at the dramatics.

She opened her eyes. "Did you see the movie *Jane Eyre* with Orson Wells and Joan Fontaine?"

"Yes."

"Did you like it?"

"Yes. I thought it represented the book very well."

"It did. But—have you seen movies of any of the modern day love stories? Or have you seen love stories made for television?"

"I...uh, haven't had time to attend movies and watch television as such, just a symphony or an opera now and then, you know that sort of thing."

"Then you don't know!" she repeated, dangerously close to tears.

"They kill romance, too?"

"Yes!"

"I can hardly believe this, Miss Bliss."

She uncurled, got up and stepped quickly over to the television and promptly put in one of the videos she had rented earlier in the day. "This is a very popular movie. It won best actress and best screenplay. Some time ago, a friend of mine asked me out to a movie. This is the one he took me to. He assured me that it was a romantic love story."

The title came on and it looked familiar to Sheldon. He probably had seen it advertised somewhere. Billie sat down and they proceeded to watch it.

Ten minutes later, Sheldon exclaimed, "Good Grief! Do they use that language in movies today?"

"Yes."

Twenty minutes later, Sheldon jumped up, thoroughly embarrassed. "Turn it off!"

"Gladly," she exclaimed through tears.

"Are you crying, Miss Bliss?" he asked, now more horrified.

"Yes," she sniffed. "See? Romance is dead!" She walked to the door and in what, to him, seemed another one of those inexplicable shifts in feminine thinking said, "Let's go have a piece of my birthday cake, Dr. Ackerman."

Dumbfounded and stunned, Sheldon followed his protege into the kitchen.

Matilda and Henry had just finished cleaning up the dessert dishes. "Why, Billie what's the matter?" Aunt Tilly asked concerned.

"We just want a piece of birthday cake, Aunt Tilly," she stated tearfully.

"Oh, yes, I'll get it right away." She scurried into the butlers pantry and retrieved it.

"Sit down, Dr. Ackerman, and you too, Billie, you can't eat standing up," growled Henry.

"Cut me a *big* piece, Aunt Tilly," Billie said, tears still trickling down her cheeks. Almost before another tear could roll down, Matilda had placed a large piece of cake before each of them.

"Please, Miss Bliss...don't cry," pleaded the bewildered and panicky professor.

"Don't take her too seriously, Dr. Ackerman," Henry said, this happens every time she watches a video or movie on television. She turns them off after only five minutes; but nevertheless, it's enough to send her into these kind of theatrics. She comes into the kitchen and cries and eats, eats and cries."

"That's right, Dr. Ackerman," Billie said, sniffling and wiping the tears off her cheeks. "And now..." she said with high drama, "you *know* my *problem*!" Another bite of cake found its way into her mouth.

Sheldon Ackerman's eyes glazed over. That he was sitting here in this bewildering situation was unbelievable; but that he was witnessing the spectacle of something that had many years ago sent him running—a weeping woman—was beyond comprehension!

He stared at the cake in front of him—certain he couldn't swallow a bite. Abruptly shoving his chair back, he stood up. "I'm sorry, Matilda, I'm afraid I can't eat this right now. I must be going."

Henry chuckled and Matilda stated in a tone that brooked no argument, "Then I'll wrap it up so you can take it home."

"Thank you," he gave her a weak smile. Avoiding any further eye contact with those tearful brown eyes, he watched impatiently as Matilda carefully wrapped up the cake in aluminum foil.

"Here you are, Dr. Ackerman. Eat the cake when you feel better."

He took the foil package. "Yes, yes, thank you." He walked out of the kitchen unaware that his charge had followed him to the door—that is, until he heard a subdued voice behind him.

"Goodnight, Dr. Ackerman."

He turned around, startled. "Oh, yes, good night, Miss Bliss." He noticed, gratefully, that the tears had dried up. He opened the door and stepped out. Billie followed him out onto the porch.

"Dr. Ackerman?"

Startled again to see that she'd followed him out, he answered, "Yes?"

"I told you I wasn't a good candidate for your project."

"So you did, Miss Bliss."

"I will be glad to drop out so that you can get someone else."

"Well uh…Miss Bliss…I just need some time to think about your uh…rather singular problem. Goodnight." He half stumbled down the steps as he beat a hasty retreat to his car.

~~~~~~~~~

Retreating to his own familiar surroundings brought Sheldon a measure of objectivity. He found that away from Miss Bliss he could think about everything more calmly—in spite of the fact that he was still shaken up over what he'd just experienced at the Bliss household. On impulse, while pacing back and forth in the kitchen, he picked up the phone to call Nettie, but immediately put it back down. Impulsiveness was not his nature; calling Nettie right now didn't feel right. What he had to do was think it all over very carefully.

The thing that disturbed Sheldon at present was—he felt responsible for Billie Bliss eating such a large piece of cake! If he hadn't asked her to show him her problem, she wouldn't have had a desire to over-eat.

Something nagged at him—oh yes—why did she tell him that she would drop out of the project? In his mind, dropping Miss Bliss from the project was not even an option. Keeping a commitment when he made one, was part of Sheldon Ackerman's honor code.

Still pacing the floor, he carefully retraced the events of the evening. He'd never seen anyone who could suffer like Miss Bliss. Somehow he had to help her. She must be wrong. Surely romance can't be dead! She has just seen the wrong movies and picked up the wrong books.

He decided right then and there to do some research himself; he would ask his female colleagues at the university about romantic movies.

This decision left Sheldon feeling much more relaxed. He went to the refrigerator and took out a carton of milk, poured himself a glass, and sat down at the table. Unwrapping the cake that Matilda so kindly sent home with him, he took a large bite, finding it as delicious as it looked.

Chapter Fourteen

Dr. Ackerman waited for his 280 class to trickle in Wednesday morning, watching especially for Miss Bliss. When she walked through the door, she avoided looking at him, going straight to her seat. He noted that her hair was pulled back and hung in one long braid down her back. She wore jeans today and a navy blue jacket with a T shirt almost the color of her hair. Yes, Miss Bliss did dress nicely. He hoped Hal, Robert and Nettie were having luck in the area of grooming with the three they were working with. He hadn't noticed. Making himself aware of female grooming in general, seemed like a Herculean task—so noting the grooming of one young lady was all he could handle.

Billie settled into her seat, pulled out a pen and notebook for notes. Josie, who always seemed to be sitting near her, leaned over and whispered.

"I hear you're one of the four chosen for the project. How is it working with ol' 'Dodds?"

"I don't really know, Josie. I haven't been in the program long enough," she whispered back. And, she reminded herself, she wasn't going to stay in it. After Dr. Ackerman left last night, she'd made up her mind to drop out and let 'ol' Dodds,' as Josie called him, off the hook.

When the class was over, Vicki, Jane and Sandy gathered around her, all smiles. "How is it going, Billie?" Vickie asked.

"How's it going with you?" she asked, hoping to avoid any further questions..

"Oh, I'm excited to be working with Mrs. Newman. She's already helped me."

"How are you both doing?" Billie asked, looking at the other two.

Jane was the first to answer, "Dr. Bittle and his wife have helped me solve a problem and have been wonderful to me. I have hopes of getting my life back on track."

"I'm happy to hear that, Jane." She looked questioningly at Sandy.

"Dr. Ozog and his wife have treated me like a daughter and have taken me under their wing. They're helping me accomplish what I've wanted to, but have been putting off."

Billie was impressed with the progress the girls were making and with the kind people who were helping them.

"What about you, Billie? How are you doing with our handsome professor? Vickie asked and the other two nodded, eager to hear her answer.

"He's been very kind also and has put in a lot of time to help me." They seemed satisfied with that answer.

Billie took so long pretending to look for something in her backpack, Vickie finally said, "Well, we've got to go, see you Friday, Billie."

"Yes, Friday, bye," she said, smiling. She watched them leave, then put the backpack over her shoulder and walked next door to Dr. Ackerman's office, hoping he was there. Seeing him through the window, she knocked.

He got up and opened the door. His eyes lit up when he saw her. "Oh, Miss Bliss, I'm glad you stopped in. I want to talk to you."

"And I want to talk to you, Dr. Ackerman."

"Oh? Please have a seat. What is it you want to talk to me about?" he asked as he seated himself behind the desk.

Billie took a deep breath. "I know how much I disturbed you last night…and I don't blame you at all, Dr. Ackerman, please understand that. But now that you know what my problem is—and know that it's hopeless—you can understand why I must drop out of the program."

"Hopeless? Why Miss Bliss, I know nothing of the sort. Of course it's not hopeless. I went home and gave it some thought and I have come up with some ideas that I'm going to work on. I'm going to *prove* to you that romance is *not* dead."

Billie blinked, shocked, then amusement flickered across her face. Did her stiff and proper professor say what she thought he said? she asked herself. "What?"

Dr. Ackerman repeated it.

Billie squelched a giggle, certain that this was totally out of character for him. "Dr. Ackerman, I've been working on this since I was eighteen years old. What can you do in a few weeks?" Suddenly distress replaced amusement; the distress so pronounced, her chin quivered.

"Please, Miss Bliss," he said, jumping up and stepping around the desk. Panic in his voice, he exclaimed, "Don't cry!" Getting hold of himself, he said in a more soothing tone while patting her shoulder, "I promise you that together we can solve your problem."

"But it isn't just my problem, it is the world's problem."

"The world?" to Sheldon, this was definitely blowing the problem out of proportion.

"Yes," she said in a small quaking voice.

Oh no, he thought, she *is* going to cry! "The world be hanged. You take care of yourself."

She stood up and looked up at him forlornly. "Myself? How can a person find romance by herself? It takes two...a man and a woman."

"Oh...yes...I forgot," he mumbled. "Uh, Miss Bliss...do uh...young men still ask you out?"

"Yes."

"Do you go out with them?"

"As I told you, I used to, but they made my problem worse, so now I turn them down."

Though feeling uneasy over this sensitive area, Sheldon bravely ventured, "I'm sorry, Miss Bliss, I don't believe I quite understand."

"I know...and I'll just cause you more discomfort, Dr. Ackerman, if I continue to try and help you understand. So I'm dropping out," she stated firmly.

"Oh, no! Miss Bliss, you must not! I have made a commitment, and I intend to keep my commitment."

Billie noticed that his eyes revealed even more distress than last night. And—she also noticed his eyes were the deepest sapphire blue eyes she'd ever seen.

"Don't you wear glasses, Dr. Ackerman?"

"Wh...what?"

"Most of the time you wear glasses in class, but you aren't wearing them now," she said, her expression turning pleasant, a small smile playing at the corners of her mouth.

Sheldon gazed down at her, bewildered. Billie Bliss was as changeable as a little child! First there was distress in her face, bringing the threat of tears, then kindness and sympathy, and now she was smiling. He wondered if he would ever understand this young woman!

"Miss Bliss, I'm nearsighted," he stated impatiently. "I put my glasses on when I'm looking at my class. I take them off when I read."

"You're irritated," she replied, the smile gone.

"Miss Bliss, you not only seem to change your emotions quickly, but you change subjects so abruptly, I can't keep up with you."

"I'm sorry."

"He scrutinized her, noticing that her brown eyes were soft and sincerely apologetic.

"All right...where were we?"

"Nowhere."

"Nowhere?" he asked, perplexed.

"But I do admire you feeling honor bound to keep a commitment, Dr. Ackerman, honor bound enough to put up with me, so I, too, will keep my commitment—that is, until you're totally convinced that my problem is unsolvable, or until you lose all patience with me." She gave him a winsome smile. "Until then, we'll continue."

"Oh...good, Miss Bliss," he said, exhaling with relief.

"Thank *you,* Dr. Ackerman. It's hard to believe that a man like you is doing this in the first place. No one has ever really tried to understand my problem, except my family."

Sheldon was at a loss for words.

Billie filled in the silence. "My mother wanted to thank you by inviting you to dinner tomorrow night, and now that we have both recommitted ourselves, can you come?"

"I uh...hardly think that would be appropriate."

"Why not?"

"Because this is not a social or a personal project, it's uh...a secular project."

"But your concern—I can feel it. It doesn't feel impersonal to me, Dr. Ackerman."

Thoughtful for a moment, his blue eyes reflected appreciation for her intuitiveness. He smiled. "I believe you're right."

"Is 6:00 PM all right?"

Sheldon's concern about the propriety of accepting the invitation soon evaporated when he thought how nice it would be to have a home cooked meal. "It is," he said finally, "thank you. And is it all right with you if we get together after dinner and work?"

"It is, Dr. Ackerman."

After Billie Bliss left the office, and after he had recovered his equanimity, Sheldon put his mind to thinking of some possible ways to prove to Miss Bliss that her problem, or as she said, the world's problem, was not what she thought it was. Nor that there was a dearth of young men out there who could fill her need for romance.

~~~~~~~~~~

After eating a TV dinner, Sheldon sat down in his favorite chair. Poised with a pen and note pad in hand, he called Nettie. Hearing her strong upbeat voice, he replied. "Hello Nettie."

"Hello, Shel, how are you?"

"Could be better."

"I'm dying of curiosity, how is everything going with your girl, Billie Bliss?"

"It's been quite an experience, Nettie. I wanted to call you for help last night, but felt it wasn't right to do so. But I did call tonight to ask you a favor."

"Oh? What is it?"

"Would you tell me how you and Don met and a brief account of your courtship?" Only silence came through the receiver. "Nettie?"

"I'm here, I just had to pick myself up from the floor."

He chuckled. "I suppose it is an unusual question coming from me."

"That's the understatement of the year. And of course, I'm extremely curious as to why you're asking me this?"

"As I said, I certainly would like to tell you and ask for some help, but you have your share of work with Miss Blume—besides, I have to respect Miss Bliss' privacy. Knowing her, however, she may tell the group."

Nettie was disappointed, but she related to Shel what he'd asked for, "Is that what you wanted to hear?"

"Yes, thank you, Nettie," he said, finishing up the notes. "One more question. Did you think that how you and Don met and how he courted you—was romantic?"

"Why, Sheldon Ackerman, what in the world is going on with you and Billie Bliss?"

Sheldon was shocked at the question. "Surely, Nettie, you don't actually mean what you inferred?"

"No...well...maybe—a little...yes."

"That sounds just like an answer Miss Bliss would give me."

She laughed. "It sounds like you're having an interesting experience with the young lady."

"As you said, that's the understatement of the year."

After he'd hung up, Sheldon was hesitant to call Molly Bittle and Sharon Ozog, knowing they would react as Nettie had. But, besides them, who did he know well enough to ask such questions? Sighing, he picked up the phone. As he had anticipated, the same questions brought the same reactions. However, this time, he was prepared. With the deftness of a boxer, he managed to dodge their natural curiosity.

Now, armed with something more concrete than guess work, he felt better able to prove Miss Bliss wrong. Feeling more optimistic, he found himself looking forward to eating dinner with the Bliss family tomorrow night.

Chapter Fifteen

Thursday evening, after showering, Sheldon put on a blue short-sleeved shirt and gray cotton pants, whistling all the while. He felt more confident meeting with Miss Bliss tonight—also the promise of a good home cooked meal had lifted his spirits considerably. He hated to cook, so his meals, most of the time, were far from satisfying.

As he drove out of the underground parking, he turned off the air conditioning in his car and rolled down the windows. It had rained the night before. The freshly watered trees, grass and plants sent moisture into the air with an imminent promise of a lovely, balmy evening. The scent of flowers and green foliage blew in, awakening youthful memories of a time when things were a lot less complicated. He whistled all the way, stopping only when the motor stopped in the Bliss driveway.

He got out. Walking briskly to the porch, he took the steps two-at-a-time, moved quickly to the door and rang the bell.

Henry answered the door. The corners of his mouth arching downward more than usual, he studied the up-beat guest before him, leaving him standing on the porch.

Sheldon cleared his throat. "Good evening, Henry."

"And condolences to you, young man, if you're here to get another dose of Billie's medicine."

Sheldon smiled. "Thank you, I may need it."

"May? No doubt about it! Come on in if you're determined to," he said, stepping aside so Sheldon could enter. "But If I were you, I would skitter out of here the minute dinner is over."

"Thank you for the advice, Henry, but I came armed tonight."

"Ha! No amount of arms is going to do you much good against the unrealistic expectations of that silly romantic girl. But come on, I've been playing chess with the old Billy goat in the library. You can watch us until dinner's ready."

Sheldon followed Henry into the library where Bill was studying the chess board.

Bill looked up and smiled. "Good evening, Sheldon. Come on in and watch me beat the tar out of this ornery cuss here."

"Thank you, Bill," Sheldon said, helping himself to a chair, which he pulled up close to the chess table. A dedicated chess player himself at one time, he soon became engrossed.

Fifteen minutes later, Will Bliss walked into the library in suit pants and a white shirt relieved of its tie. "Well, good evening, Sheldon."

Sheldon scooted back his chair and stood up. "Good evening, Sir."

"Margaret sent me in to tell you it's time for us to gather in the dining room."

The three men followed Will into the dining room and were instructed where to sit. The three women came in, each carrying food to be placed upon the table. After the greetings were over and all were seated, Will suggested that they bow their heads while he said grace.

Sheldon's mouth watered as he eyed the hot rolls, fried chicken, mashed potatoes and gravy. "This meal looks wonderful, Mrs. Bliss. I intensely dislike my own cooking.

"Please call me Margaret, Dr. Ackerman."

"Thank you, Margaret, please call me Sheldon."

"Actually, Sheldon," Margaret said, "the meal is a community effort. Matilda made the rolls, Will mashed the potatoes and Billie made the apple pies."

Billie, trying to stay cool had again pulled her hair up off her neck into a clip and wore a light blue cotton dress with an empire-waist, which hid her figure.

Sheldon noticed that Billie looked very attractive. If we can just get her problem solved, he mused, she is most certainly on the road to success.

Pulling his eyes off Billie, he asked, "Who made the birthday cake you sent home with me, Matilda? It was delicious."

"I'm glad you enjoyed it, Sheldon," she said, pleased. "That's Margaret's specialty."

"How long have you taught at Fairfield College, Sheldon?" Billie's father asked.

"Three years."

"And where did you teach before that?"

"I didn't. I've been in the business world all my adult life, until I began teaching."

Hearing this, Henry blurted out, "Well, it's good to see an educator who has something between his ears besides book learning."

Sheldon acknowledged his off-handed compliment with a smile then turned to Will. "And what do you do, Will?"

"I own two hardware stores and one feed store."

This launched the two men into a discussion of business growth, profits etc. Billie, who was seated across from Dr. Ackerman, listened to him and her father with great interest. No wonder her professor was so brilliant at teaching business, she thought. He's apparently had a lot of practical experience.

As dinner progressed to the dessert, Sheldon complimented each one's contribution to the meal; then stunned the family by an unexpected question.

"Margaret, how did you and Will meet?"

Billie, with a fork full of pie halfway to her mouth, jerked her head up and stared at him, shocked. This certainly wasn't the Dr. Ackerman she thought she knew!

Her mother, recovering from her surprise, smiled and looked very pleased. "It has been a while since I related it, Sheldon, but," a dreamy expression came over her face, "I remember it as if were yesterday. Will and I were both attending Fairfield when it was a very small college. I was helping to put myself through school by working as a waitress at a malt and sandwich shop near the campus. It was a hangout for the college students. One day, this tall, handsome auburn-haired young man came in with three girls." She smiled at her husband and then continued. "The minute I saw him, my heart skipped a beat. The girls seemed mesmerized, hanging on every word he said. I know it sounds irrational, but I found myself resenting them.

"I had to wait on them, and I was so nervous I could hardly concentrate on their orders. They all ordered sandwiches and a malt." Margaret heard her husband chuckle. She smiled at him, then continued, "When I served them, I was so nervous, I dumped the sandwich right in his lap."

Billie found herself laughing even though she had heard the story many times. She glanced at her professor and saw that he, too, was enjoying it.

"Needless to say," Margaret continued, "I apologized and made him another sandwich. The next time he came in, he had two different girls with him and they all ordered malts. When I served him, I knocked over his malt." Everyone at the table laughed. "I was so flustered, I could hardly wipe it up. He was so nice about it and joked with me. The next time he came in, he was alone. He ordered french fries and a malt. This time, I was determined I wasn't going to spill anything. I was very careful, but somehow I managed to tip the french fries right into his lap." Margaret put her hands over her face laughing with the rest. "You finish the story, Will."

He chuckled and began, "You see, Sheldon, from the time she tipped over my malt, I was smitten. I came in alone the third time, hoping she'd spill something again because I had planned my tactic. I was delighted when she tipped the french fries into my lap. When that happened, this is how it went:

"'Miss,' I said in a stern voice, 'would you please tell me your name?'

"'Please...I told you I am sorry. I...I won't let it happen again.'

"'All I'm asking for is your name.'

"'If I give it to you, are you going to complain to my boss?'

"'No. It's just that I can't talk to you without a name.'

"She was still nervous, but she told me that it was Margaret Gray. I said, 'Thank you, Miss Gray, my name is Will Bliss, now would you be so kind as to tell me how many nights you work?'

"'Six.'

"'What are your hours, Miss Gray?'

"She began to be suspicious. 'Why do you want to know, Mr. Bliss?'

"'Answer me please, Miss Gray or I'll have to go to your boss', I said. She was beginning to get quite put out with me by now.

"'My hours are 6:30 to 8:30 PM Monday through Saturday, Mr. Bliss. Now, I have to get back to work.'

"'Please give me one more minute, Miss Gray. May I have a date tomorrow night at 5:30 to buy you a sandwich and a malt right here?'

"She was so shocked, she was speechless for a moment, then she asked abruptly, 'Why?'

"I answered, 'Because bringing you here on a date and letting some one else wait on us is the only way I can eat here without getting food dumped on me!'"

Sheldon laughed. "Very clever, Will."

"And very romantic," sighed Billie.

Sheldon smiled. It was going even better than he'd planned.

~~~~~~~~~~

At Billie's request, she and her professor were seated on the back porch. She chose to sit in the porch swing, while Sheldon sat on a comfortable patio chair.

How pleasant, he thought. The balmy evening air brought with it the comforting smell of fresh mown lawns, and the delicate scent of roses, mixed with warm moist earth.

"Dr. Ackerman?" Billie questioned, breaking into his thoughts.

"Yes, Miss Bliss?"

"You and everyone in this household are calling each other by first names, but you continue to call me Miss Bliss. You may call me Billie, if you like. I know you have to be more formal in the classroom, but since we'll be working together for some time, in these private circumstances, it just seems more natural."

He looked perplexed. "I've been wanting to ask, for some time now, why your parents named you Billie?"

Her brown eyes twinkled and a little smile played around her lips. "I'll bet you think that my father wanted to name me Billie because he wanted a boy."

"I think one might assume that, yes."

"That isn't the case. Papa was thrilled to have a girl, even knowing that mother couldn't have anymore children. It was my mother who named me Billie, feeling sad that he couldn't have a boy to carry on his name."

Dr. Ackerman still looked perplexed. "That was very kind of her, but Billie doesn't fit you," he said flatly. "I agree that the formality could be done away with under these circumstances, but I wouldn't know what to call you since I intensely dislike the name Billie—for you, that is."

"Oh dear, I don't have a middle name."

They both thought about it for a couple of minutes. Sheldon studied her as she swung gently back and forth on the swing, remembering the dreamy expression he'd seen on her face when talking about that elusive thing called romance. Suddenly he smiled.

"Bliss fits you."

She smiled and nodded. "You may call me that if you wish."

"Bliss it is," he said.

"Shall I continue to call you Dr. Ackerman?"

"Well, Miss Bliss, I mean, Bliss, I am quite a bit older than you and I am your professor. It's important that we maintain that relationship."

"Why?"

"Because…uh…comradery between teacher and pupil isn't wise."

"Why?"

"Miss Bliss…er Bliss, I…oh, never mind. It seems whenever we are at odds, logic escapes me. You may call me Sheldon in private, and I assure you in private only."

"Sheldon doesn't fit you."

Shocked, then annoyed he stated emphatically, "I consider Sheldon a very fitting name for myself."

"I admit that it's a very nice and dignified name, but it's humorless."

"Humorless, Miss Bliss?"

"Bliss," she reminded him.

"There are times when Miss Bliss fits you better…and now is one of them."

She smiled. He fumed.

Finally he asked, "And what would you call me, Miss Bliss, that is not humorless?"

"Dodds."

"Dodds?" he questioned, totally surprised. "That's not only my middle name—it's my mother's maiden name."

"It is? How much nicer then that I call you Dodds."

Sheldon had serious doubts about that, but said, "Suit yourself, then Miss...I mean Bliss." He shook his head. "This is all going to take some getting used to," he muttered.

"Now that we have that out of the way," Billie said brightly, "Where do we start tonight?"

"The first thing is to remind you that tomorrow night, Friday, we are meeting with the Committee at 7:00 at the Franklin lounge."

"Yes, I remember."

"And, uh, Bliss, you dress nicely so I can't tell if you've...uh...gained or lost. As you know," he said, feeling uncomfortable about bringing it up, "We are to be working on it."

"Of course we are. I have been walking every morning as Nettie suggested, and I have always eaten nutritiously. I learned that from my Mother."

"Have...have you lost weight?"

"Yes. One pound...but that's just a start toward getting to where I was before I binged out on my birthday cake."

"Oh," he said, looking disappointed.

"But, Nettie taught me that it isn't pounds we should worry about anyway. We're supposed to lose inches, and I'll let you know when it's best for you to know."

"Good," he said, relieved that the subject was out of the way. "Now," he began, putting his elbows on his knees and tapping his finger tips together in the gesture she was coming to know so well. "I've been doing some research."

"On what?"

He felt self conscious, "On...uh...romance."

Her eyes twinkling with amusement, she smiled. "How did you do that?"

"Listen, and I'll tell you." He related the story of Molly and Robert Bittle's courtship, watching her closely. He noticed that she reacted as he expected, her eyes, animated one minute, wistful the next. Then he repeated Hal and Sharon Ozog's and Nettie and Don Newman's courtships.

Billie clapped her hands and sighed. "How romantic!"

"I rest my case...Bliss," making a conscious effort to call her that. "There you are—romance is *not* dead."

Billie's face fell. "But that was *then,* it's not that way *now.*"

Sheldon felt frustrated and let down. "Well...don't you have friends your age who are married?" She nodded. "Have you asked them about their courtships?"

"Yes. And after hearing some, I don't want to hear the rest," she said, her face sad. "And just recently, a friend of mine got married and her story is even worse." The sadness turned into anguish so quickly, Sheldon jumped up.

"Please, don't get upset, Miss Bliss," he said, forgetting again, "I just can't believe there aren't modern courtships that are romantic....uh, I'm afraid I have to ask what makes it worse?"

Tears threatened, "I would be embarrassed to tell you. I couldn't, anymore than I could tell you about the movies. All I can say is, modern courtships are not enjoyable to listen to like the Bittles and the Ozogs and the Newmans."

Finding himself at first shocked then doubtful that things could really be this bad, he sat down on his heels before her and looked into her eyes, "Please, don't let yourself be upset, I will interview some young students of mine who are married. I'm sure I can show you that romance in this day and age is alive and well."

"You can?" she asked, wanting it to be so for his sake.

"Yes." Relieved that she looked hopeful, he stood up. "Now, before I go, what are we going to tell the group tomorrow night about...you know...your...uh problem?"

Chapter Sixteen

The telephone lines between Nettie Newman, Molly Bittle and Sharon Ozog were buzzing; the subject was 'what is going on with Sheldon Ackerman?' After all, it isn't every day that a thirty-eight-year-old bachelor feels compelled to interview three older women about their courtships.

~~~~~~~~~~

By the time Sheldon drove into the Franklin building parking lot, Friday evening, he was feeling very apprehensive. Miss…Bliss, he silently corrected himself, had told him not to worry, that she would think of something to say to the group. This, in and of itself, made him nervous. Aware of how confusing Bliss' account of things could be, he drew in a gulp of air and blew it out.

He was late; something he detested. A long distance business call had detained him. He pulled his long legs out of the car and moved rapidly toward the Franklin building. When he walked in, the group was all there, seated around the conference table, waiting for him. Stepping in quickly and taking his place, he looked around, consternation on his face.

"I apologize for being late."

Robert chuckled. "Thank you for that apology, Dr. Ackerman, we've never known you to be late before. It's nice to know that you're as human as the rest of us."

This seemed to amuse the rest of the group, but caused Sheldon to flush. He didn't know whether or not he appreciated this kind of humor in front of his students. What ribbing he'd taken before from the DeePees had been in private. Well, he reflected, he'd asked for it when he invited these three to participate in the project. He managed a brief smile and waited for their amusement to subside.

"Now that I've provided a good time for all of you," he said with a touch of asperity, "shall we begin the meeting?"

"I'm ready to take the minutes. Dr. Ackerman," Nettie said, smiling, her pen poised over a pad. It had been agreed that since Nettie knew shorthand from her secretarial days, she would take the minutes.

Sheldon welcomed them to the first of the formal group meetings of *Project Success.* He suggested that they begin with each of the girls reporting how they felt about the project so far. He called on Vickie Blume, Sandra Potter and Jane Bentley, in that order, suggesting the informality of remaining in their seats while doing so.

The committee sat back and listened while the girls expressed their gratitude for what was being done for them and how kind they'd been treated by their support counselors.

Sheldon was gratified by their remarks. He had not expected such positive results so soon and it immediately reinforced his hope for the project—which had been waxing and waning of late. It also eased his apprehension somewhat over what Billie Bliss might report.

"Miss Bliss, may we hear from you now?"

"I'm afraid that I'm the maverick of the group," she began, "I'm a hopeless case for *Project Success,* but Dr. Ackerman is the kindest and most caring man I have ever known." Her class mates stared at her wide-eyed, wondering if she was really talking about their professor. "He's determined...no, he's committed to proving that I'm not a hopeless case. He's willing to give the time no matter how long it takes, and is willing to do whatever it takes."

There was silence around the table, each waiting expectantly for her to go on.

"That's all I have to say." Billie concluded abruptly.

Nettie was disappointed. Billie hadn't divulged anything she could sink her teeth into. Instead, Billie had managed to make her more intrigued and curious over what was going on. In fact, everyone was curious, everyone, that is, except Sheldon. He was speechless. This was the second time Bliss had mentioned that he was kind and caring, but tonight she had said he was the kindest and most caring man she'd ever known! How could this be true, he wondered? But deep inside, it pleased him more than he cared to admit.

Realizing all eyes were upon him, waiting, he cleared his throat. "Thank you, girls, for your reports. Now, I would like Dr. Bittle, Mrs. Newman and Dr. Ozog to say a few words."

These three each expressed appreciation for the girl's comments, remarking that it was helpful to hear such encouraging feedback so early in the program.

Sheldon closed the meeting, thanking everyone for coming and participating and then encouraged the girls to continue striving toward their goals.

As everyone prepared to leave, Jane, Sandra and Vickie gathered around Billie, peppering her with questions, which she neatly sidestepped by promising details when there was a conclusion one way or another.

When the three interrogators left, Sheldon stepped over to Billie. "Miss Bliss, is Monday evening a good time for our next meeting?"

She thought about it, then said, "Yes. Shall we meet at my home again?"

"I'm wondering if that would be taking advantage of your family's kindness."

"You can say that after meeting my family?" she asked, smiling.

He smiled back. "I agree that they are a very interesting, warm and hospitable family, but…"

"There aren't any 'buts,' Dr. Ackerman. You might as well add 'curious' to those adjectives describing my family. They like to be in on everything that is happening to me."

Still smiling, he said, "All right then, 7:00 Monday at your home. And thank you. I enjoy your family. It's been a long time since I had one."

"Oh? Your parents aren't living?"

"No. My mother died ten years ago and my grieving father died a year later in a car accident. He was going downhill healthwise after my mother died anyway, so the accident just took him a little sooner."

"I'm so sorry; you really have had a lonely life."

He felt disconcerted. He hadn't thought his life so lonely. Yet, here she was, looking up at him with those large brown eyes filled with tender and compelling empathy for him.

~~~~~~~~~~

Saturday morning after planning his lectures for the 280 class next week and grading exam papers for his other class, he pulled out the telephone list of his colleagues at Fairfield College. He scanned through the list, writing down numbers of three married women colleagues he knew well enough to ask the names of their favorite romantic video movies. Normally, he might have asked Nettie, Molly or Sharon, but he hesitated to provide more fodder for their curiosity.

Feeling a little timid and apprehensive, he wondered how his female colleagues would react to his request. Nevertheless, he began phoning with pad and pen in hand. To his surprise and relief, none of the women indicated in any way that his request was odd or unusual.

After lunch, with the list of movies in hand, he drove to and entered a video rental store for the first time in his life. He looked around in amazement at all the videos. This had all happened right under his nose, and he'd been totally unaware. Feeling like the novice that he was, he walked around looking at the covers and titles. Once in a while there was a title that sounded familiar, probably from a commercial on the television seen when he was flipping to a news channel or to stock market reports.

Above the rows, he noticed, there were signs indicating the types of movies underneath. Finally, finding the sign that said ROMANCE, he looked at his list and began searching. Some of the covers were distasteful to him, but most of them weren't, which seemed hopeful. He found three of the movies on his list and chose two others that looked like they might be 'romantic'.

When the annoying procedure of acquiring a video card was all taken care of and he'd paid for them, he moved to the indicated pick up place near the door. He had just picked up all five videos and placed them under his arm when behind him he heard a female voice.

"Hello, Dr. Ackerman."

He was so startled, one of the videos dropped out from under his arm. He turned to see who had spoken, but was greeted only by the back of the head of a young woman picking it up. As she stood up, he saw that it was Vickie Blume! She was staring at the video, her eyes wide, her mouth open.

Sheldon Ackerman flushed furiously, totally embarrassed to have one of his students see him in here, let alone see the kind of videos he was renting! It hadn't entered his head that someone in one of his classes would see him. He'd been so amazed over the number of videos available, that he had been oblivious to anyone else in the store.

"Are you renting this for yourself, Dr. Ackerman?" Vickie Blume asked bluntly, wide-eyed curiosity on her face.

Even more embarrassed, he nodded as he took the video from her hand.

"Do you know anything about that video?" she asked. For some reason she didn't think so.

"I'm afraid I don't."

"I heard it was the steamiest movie yet."

He looked at it. It was one of the benign looking ones he himself had chosen. "Good Grief!" He dropped it back down where he'd picked it up.

"No, Dr. Ackerman, don't put it there, you won't get credit for returning it," she said, picking it up and thrusting it into his reluctant hand. Then picking up her own rented videos, she said, "Come, I'll show you where the night drop is."

They walked outside, and she pointed to it. He dropped it in as if it were a snake about to bite him.

"You haven't been to a video store for a long time have you, Dr. Ackerman?"

"Uh...no, I haven't, Miss Blume," he began, still feeling flustered. "But I want to remind you that you signed an agreement not to discuss anything outside of the group concerning the project."

Her eyes widened in shock again. "You rented these videos for the project?"

This usually very careful man, was horrified at his careless remark. His face felt hot. He couldn't believe he'd blurted out such information. "I know what this looks like, Miss Blume, but I assure you, it is not what it looks like."

"I believe you, Dr. Ackerman." She knew that if it had been anyone but Dr. Ackerman, she wouldn't believe it.

"Thank you, Miss Blume," he said with heartfelt relief. "I'll see you in class on Monday." With that, he hurried to his car and dropped the offending videos on the seat, got in and started the car.

Unknown to Sheldon, another pair of eyes had been watching him as he picked out and rented the videos—Miss Lora Lemmon. She now watched him through the window of the store. When both Dr. Ackerman and Vickie Blume had driven off, she walked out of the store, a sly smile on her face.

As Sheldon drove home, another unsettling thought came to him— he would now have to view these videos before taking them with him to meet with Bliss, Monday night.

The phone was ringing as he walked into his condominium. He rushed over, picked it up and learned there was a crisis in his holding company, one which he had to handle in person. He'd have to drive to Claytonville's small airport and take a commuter plane as soon as possible to Springfield, then catch a flight on a regular airline to St. Louis. He couldn't possibly get back until late Sunday night or early Monday morning.

Meanwhile, Vickie Blume was tickled. She had agreed not to discuss anything concerning *Project Success* with anyone outside the group...but she *could* talk to anyone in the group. And did she ever have a juicy tidbit to share with her fellow projectees!

Chapter Seventeen

Everyone in the 280 class Monday morning was looking at each other in astonishment. It was ten minutes after starting time, and their usually punctilious professor was not there. Billie was particularly concerned. This was not at all like Dodds.

Vickie Blume, Sandra Potter and Jane Bentley were throwing glances at each other, after which their eyes focused on Billie, then again at each other, smiling over the titillating news that Vickie had wasted no time in disseminating. Lora Lemmon, with the same tidbit of juicy knowledge, sat in her usual place near the front, smiling smugly.

Five minutes later, Dr. Ackerman breathlessly walked through the door and stood before them, his tie off center, his suit rumpled. The class stared at the unusual spectacle, wondering with curiosity what could have happened to cause this meticulously neat man to come to class in this condition.

Pulling his glasses from his pocket Dr. Ackerman studied the surprised faces before him. "I apologize for being late. It's regrettable that time has been wasted." And without offering any further explanation, he launched into his lecture.

~~~~~~~~~~

The rest of the day proved to be so full Sheldon didn't have time to preview the videos he'd rented. He'd had several counseling sessions with students and a faculty meeting which ran him so late into the evening, he couldn't fix himself more than a sandwich before showering and getting ready for his meeting with Bliss.

When he was ready, he eyed the videos. Without them he had nothing to show Bliss, no reason for the meeting. Feeling apprehensive about showing them to Bliss before he had seen them himself, he decided to ask *her*. Together they would decide whether or not to view them. Placing them in his brief case, he left.

Standing on the Bliss porch feeling off kilter after his hectic weekend, he wondered what kind of an evening was ahead of him. He took a deep breath and pushed the doorbell.

Margaret Bliss answered the door. "Good evening, Sheldon," she said smiling. "Come in. It's nice to see you."

"Thank you, Margaret," he said, feeling more relaxed after being greeted by this gracious and serene woman.

She led him into the front room and invited him to sit down. "When you and Billie are through with your meeting tonight, Sheldon, we have some blueberry pie and ice cream for you both."

"And Mother is famous for her blueberry pie," stated Billie as she entered.

"Sounds good, Margaret, thank you." He watched Margaret walk away, straight shouldered and dignified.

"Good evening, Dodds," Billie said, grinning. "You still look as if your weekend was less than orderly."

"I do?" he asked, surprised at her intuitiveness.

"You do."

"It's probably because I don't know how prepared I am tonight. I have some videos in my briefcase, uh...some romances that several women colleagues of mine said were, and I quote: 'Wonderful romances.'"

Billie's eyes widened with surprise. "It sounds like you are prepared."

"But I didn't get to preview them, so I'm nervous about showing them."

Billie smiled at the thought of her professor previewing romances. He was certainly going the extra mile. "Let me see them, maybe I can help."

He reluctantly opened his briefcase and pulled out all four and handed her one. Shaking her head sadly, she handed it back to him. The next one he handed to her, was one of the two he'd chosen on his own. He held his breath and watched her expressive face.

She blinked as she looked at the video. "Someone recommended this?" she asked, shocked.

"No, I chose it myself because the cover and name sounded nice and uh...harmless," he replied miserably. He took it from her and shoved it back into the briefcase. He picked up the third one, but just held it in his hand as he showed it to her. She frowned sadly and shook her head. More miserable than ever, he picked up the last one.

Her expression changed. "I don't know anything about this one."

"One of my colleagues said it was her favorite romantic movie of all time," he said tentatively, afraid to hope that it was any better than the others.

Billie leaned over and put her hand upon his bare forearm. "Don't be so concerned, Dodds. If this one isn't a good one, we'll soon know and we can turn it off." She smiled. "I appreciate your efforts to find one for me."

The touch of her hand was soothing, and he relaxed. "Thank you," he breathed. "I guess we might as well get it over with. Let's go look at it."

Sheldon was amazed that they hadn't run into Matilda or any other member of the family as they walked down the hall to the television room.

Billie turned on the television and VCR and shoved the video in. She sat down in the chair and Sheldon walked to the couch, but just stood there tensely staring at the screen.

"Please be seated, Dodds, and try to relax," Billie said, her eyes filled with amusement. "I have the control in my hand. I'll turn it off the minute you say."

"Oh, yes, thank you," he said sitting down stiffly.

The title of the movie appeared, listing the names of the popular and well-known stars. The movie began. Beautiful music came from the speakers and exotic scenery filled the screen. Sheldon began to relax a little, allowing himself to enjoy what promised to be a good movie. Fifteen minutes later, the leading man and leading lady, having met just five minutes before, began to get a little affectionate. The woman gave the man a suggestive look and the man immediately grabbed her and kissed her—no, Sheldon thought, that wasn't a kiss! Revulsion swept over him. He jumped up.

"Turn it off!"

Billie turned it off.

"Good grief, Bliss! What were they doing? Trying to swab each other's tonsils?"

Her anguished expression turned to one of amusement and she giggled. "I'm sure that's what they were doing, Dodds. They certainly were *not kissing!*"

Sheldon paced around the room, anger building up in him. "Why...why there was no drama in that fifteen minutes. No building up of the relationship, no suspense, just meeting and then the woman throwing herself at him in an aggressive manner and the man simply responding to her sexual aggression."

Billie's eyes followed the pacing man. "What if..." she began hesitantly, "in this movie they had built up the suspense of their relationship, would you like it any better?"

"No! They couldn't build it up enough for me to like it."

She sighed in relief. "Then they stole your emotions, too?"

He stopped pacing long enough to ask, "Stole my emotions? What do you mean?"

"You know when you're watching a romantic movie where the man and woman get to know each other, and the suspense of their love grows and finally culminates in—a *real kiss,* and then how your emotions soar with it, making you feel the joy of their love?" She sighed, staring into space, a dreamy expression in her eyes. "You know, all that emotion you feel at that time?" She looked over at him, expectantly, but could see by his blank expression that he didn't understand, so trying to explain further, she went on, "You see, Dodds, like you said, in this movie, there was no time to build up emotion, but even if there had been time, what they did, killed my emotion. Didn't they kill yours, too?"

Sheldon tried to understand, wanting to understand, but he knew it was apparent to her that he didn't. "I had plenty of emotion, Bliss. It was disgust and anger. But...somehow I don't think that's what you meant. It has been a long time since I've seen what you would call a romantic movie. In fact, I'm not sure what a romantic movie is. But one thing I can say for certain, this movie," he pointed his finger vigorously at the VCR, "is not one!" He began pacing again, then some minutes later he said, "So far it appears, and mind you, I said it only appears that you're right—that romance is dead." In three steps he was over at the VCR ejecting the video, then walking to the couch, he sat down, opened his briefcase, grabbed the cover, shoved the video in and threw it back into the briefcase.

Anger compelled him to tell her more, "I also rented another movie that looked benign." He told her the name of it. "Do you know anything about it?"

She was shocked. "I've heard about it. Where is it?"

Someone told me what it was, so I shoved it in the night drop."

"But...but you didn't know, Dodds."

"No, I didn't know what has been happening right under my nose. I've been burying my head in the sand for years!" He jumped up and began pacing again. "I can't believe what has happened to society." His dark brows furrowed as his discomfort mounted.

He stopped suddenly, picked up the briefcase in his left hand and grabbed Billie's hand with his right. "Come, Bliss, I feel the need of a big piece of berry pie a la mode." Dropping his briefcase long enough to open the door, still holding tightly to Billie's hand, he walked rapidly down the hall, dragging her along with him.

No one was in the kitchen, but on the kitchen counter was the waiting pie. Sheldon let go of Billie's hand and plunked himself down at the table, while a dazed Billie got some plates and forks out.

"How big a piece, Dodds?"

"Big!"

She obediently cut a large piece for him and a small piece for herself. Opening the freezer and pulling out the ice cream, she then scooped out several large hunks for Dodds and a small one for herself.

"Thank you," he mumbled, still frowning morosely as she placed the large concoction before him. He began eating automatically, staring at some invisible spot in the middle of the table.

Henry, who knew the pair had been watching another video, ambled into the kitchen expecting to see the usual scene. He stopped short, staring at the unexpected sight before him. Billie, a serene expression upon her face, was taking small mincing bites from a very small piece of pie, while Sheldon was glowering and wolfing down a large piece.

"What happened to the 'odd couple?' Looks to me like you two decided to switch places."

"Uh...what?" Sheldon asked, trying to break out of his dejection.

Henry perversely pleased, repeated the question.

Sheldon was puzzled, "What do you mean, Henry?"

Henry gave him a sardonic smile while pointing to Sheldon's plate and then to Billie's. Sheldon looked at Billie's small partially eaten pie, surprised, then looked up into her tranquil face. He was totally amazed. Where were the tears and grief that were so evident last time? *He* was the one who was agitated, she was the composed one. They *had* switched roles! All he could do was stare at Billie questioningly.

"Are you both wondering why I'm not in tears?"

Both men nodded.

"Because," she smiled affectionately at her professor, "Dodds took my 'hot potato' and right now, at least, he's juggling it for me."

A slow smile spread across Sheldon's face. "I...guess I am." He studied her in wonder. "Maybe we have the answer here."

"I wish it were that simple," sighed Billie. "Besides, even if it were that simple, I'm afraid that before long, you'd get very tired of juggling."

Her statement brought an idea to Sheldon's mind, an idea that might prove worth acting upon. It was perfectly obvious what Bliss needed. It was a husband to carry her 'hot potato!'

He finished his pie in silence, noticing for the first time how good it was. "Excellent pie, excellent."

"It is at that," Henry said, walking over to the counter and cutting himself another piece.

The three ate in silence. When Sheldon finished, he stood up abruptly. "If you two will excuse me, I'll be going. Nice to see you, Henry."

Before Henry could swallow his mouthful of pie, Sheldon was out of the kitchen with Billie running after him. As they reached the front door, he turned to his charge who, he knew, had followed him.

"Bliss?"

"Yes, Dodds?" she said, looking up at him.

He noticed, with some disquiet, how expressive and warm her large brown eyes were. "Uh...would you allow me to juggle your 'hot potato' for a while longer?"

"You really want to do this for me?"

"I do."

"Thank you," she said, smiling.

Her smile, Sheldon noted, was the most winsome smile he'd ever seen on a young woman.

Chapter Eighteen

Ever since Saturday, Vickie Blume had been bursting with curiosity and speculation over the possible relationship and activities going on between Billie Bliss and their handsome professor. Finally, Vickie spilled the news to Nettie Newman Tuesday afternoon during their meeting. Vickie could tell that Nettie was shocked, even though she tried to hide it.

"This is most unusual, Vickie," Nettie said, trying to sound casual.

"It certainly isn't like Dr. Ackerman is it?" she giggled.

"Not at all. However, I'm sure there's a good reason for it, but I do hope you'll keep this to yourself, Vickie. Remember, you signed an agreement not to divulge any information about the Project to anyone so that other girls can participate in a later extension of it."

"I remember, but" she confessed, "I did tell Sandy and Jane. But they promised not to tell anyone."

"Oh? Well then I need to call and remind them of their promise," she said, as if it were of no real consequence.

After her meeting with Vickie, Nettie could hardly hold herself back from calling the Bittles and the Ozogs. Why would Sheldon rent those kind of videos for the project? She asked herself. Whatever could be going on with him and Billie? Reluctantly, she decided not to pursue it—for now anyway, and wait and see. After all, she knew Sheldon well enough to know that everything was on the up and up. It was, wasn't it?

~~~~~~~~~~~

Lora Lemmon drove her old blue 1972 Volkswagon toward the west side of Claytonville, pulled into the parking lot of Phillip's Pharmacy and parked. It was the first of August and the hot muggy air was smothering, sapping her energy as she shuffled into the building and up to the pharmacy counter.

"May I help you?" the pharmacist asked.

"Do you have two prescriptions for Ella Lemmon?"

He turned and searched through the already filled prescriptions and brought two over to her. "That will be $43.95."

Lora, feeling resentment toward her mother, searched through her purse and pulled out a worn looking wallet. Withdrawing forty-five dollars she handed it to him. She received the change, put it into her wallet and took the white sack from him, retreating to her car, feeling even more tired.

The resentment still broiling inside her, she drove six blocks and turned into the graveled driveway of her home. She remained in the car thinking, remembering how her mother, rummaging through her dresser drawers, had found the two hundred dollars that Dr. Ackerman's benefactor had donated to each of the students of the 280 class who had filled out the form. Her mother had tearfully accosted her and accused her of attempting to hide this windfall, complaining that she needed more medicine.

Lora was twenty-five years old and feeling desperate to leave home. The two hundred dollars would have helped toward the goal of living in her own apartment, away from her mother. For two years now, she'd been a part time student at Fairfield College while working at a fast food place almost full time. Lately, she had to support both herself and her mother.

She studied the small, dilapidated, wood-clad house in front of her with its side-gabled roof, narrow windows and small covered entry porch. It needed paint and a new roof. The yard, with its overgrown lawn, several spindly rose bushes and two overgrown hickory trees, needed tending and watering. Self-pity almost choked her as she thought of Billie Bliss' big beautiful home.

"It isn't fair," she mumbled. "It just isn't fair!"

She opened the door and got out. Her legs felt weighted down as she walked to the front porch. She knew, before she opened the door, where her mother would be. She was right. The soft, flabby hulk of Ella Lemmon was half reclining on the couch watching some soap operas she'd taped previously, so she could sleep in.

Like others who hid from life, Ella Lemmon kept the blinds perpetually drawn. Prescriptions and over-the-counter medicines cluttered the lamp table. The small coffee table in front of the couch, was crowded with the remains of snacks and meals from several days.

Engrossed in the television, Ella Lemmon didn't hear her daughter enter the house, and it wasn't until Lora shoved the white sack under her nose that she became aware.

"What took you so long, Lora?" she whined, "I needed these prescriptions."

"It was the best I could do, Ma. "Turning abruptly, she went toward the kitchen just off the front room. She stopped at the door and groaned at the sight of dirty dishes everywhere.

"Ma! You promised you'd clean up the kitchen if I bought you those prescriptions."

"I will, Lora, I will. It's just that I've had another migraine today."

Lora bit her tongue to keep from lashing out at her mother, whose aches and pains seemed to come and go conveniently. Deciding to eat at work and let her mother fend for herself in this filthy kitchen, she went into the bedroom, and lay down on the bed. She desperately needed a nap before going to work, but her mind wouldn't let her. Ever since Saturday, she couldn't quit thinking about Dr. Ackerman. In her mind, he was the last person in the world who would rent those kind of videos. Yet he had!

As she lay there, her thoughts went back to the day she signed up for Dr. Ackerman's class. She'd hit bottom. Her hopes of ever pulling herself up and out of the mire were dashed when her mother informed her the day before, that she probably would never be able to go back to work.

From the very first day of class, Lora noticed Billie Bliss. She noticed with envy how beautiful she was. Her hair was thick and glossy, unlike her own stringy, mousy hair. The only thing that made her feel better was—Billie Bliss was a little overweight, too. However, it wasn't long before she noticed that Billie apparently had the money to buy beautiful clothes with which to hide it. This was the last straw. Her hopelessness turned into overwhelming pessimism. When Billie was chosen as one of the four girls to participate in the project, the envy turned into something Lora had never felt before, jealousy.

One day, on impulse, she followed Billie home. She was living where she herself wanted to—in a nice little apartment. She wanted to see inside, so she parked the car, walked around to the back and knocked on the door on the pretext of asking her if she knew of another apartment like this one.

Lora hadn't expected Billie to be so nice. It mitigated the jealously somewhat, but not for long, however, for Billie invited her in and Lora saw that her apartment was just the kind she herself wanted, and decorated just as she would decorate if she had the money. It wasn't fair! She also learned that day, that Billie's parents lived only three blocks from her apartment at 303 Maple Ave. Right after she left Billie's place, she drove past the Bliss home. It took her breath away. It was a beautiful old home three stories high. The yard was beautifully landscaped and kept—no doubt they had a gardener. Why did Dr. Ackerman choose Billie? she thought bitterly; she didn't need the money!

All of a sudden, a thought struck her. Could those videos Dr. Ackerman rented have anything to do with Billie? She had learned from Vickie Blume that he was the one who was counseling Billie. The idea was tantalizing. If by any chance it was true, what could she do with the information? What should she do? At the moment, she didn't know, but, she mused, this kind of juicy information might come in handy some time.

Wednesday after class, Billie knocked on Dr. Ackerman's office door. She could see him through the blinds, his head studiously bent over something as he yelled, "Come in."

Billie opened the door and stepped in. "Good morning, Dr. Ackerman."

He looked up. "Bliss!" he exclaimed, his face lighting up."I mean, Miss Bliss," he corrected himself and grinned. "It's nice of you to drop in." For some reason her presence brought to his mind snatches from the poem *"Pippa Passes"* by Robert Browning: "Pippa passes…God's in his heaven—All's right with the world!"

Greatly pleased at his reaction, Billie said, "It's nice to drop in, Dr. Ackerman. How are your arms?"

He looked puzzled. "My arms?"

"Are they sore from juggling?"

"Oh." He chuckled. "Not a bit sore. I'm very muscular and strong you see."

Billie giggled. "I'm glad of that. My arms needed a rest. I came in to invite you to my home tonight or tomorrow night to see one or two of my collection of romantic movies, so that you can learn what a romantic movie is."

"Oh?" He smiled. "That sounds like a logical and sensible thing to do at this time. I do need to refresh my memory on the subject. I think that it had better be tonight because I have several appointments tomorrow evening here in my office concerning the issue…of…uh romance."

She blinked, "You do? I appreciate all the work you're going to Dodds…I mean Dr. Ackerman," she corrected herself, remembering they were here at school. "Can you tell me any more? As you might guess, I'm very curious about it."

He smiled, "Not yet…maybe later."

She pouted a moment, then asked him what time he'd like to come over. They both decided that the usual time of seven o'clock was convenient for both of them.

~~~~~~~~~~

Lora Lemmon's life all of a sudden changed from drab and depressing to exciting. She had an agenda. She decided to follow both Billie and Dr. Ackerman as much as she could. After all, she convinced herself, she had to protect the reputation of Fairfield University didn't she? She even decided that if she had to cut her work hours to do so, she would. Was it a coincidence that her energy returned? she wondered.

Tonight, Wednesday, was her night off. At 5:00 o'clock she grabbed a sandwich from home, leaving her mother complaining about how thoughtless she was to leave her alone on the one night she could stay home and keep her company. With an armful of studies, she got into the car and drove close to Billie's apartment, parking where she could see anyone coming or going. Soon, she found out that her intention to study while sleuthing didn't work. She couldn't seem to concentrate on both at the same time—probably because one was so much more interesting than the other.

At six forty-five, she saw Billie's car back out of the driveway and turn left. She followed at a safe distance, feeling what she thought must be the excitement a private investigator feels. Maybe she should become one, she mused, a smile on her face.

Disappointed that Billie's destination turned out to be her parents home, Lora decided, nevertheless, to park up the block and wait for a few minutes. About three minutes to seven, a car drove into the Bliss driveway. Dr. Ackerman got out! Now, she knew his car. Her excitement soon fizzled, however, realizing that it all looked very proper. Now what was she going to do? Still keyed-up, she couldn't face going home so soon. Telling herself that this was just the life of a PI and that something was bound to turn up, she decided to go to a movie.

Chapter Nineteen

Billie seated herself on the couch where Sheldon usually sat, so he went for the chair.

"No, Dodds, sit here," she patted a spot on the couch beside her. "We both can see the television better from here."

He felt nervous about sitting next to her. "Uh…do you think that's appropriate, Bliss?" he asked, hoping she would agree that it wasn't.

"Of course it is. And besides, I trust you to act appropriately at all times."

"All right," he said sitting down stiffly beside her.

"Relax, Dodds, I promise I won't bite," she said grinning at him.

He didn't really know how he could relax, but he sat back and tried anyway. A knock came at the door.

"Come in," Billie said.

Matilda appeared in the doorway and smiled. "Hello, Sheldon, how are you?"

"I'm fine Matilda, it's good to see you."

"Since you two are going to watch a movie, I came to see if you would like some popcorn?"

"Oh, Aunt Tilly, how nice of you. I would like some, would you, Dodds?"

He noted that Billie's eyes were as excited as a little child's. In fact, he found himself looking forward to eating popcorn while watching the movie. "Yes, I would like some, Matilda. Thank you."

Billie turned to him. "Which movie do you want to see, *Jane Eyre* or *It Happened One Night*?"

"I can't remember either one very well, you choose."

"All right, I choose…*It Happened One Night*, starring Clark Gable and Claudette Colbert," she said jumping up and putting it into the VCR. With the control in her hand, she sat down beside him, smiling. "Shall we wait for the popcorn or start?" It turned out to be a moot question, as Matilda appeared at the door carrying a tray of popcorn and two mugs of cold root beer.

"However did you do that so fast, Aunt Tilly?" Billie asked.

She smiled. "I already had it popped."

Sheldon chuckled. "I don't think we could manage without you, Matilda."

"Now don't try to butter me up, Sheldon," she said, "there's enough on the popcorn." Smiling happily, she placed the tray on the small coffee table in front of them. "Have a good time. I'm glad that you're watching one of Billie's favorites instead of one of those others."

"Me too, Matilda," he said, nodding vigorously.

After her aunt left, Billie curled up on the couch and turned on the television and VCR.

The movie captured Sheldon's interest immediately, but he was intensely aware of Billie's presence next to him. Soon, however, he began to feel at ease. The popcorn and root beer tasted good, bringing nostalgic memories of his mom, dad and himself all three munching on popcorn and drinking pop while enjoying a movie together.

Billie giggled over a scene. She looked over at Sheldon and together they enjoyed the humor of it. The professor had to remind himself that he was here not just to enjoy it, but to understand the young woman next to him, and understand the subtle essence of romance—which was so important to her.

The movie was familiar to Sheldon, but it had been so long since he'd seen it, it was like seeing it for the first time. When the unmarried couple had to stay in a motel room together because of lack of funds, he found himself intensely intrigued with the morality and honor of the leading man, played by Clark Gable, and with the cleverness of his solution to their problem. How refreshing after those other videos he and Bliss had momentarily watched!

As the movie ended, they turned towards each other and Billie sighed, "It was over just too quickly, Dodds."

"I enjoyed it very much, Bliss, thank you for the invitation."

She looked at her watch. "It's too late to watch *Jane Eyre* now," she said, disappointed, "but maybe another time?"

"Yes," he smiled, "another time. But I'm a little confused, Bliss, you mentioned emotions culminating in a kiss—there wasn't a kiss in this movie."

"I know," she replied in a small breathy voice, "but it seemed like it. And it certainly didn't make it any less romantic, did it?"

Sheldon couldn't help smiling. They both sat there silent, engrossed in their own thoughts for several moments, then Sheldon rose abruptly.

"Well, it's time for me to leave so that you may get home, Bliss or are you staying here tonight?"

"I need to go to my apartment. If I start staying overnight, my family will begin asking me to stay another night and another until I'd find myself living here again."

They walked slowly toward the front door and out onto the front porch. The warm August evening, lit by a full moon, was filled with the pungent scent of roses.

"I love summer, Dodds, it in itself is romantic to me. But then," she added thoughtfully, "so is fall with its kaleidoscope colors and feeling of excitement for the new season, and wintery nights when large snowflakes fall lightly and the night is still and shimmering white."

"In other words all year round, around the clock, you find romance—so don't let it go, Bliss, hang on to it—and to hope." He curled his forefinger under her chin, lifting her face to his, he studied her a moment, his eyes, warm and appreciative, twinkled with delight. "How can romance be dead if it's alive in you? Good night, Bliss." With that he briskly descended the steps, crossed the short distance to his car. He waved at her and got in.

Billie watched him drive away, leaving her feeling a little lonely after such a fulfilling evening. Her professor was trying so hard to understand her and her needs. At the moment, however, it was difficult to think of him as her professor, even though he was just working on the Project. He'd become more than that, he had become her friend.

Driving home, Sheldon offered congratulations to himself. He'd been right. What Bliss needed was a husband!

When he entered his condominium, the palpable emptiness of it surrounded him like a cold whirling eddy. In the past when that feeling came, he just buried himself in work and making money. But here he was, his fortune made and he was teaching. What could he do to fill his mind and energies now? He was a focused man, used to getting done what needed to be done at the moment, with the ability to totally immerse himself in the issue at hand. His focus now was the Project—four human beings, helping them achieve their goals. His particular responsibility was one of those four—Bliss—but it wasn't the same as making money; he couldn't shake and move and make things happen as he could in the business world. He was in alien territory. Hal Ozog's words came to mind: "You manage your life better than all three of us. But—you see, in addition to our professions, we have a spouse, children and like me, grandchildren who are all added to the equation, and they really can't be *managed.*" Amen! he said to himself. He felt like a fish out of water, trying to swim on dry ground.

His mind and energies already focused on Bliss, he admitted to himself, somewhat uncomfortably, that his desire to help her had intensified to the point of excitement rivaling that which he usually felt when closing a business deal. Now that he was at this fever pitch, what was he to do?

He found himself staring out the window at the twinkling lights of Claytonville, each set of lights encompassing a family. An emotion came over him that he had, consciously at least, fended off through the years—loneliness. He shook his head. It must have been the movie, the popcorn, the nostalgia of it all.

Wishing he could talk to his mother, he walked over to the bookcase and browsed through some of her books. His mother, a feminine, gentle woman with blue eyes and dark hair, was a reader. Many times after school, he found her sitting by the window, a book in her hand. One day in particular came to his mind.

"Read it out loud to me, Mama," he remembered saying to her after coming home from school and finding her in the familiar setting. He was nine years old and had been read to by his mother ever since he could remember. She began reading.

"That's a poem about mushy love," he had exclaimed in disgust. "Never mind, Mom, I'm going out to play."

He realized for the first time that many of her books were poetry books. He remembered seeing these in her hand most often. He pulled out an old book of poetry by Lord Byron, went over to his favorite chair, opened the book gingerly and began reading.

"She walks in beauty, like the night
  Of cloudless climes and starry skies;
And all that's best of dark and bright
  Meet in her aspect and her eyes...."

Chapter Twenty

Thursday afternoon, Sheldon greeted the young man who walked into his office, shaking his hand across the desk. "It's good to see you Sherman. Have a seat."

"It's good to see you, Dr. Ackerman. I'm glad you called me in to visit, because this is my last semester here. I'm going to get my doctorate later since my girlfriend, Gail, and I are going to bum around the beaches in California for a while."

"Your girlfriend? I...I thought you two were married."

"Naw, we want to wait a year or two."

"But...didn't you live in an apartment together?"

"Sure did," he grinned. Noticing the shock on the professor's face, it was his turn to react. "Don't tell me you're prudish about that? This is the new millennium, Doc, remember?"

"Yes...I remember," he answered slowly.

Arranging for three of his most promising *married* students from last winter to come in for a visit, he planned to casually ask about their courtships. This was one of the ideas that had come to him. Now, he cut the visit short, asking only a few questions and wishing Sherman well. He was deeply disappointed over the young man's lack of ambition and lack of commitment.

Feeling more than irritated, his mood was a little testy when Evan came in. After the greetings were over, Sheldon asked him in an abrupt manner about his studies and goals. The young man, disconcerted by the professor's unusual behavior, stumbled all over himself, assuring Dr. Ackerman that he was determined to get his masters in business and that he would be taking classes from him next year.

"Good. Now how is your wife?"

"My wife?" he asked surprised.

"That's what I said."

"We're divorced. It didn't take us long to learn we weren't suited for each other."

"Tell me about your courtship—maybe it should have lasted longer so you could get to know each other better."

"Well, I don't know if you would call it a courtship or not. We'd gone to a couple of movies together, then I found her in my bed one night—so in a week or so we decided to get married."

Sheldon bit his tongue. After all, it wasn't his place to lecture or censure. Instead, he muttered some encouragement and excused him.

He waited for his next and last appointment, tapping his fingers together, frowning, seeing in his mind's eye the mounting evidence in favor of Bliss' conclusion about romance. By the time Morris arrived, he was feeling angry about the whole thing—Project and all!

"I know I'm early, Dr. Ackerman, but…"

Sheldon looked up. "Sit down, Morris. No matter," he snapped.

"Is anything wrong, Dr. Ackerman?"

"Yes, there's a great deal wrong."

"Shall I come back another time?"

Sheldon realized he was taking out his frustration on the young man in front of him. "No, now is fine. I'm sorry for being short, Morris. How are you?" After a few more questions and answers, he asked him about his wife.

The young man smiled. "She's fine. We're going to have a baby."

Sheldon felt some relief. "Congratulations." After the discussion about Morris' coming fatherhood and his career, he led into questions about his courtship.

Morris told how he and his wife met and how they got to know each other. Sheldon smiled. He felt that it might sound romantic to Bliss. At least, one out of three says something, he thought to himself—then the thunderbolt came.

"And when she found she was pregnant," Morris continued, "we decided we better get married. I'm glad we did, because after a couple of months of marriage, we both realized we loved each other."

Sheldon paled.

"Dr. Ackerman, you don't look well at all. Maybe I'd better come back another time."

"Thank you Morris, another time would be better."

Sheldon sat at his desk a long time after Morris had gone, stunned and shaken, the burden of proof laying heavier on his shoulders.

Finally, he wondered if he needed to ask ten students, rather than just three. Maybe the odds would be better. But he knew he didn't have the stomach for it. If these young men were typical of what Bliss could expect as potential husband material, it was no wonder she felt romance was dead! Maybe there wasn't anyone out there good enough for her.

His gloom deepened when he remembered the Project meeting tomorrow night. Bliss could not report any success. He was feeling less hopeful she ever could, with his help anyway. He got up from the desk and paced around the small room trying to deal with these unsettling thoughts. Why did Nettie, Hal and Robert insist that he be the one to support Bliss? But...could he do any better with any one of the other three? No. He should have gotten a fourth person to take his place and not be personally involved! How did he ever think he could do it, a bachelor of many years with no real life experience?

Commitment or no, he needed to get someone else to take his place with Bliss. He decided to go see her immediately and tell her so. Conscious that this was an impulsive reaction, he stuck by the decision anyway. What did it matter? He hadn't been himself since the day Miss Billie Bliss first stepped into his office!

Grabbing his suit coat, throwing it over his arm, he headed for the door, then stopped. He didn't know where she lived. Going back to the desk, he looked through his records and found the address of her apartment, assuring himself that it didn't matter whether it looked proper or not. He was quitting! He locked up the office and strode briskly down the hall. Hearing a quick shuffling sound behind him, he turned. It was Miss Lemmon.

"Good evening, Miss Lemmon." Glancing at his watch, he saw that it was 5:00. "Do you have a class this late?"

Lora, breathless and flustered, stared at him, trying to think of an explanation as to why she was there at this hour. "Uh...no, I just...needed to check on something," she replied lamely.

"Oh...well, goodnight then, Miss Lemmon."

"Good night, Dr. Ackerman."

He resumed his brisk walk toward the exit. When almost to the door, he heard heavy breathing behind him. He turned and once more saw the flushed face of Lora Lemmon. "What is it, Miss Lemmon, are you late for something?"

"I uh…no," she said, shifting the heavy back pack to the other shoulder, "I just want to uh…get home."

"Oh. Well, goodnight again, see you in class tomorrow." He stepped quickly to his car which was parked conveniently close in faculty parking.

Lora trotted as fast as she could to the other side of the parking lot where her car was parked, the back pack bouncing uncomfortably against her hip. She felt irritated at herself for not remaining in the car to wait for Dr. Ackerman! Unlocking the car, she dropped her pack into the seat and heaved her tired body in behind the wheel. Starting the car, she shoved the stick shift into reverse, backed out, then shoving it into gear the car lurched forward past the parked cars. She was so intent on catching up with Dr. Ackerman she was unaware of another car in the adjoining exit. Making a sharp left turn heading toward the south exit, she suddenly slammed on the brakes. The other car having made a right turn leading to the same exit, loomed directly in front of her. It was too late. Despite the simultaneous screeching of brakes, their front bumpers hit. Both drivers sat there momentarily stunned, then the driver of the five year old Buick Le Sabre, got out to inspect the damage. Lora was horrified. It was Dr. Ackerman!

"Oh no!" she gasped. She got out and looked at the bumpers.

Sheldon looked over at the other driver. "I don't see," he began, then stopped. "Miss Lemmon!" They stared at each other. He blinked a couple of times…"Didn't I just see you back at the…"

"Yes," she mumbled.

"How did you get here so fast?" .

She shrugged her shoulders miserably.

"And why were you driving so fast?" he asked irately.

"I…uh…I didn't realize how uh…fast I was going."

Sheldon sucked in a deep breath…letting it out slowly, trying to calm his rising impatience. "You should be more careful, Miss Lemmon. You are fortunate that my brakes are good as well as my reflexes because I can't see any damage to either of our cars."

"I'm certainly glad to hear that, Dr. Ackerman," she breathed out, greatly relieved.

"Well, as I said twice before, I bid you good night." He got back into the car, backed up, drove around the Volkswagon, and exited the lot.

Lora got into her car as quickly as she could. "Darn! Now he knows my car. How stupid of me," she chastised herself loudly. "Oh well," she said with grim determination, "I'll just have to be more careful."

Sheldon shook his head over the strange coincidence; running into Miss Lemmon three times and, literally—on the third. Soon, however, his mind became engrossed with the matter at hand until he glanced into the rear view mirror just before turning a corner. Had he seen a blue Volkswagon? No. He mentally shook himself and dismissed the thought.

Finding Bliss's street just off the campus, he stopped in front of the appropriate house, trying to figure out where the apartment was. He noticed Bliss's car parked in back in plain view of the street. Parking against the curb, he crossed the street. Quelling a feeling of trepidation, he walked down the driveway to the back of the house. Seeing Bliss's apartment number above a small porch, he stepped up onto it and knocked. The door opened. Startled, Billie gaped at him.

"Why...Dodds! This is a surprise."

"I need to talk to you, and it can't wait."

"Oh? Would you like to come in?" she asked hesitantly.

"Yes, I would," he stated resolutely, stepping inside.

As Billie closed the door behind him, he looked around. "A charming place...looks like you," he muttered glumly.

"Please have a seat, Dodds."

"Thank you." Even in his dour mood, his nose detected something cooking that smelled very good.

The phone rang. "Will you excuse me, Dodds?"

"All right," he said, feeling irritated at the interruption.

"Hello?....Oh, hello, Jordan....I have to go, I have a guest....no....no it isn't....no I have plans for this weekend....please Jordan, I do have to go....I'll talk to you later....goodbye Jordan." She hung up abruptly and smiled at her guest.

"I'm so glad you dropped by. I want to tell you how well I'm doing with my weight...I mean inches. Just having you try to understand my feelings about everything has helped me so much."

"It has?" Though surprised and more than pleased at this news, he was acutely aware of the purpose of his visit. Determined not to be deterred, he said, "However...I..."

"Oh, please excuse me," I have to get my scalloped potatoes out of the oven."

Sheldon watched her open the oven and pull out the casserole dish and place it on top of the stove. She was wearing a large white T shirt and cut off jeans. Her hair was pulled up into a pony tail, making her look like a little girl. Sheldon realized, with some disquiet, that no matter what she wore or how she wore her hair, she looked—lovely.

"Would you do me a favor, Dodds?" she asked, smiling one of those special Bliss smiles, as he was beginning to think of them.

"What is it?" he asked, wariness in his voice.

"Have dinner with me. I've made plenty, because I like leftovers."

"I don't think that would be wise, Bliss."

"Why? The wise thing is not to be here at all, but since you are here, please stay. I owe you so much—and besides, I like your company," she said, softly, her brown eyes entreating.

All of a sudden, Sheldon felt like his spine was made of putty. He couldn't think of an appropriate rebuttal to the invitation and what's more, he realized—he didn't want to. "All right, thank you. It smells so good, I'm afraid I can't resist."

Before long, they were seated together at the small table, enjoying a meal of filet of sole, scalloped potatoes and coleslaw. He helped himself to a slice of whole grain bread and buttered it.

"This is a delicious meal, Bliss."

"Thank you," she smiled. "It's so nice to have someone to eat with for a change."

"You certainly eat well."

Billie sighed, a wistful expression replacing the smile. "Oh, but it's so hard to cook and eat well when it's only me I'm cooking for. That's why I make a lot, so I can eat leftovers."

"Now, you won't have leftovers. I would like to make it up to you by taking you out to dinner at the Maple Woods Country..." He stopped, his fork in mid-air, shocked at what had just come out of his mouth. Noticing Bliss gazing at him wide eyed, apparently in shock herself, he smiled nervously, feeling foolish. "Sorry. I mean, it would be nice to be able to take you to dinner to make up for my eating up what would be leftovers for you," he finished lamely.

Billie's laugh sounded musical. "Thank you, Dodds. It's very nice of you to want to take me to the country club for dinner. I hear the food is delicious there."

They continued eating, while exchanging pleasant conversation about the class, the university and her family. Sheldon noted that Bliss seemed happier than he'd ever seen her in the short time he'd known her, but wondered if it could last. It was then that he realized he had completely forgotten why he'd come to talk to her—and Bliss, usually so curious, hadn't even asked. The phone rang.

Billie frowned in irritation as she got up and answered it. "Hello? Mike?....Oh yes, I remember, Drew introduced us this morning....I'm sorry, Mike, but I don't go out with someone I hardly know....What do you mean you've heard about my reputation? I see....I guess it's true....Mike, I really can't talk now, I have a guest....All right....Thank you for the invitation any way....Goodbye." She hung up and removed the phone from its cradle. "There! We won't have any more interruptions," she said to Sheldon, a conspiratorial smile on her face.

Sheldon had been listening with great interest. Apparently Bliss was sought after by the young men, if tonight was any indication at least, but then—this didn't surprise him. For some reason, he felt a nudge of hope. Maybe he was wrong, maybe there was someone out there for her.

"Those calls...how often do you get those kind?" he asked, hopefully.

"Too often. I can't get my studies done sometimes unless I take the phone off the hook."

"Why aren't you accepting any of the young men who call?"

She looked at him puzzled, "You already know why, Dodds."

"Oh, yes...yes, I do, it's just that you are doomed to such a lonely life if you don't get married, Bliss." He was sure now he was on the right track.

She nodded her head thoughtfully. An expression of great sympathy appeared on her face. "And you know how lonely don't you, Dodds?" She reached over and took one of his hands in both hers. "I haven't been able to take my mind off you lately, thinking how lonely you must have been all these years—no parents, no loving wife and no children. Oh dear, dear, Dodds—we must find a wife for you."

How did this happen? he asked himself. He pulled his hand away, horrified. Backing his chair away from the table, he stood up abruptly. "Good Grief, Bliss! How did the conversation get turned on me?"

Billie also stood up. Stepping around the table, she looked up at him. "Why do you react this way, Dodds? You know you've been lonely. I know you didn't mean to be a bachelor. Maybe you were shy or got your heart broken or something and just immersed yourself in your work so completely you quit trying to find a wife and..."

"Stop! We were talking about *your* life becoming lonely, not *mine*."

"I know," she said gently, "but right now I'm more concerned about your life, and lately that's all I've been able to think about, so I suggest we work on you for a while." She noticed his mouth working, obviously trying to form words that wouldn't come. "Please Dodds, I promise you that I'm making progress in many ways and while I'm progressing, we can work on finding you a wife."

Sheldon grabbed her shoulders to shake her, but immediately got hold of himself. Still gripping her firmly, his voice harsh, he stated, "Miss Bliss, the Project is for you not me." Then desperately, he advanced the only argument he could think of. "How do you think the benefactor of Fairfield University would react if the Project took a U turn to me?"

She closed her eyes a moment, feeling the grip of his hands on her shoulders, very aware of how strong they felt. Opening her eyes she rushed on breathlessly, "I think he would like that very much since you're trying so hard to help your students. You see, Dodds, I'm sure he'd realize that if you're happily married, not lonely any more, you can help your students even more."

He was speechless. Unable to get back on track, he had another urge to shake her. Instead he dropped his hands and quickly stepped to the door. "Good night, Miss Bliss. Thank you for the dinner."

He opened the door, ran down the steps, down the driveway and across the street to his car, aware that Billie was following him. He unlocked the car and was about to open it when Billie reached him.

"I'm sorry for offending you, Dodds," she said in a tremulous voice.

"I'm not offended, I'm frustrated," he stated bluntly.

"Oh please, Dodds, don't be frustrated."

Sheldon gazed down at her and saw tears glistening in her beautiful eyes. Suddenly, he felt ashamed of his perfectly logical and totally justifiable behavior. He couldn't resist her. Those eyes, that voice, those tears. His hand went out toward her, then abruptly withdrew. "All right, Bliss, I'll go home and try to get 'unfrustrated'," he said, a faint smile hovering about his lips.

Relief flooded her features. She smiled, "Thank you, Dodds. See you tomorrow in class—and thank you for not letting me eat alone." With that, she ran across the street, then turned and waved. Sheldon waved back and drove off. She walked slowly up the driveway enjoying the lovely evening. A rustle in the bushes behind her apartment made her look in that direction. Realizing that there wasn't a breeze, she wondered if it was an animal of some kind. She waited and listened...

Why doesn't she go inside? thought Lora, desperately. She needed to get out of the bushes! The convenient mound of dirt she'd found to sit on turned out to be an ant hill, discovering too late that the tickling on her legs were ants! She saw Billie study the bushes just after she'd tried to brush the stinging little insects off—so the fear that Billie would come over and investigate if she moved the bushes again, held her immobile. And now they were crawling on her arms! She squelched a scream. The idea to hide in the bushes so she could really spy on Dr. Ackerman and Billie had resulted in disaster. When she'd realized her predicament, it was too late. Dr. Ackerman came out the door with Billie following him. There was no way to escape without being seen by both of them. She would rather die of ant bites.

"Oh no!" Lora whispered, Billie was sitting down on the steps. She now felt the ants crawling on her neck! A voiceless, strangling sound issued from her throat as she tried to brush them off without rustling the bushes. Mounting hysteria burst out in short silent gasps.

At last, Billie stood up and went inside. Immediately, Lora crawled along through the bushes, oblivious to the scratches, squeezing through until she reached the place where she'd entered—the growth that was out of view of Billie's front window. Extricating herself, she ran down the driveway and up the walk toward her car as fast as she could, while squirming and brushing ants off her face, neck, arms. When finally around the corner, she realized that not only were the ants inside her pants, they were inside her shirt! Small shuddering screams escaped as she brushed and shook herself vigorously. She couldn't disrobe right here; she had to get home as fast as she could. Unlocking her car, she got in, turned on the key and shoved the stick shift into gear. The car lurched forward, weaving from side to side as she wiggled and squirmed.

After pressing the gas peddle to the floor for several blocks, she heard a siren behind her. Glancing in the rear view mirror she saw a policeman on a motorcycle. "Oh no!" she groaned, pulling over to the side. Unable to wait for the policeman to come to her, she got out, shaking herself, jumping up and down, gasping and shuddering. The startled young policeman approached her.

"Oh please," she implored him, "I just sat on top of an ant pile and ants are even down inside. I have to get home and take off my clothes!" she exclaimed, jigging up and down, tugging at various parts of her anatomy, "unless you want me to disrobe right here."

"Oh no, Miss…no!" He quickly assessed the red bites on her face, neck and arms. "Don't disrobe, I'll lead you home on my motorcycle, sirens and all."

"Th…thank you, officer!"

Had Lora not been so excruciatingly miserable, she would have found this a great adventure roaring down the highway as fast as her little Volkswagon could go, with the sirens of the policeman ahead screaming for the cars to move aside—just for her.

Ella Lemmon heard the sirens as they got closer. She peered out through the blinds and got the shock of her life. She saw Lora speeding down the road—chasing a policeman!

Chapter Twenty-One

The minute Sheldon entered his condo, he walked over to the phone and called Nettie.

"Hello?" came the cheerful voice.

"Nettie, help! I need some help."

"Good. I'm dying to know what's going on with you and Billie Bliss. What can I do for you?"

"I wish I could tell you everything, but I can't. I'm in deep water, Nettie! Females are so unpredictable, so confusing so…"

"Shel, stop. Just tell me the bottom line and we'll back up if we have to."

"Bliss is…oh, I need to tell you, we've decided to be less formal in private. She calls me Dodds and I call her Bliss."

"Oh? Why do you call her Bliss rather than Billie?"

"Billie doesn't fit her at all."

Nettie smiled, wondering why he felt that way. "Go on, Shel."

"Tonight, out of the blue, this girl told me that she'd been thinking about me, how lonely I must've been through the years, and she wants us to work together to find me…uh a wife!"

Surprised, Nettie's silence lasted only a moment before she laughed. "Good for her."

"I knew you'd like to hear that, Nettie, but tell me how to get her off this kick. I let her know that it's not a subject to consider or even discuss. But what if she thinks it will save my soul and refuses to let it go—what should I do, what shall I say?"

"I wouldn't worry about it, Sheldon, she seems like a sensitive girl. I don't think she'll mention it again, unless you provoke her into it by something you say."

Sheldon thought this over. "Maybe you're right. I hope you are. You know…I think I'll beat her to the punch. This brings me to the main reason I called. Could you stay after the meeting tomorrow night for about fifteen or twenty minutes? I need to talk to all three of you about something."

"Sure can, Shel."

"Thanks, Nettie, I'll call Robert and Hal. Goodnight, I'll see you soon."

~~~~~~~~~~

Friday morning, when Sheldon walked into his class three minutes to ten, he found all the class members gathered around someone, laughing and chattering. He could see Bliss' shiny auburn hair in the group and wondered what could be so interesting.

Lora Lemmon was eating it up—all this attention! One by one, the class members had walked over to her, aghast at the condition of her face and arms, asking question after question. She was more than eager to tell of her adventure with the policeman, but was carefully vague as to how she came to sit on top of an ant hill—and why she had to sit there long enough for them to crawl all over her. All the girls assured her that they'd never heard anything so funny. Lora then informed them that even through the stinging and smarting, she'd noticed how good looking the young policeman was, describing his nice blue eyes, sandy blonde hair and broad shoulders. She told them how he'd gallantly made her promise to go to a clinic and have a doctor check her over, suggesting that maybe she needed a shot of some kind to counteract the poison from the ant bites. Lora, gratified at the reaction she was getting, beamed.

Dr. Ackerman cleared his throat, suggesting it was time for class to start. As the group dispersed, he saw who was creating the interest— Miss Lemmon! For several days of late, Lora Lemmon seemed different; the perpetual sour expression had changed to an all-knowing, smug one. He couldn't decide which one he disliked the most. But today, something was wrong with her.

"Miss Lemmon, would you please come up to the desk?"

"Yes, Dr. Ackerman?"

He studied the red spots all over her face and arms, as well as some scratches here and there. "Do you have the measles, Miss Lemmon?" he asked concerned.

"Oh no, these are ant bites."

"How...how in the world did this happen?"

"I sat on top of an ant pile."

"Good grief, girl, surely you could tell that it was an ant hill."

Lora Lemmon stuttered, hedged, then turned as red as a turkey wattle.

~~~~~~~~~~

Six-fifty-five was cutting it too close, Sheldon thought, as he drove into the Franklin Building parking lot. He preferred to be slightly early for every appointment. At six-fifteen, Atwood had chosen to have a conference concerning the Project, and the dean had never been known for his conciseness—so here he was—crunched for time. Finding the faculty parking taken up, he backed around and headed toward a vacant space he'd seen coming in. As he turned right he jammed on his brakes, and the driver facing him did the same. The jolt was hard and both drivers sat there stunned. Sheldon blinked a couple of times as he stared at the car in front of him. It couldn't be, he thought—but it was. It was Miss Lemmon again! He got out of the car and stared at the bumpers. One side of her front bumper was lodged under his.

Lora couldn't believe it. "Not again!" she groaned. The last thing she wanted to do was get out and face Dr. Ackerman, but he was angrily motioning her to do so.

Reluctantly, Lora got out. She stepped over to him, looked at the locked bumpers, gave him a mortified glance and lowered her head.

He began slowly, trying to control his anger, "Why, Miss Lemmon, were you driving recklessly again?"

Her head still down, she mumbled, "I was turning left."

"Miss Lemmon, I think you need to go back to Drivers Ed. In a parking lot, it's very important that you drive slowly and watch where you're going."

"I know…but I…uh was in a hurry."

"Why? What are you doing here?" he asked suspiciously. He was feeling hexed by Lora Lemmon. Everywhere he went of late, there she was!

She turned red again, trying desperately to think of an excuse for being in the parking lot of the Franklin building—and why she was in a hurry. "I…I have to get to work."

"Where do you work, Miss Lemmon?"

She fidgeted and scratched at an ant bite. "Uh...uh at a fast food place on Syracuse and Main."

His eyes bore into her unmercifully. "So then—why are you *here*?"

"I uh...I guess I was lost...or something," she mumbled, her voice trailing off.

"Lost? How could you be Lost, Miss Lemmon? Do you realize you've made me late for an important meeting? Help me lift this bumper off yours."

Grateful he didn't make her answer that question, she helped him tug on the bumpers.

"No, Miss Lemmon! Don't lift up on your bumper, lift up on mine," he barked, stopping to loosen his tie and remove his coat.

"Oh...of course, it's just that I'm so...so flustered."

They both worked at it for five minutes and couldn't dislodge them. Sheldon looked at his watch.

Miss Lemmon, I must go into my meeting. There is a phone there, I'll call a wrecker and have him come out. You'll have to remain here with the cars and wait for him."

"Yes, Dr. Ackerman," she said in a small miserable voice. She watched him go. "Dang it!" she shouted at herself when he was out of ear shot.

Sheldon was sweating profusely as he ran to the building. The fact that it was blistering hot and humid didn't help his disposition at all.

The disheveled professor entered the lounge, and all heads turned in his direction, taken back by his flushed and angry face.

Nettie looked at her watch and saw that it was seven fifteen. "What happened, Dr. Ackerman?" she asked, concerned.

"I'm being hexed!" he mumbled under his breath.

"What did you say?" she asked.

"Had a little accident out in the parking lot. Would you all excuse me while I call a wrecker? I'll be with you soon."

"Are you hurt, would you like to postpone the meeting?" Hal asked.

Sheldon shook his head. Holding the phone in a death grip, he told the wrecker where to find the cars and afterwards where to find him. He walked over and sat down, leaving his coat over the chair. "Well," he smiled half heartedly, "did you start without me?"

"No, we were waiting for our punctual professor," Robert chided, a twinkle in his eyes. Every one laughed, including Sheldon.

The tension released somewhat, his fingers uncurled from their subconscious grip on Lora Lemmon's neck. "Nice timing, Dr. Bittle. Sorry again for making you wait."

The meeting proceeded as last Friday—the girls reporting and the counselors responding. The girls were progressing nicely and still very hopeful, but the surprise came when Billie Bliss reported. She stood up, removed her jacket and whirled around. Every one gasped, except Sheldon who just stared in disbelief. The inches had just melted away!

"How…how did that happen so fast?" asked a dumbfounded Vickie Blume.

"Well, it really wasn't as fast as it looks. You see, it began almost as soon as Dr. Ackerman started working with me, but I wanted to make sure they would stay off so I just kept wearing the same clothes—until now."

"Tell us, Miss Bliss," Nettie asked, "have you exercised everyday and eaten right all the while?"

"I have. But the main reason for my success is…" her eyes, filling with warmth and gratitude, she looked over at her friend and professor, "that Dr. Ackerman has helped me in a way no one else could have."

The gaze of the whole group focused on Sheldon questioningly. He felt a deep flush work its way from his neck to his forehead.

Robert Bittle, smiling, his eyes twinkling, asked, "I think we could all use a few pointers here. Could you tell us, Miss Bliss, *how* he helped you?"

"How many weeks do you have?"

Sheldon's deep guttural laugh, that clearly said—now it's your turn to be confused—caused heads to focus on him again, waiting, until Nettie spoke and they swivelled back to her. "Will it really take that long, Billie?"

"It took a while for Dr. Ackerman to understand my problem, and you would surely have to understand before I could explain how he's helped me."

Sheldon quickly stood up and cleared his throat. "I think we should hear from the support counselors now, and I'll be the first. Miss Bliss gives me the credit, but I assure you, it's really her efforts that have produced the physical effects you see. She has worked at it very hard. Now may we hear from the rest of you?"

~~~~~~~~~~

The meeting over, the girls excused, the Committee seated themselves in the softer chairs for the meeting with Sheldon. The wrecker had come and gone. Sheldon had parked his car and assured Miss Lemmon that there was no damage, but told her if there was a next time, he'd call the police to take a look. Her reply more than puzzled him. "If there is a next time, Dr. Ackerman, will you please request Officer Bates?" He found himself shaking his head over the question, and—over all the episodes with Miss Lemmon.

"What is it, Shel?" asked Nettie as she watched him.

"Oh, nothing—at least I hope it's nothing. Well, now I'll explain why I asked you to stay for a few minutes. I need your help."

"It doesn't look like you need our help," Hal said, smiling. "Miss Bliss is literally glowing, as well as looking much better."

"But it won't last, Hal, I assure you. Her problem is just temporarily on hold."

Robert expelled a breath of exasperation. "Come on, Sheldon, tell us what her problem is?"

Sheldon chuckled. "How many weeks do you have?"

"You can't be serious," Robert replied, his voice thick with skepticism.

"I am, Robert. I wish I could explain it, but it isn't my place to try. I hope Bliss will be able to soon, and I hope all of you will be able to understand it sooner than I did."

"I'm afraid if Billie does the explaining, we won't," Nettie stated, smiling.

Sheldon returned her smile, nodding. "Maybe when the time comes, I can help. Now, folks, I have only one more idea to help Bliss with her problem."

"Bliss?" questioned Robert. "That's the second time you called her by her last name."

"The name Billie doesn't suit her."

Robert's brows arched, and the three glanced at one another. Sheldon gave them a sardonic smile. "All right, you three, it's not what you think." He cleared his throat nervously. "Now—to get to the reason I asked you stay for a few minutes. Billie Bliss has decided not to get married. All I can say is—she has become disillusioned in young men. However, I know that if a nice old-fashioned young man came along whose values matched hers, she would change her mind and her problem would be solved."

"Oh? Let me get this straight," Nettie said. "*You* want to find a husband for *her,* and *she* wants to find a wife for *you*?"

"What?" Robert blurted out.

Nettie filled the other two in on Sheldon's Wednesday night call. Sheldon leaned upon his knees, tapping his fingers together, trying to be patient. Robert raised his brows again, and Hal chuckled.

Nettie leaned toward him, curious. "What is it you want from *us,* Shel?"

"I want all of you to help me find that old-fashioned boy for Bliss."

Time crawled by as the three silently digested what each thought was an absurd request.

A look of smugness on her face, Nettie said, "I thought only we women were accused of being matchmakers."

"Now—you know how desperate I feel!" Sheldon exclaimed. "Wednesday afternoon I had decided to pull out of the Project and find some one else to be a support counselor to Billie Bliss."

The three began to take Sheldon seriously. Reneging on a commitment was not his style.

"What changed your mind, Sheldon?" Hal asked.

Thoughtful a moment, he answered. "You know...I'm not quite sure. Well, how about it?" he asked, looking at each of them.

Robert shook his head. "I would like to help you out, Sheldon, but I wouldn't touch it with that proverbial ten foot pole."

"I think I'll pass, too," Hal said.

"You aren't going to bale out on me, too, are you, Nettie?" he implored, looking like a man fearful of his immediate demise.

"Shel, I think I've been the most avid matchmaker in the history of Claytonville, but a few years ago I got burned and I promised my husband I would swear off matchmaking."

Gloom settled over Sheldon like a sweaty horse blanket. "I guess I'm on my own...."

Chapter Twenty-Two

Sheldon, ready for bed, wandered around aimlessly trying to come up with a way to find a worthy young man for Bliss. The exercise of coming up with and rejecting one idea after another, left him feeling totally exhausted, nevertheless, he couldn't turn off his mind.

The progress Bliss had made in her weight management was amazing—but at the moment what he really cared about was—she seemed happier. Though realizing that cheerfulness was her natural disposition, Sheldon agreed with Hal. Recently she literally glowed—and he desperately wanted to keep her feeling this way! He needed to buy time. After a few more paces around the room, the obvious hit him. "That's it!" he exclaimed aloud. It was an idea for buying time, while at the same time giving him opportunity to learn more about that subtle essence Bliss called romance.

Checking his watch, he saw that it wasn't quite ten o'clock, so taking a chance that Bliss wouldn't be in bed, he called her. It rang and rang. He was about to hang up when she answered with a breathy hello.

"This is Dodds, did you just walk in?"

"Yes, I've been over visiting my family. They all asked about you and asked when you were coming over for dinner again."

"Well, that brings me to the reason I called. I would like to see more of your favorite movies."

"You would? Oh, that would be wonderful."

Sheldon noted that she sounded as excited as a child about to participate in Christmas. He wondered why, since she must have seen all of the movies several times.

"Since tomorrow's Saturday, we could see a couple of them if you came over in the afternoon. We could watch one before dinner and one after."

I have a better idea. How about me taking you and your whole family out to the Maplewood Country Club for dinner tomorrow night after watching the first movie? Then we can go back and watch another one if there's time?"

There was silence. "Bliss? What is it?"

"I don't know what a professor at Fairfield University makes, but I was surprised that you could even afford to belong to the country club, let alone take our whole family out."

"You forget, Bliss, I was in business for years before becoming a professor. I have a few investments that supplement my income from the university."

"Oh. Then I accept for my whole family. I'm so excited, thank you, Dodds."

"It's my pleasure, Bliss."

"And, Dodds, let's watch a couple of romantic comedies. You seemed rather down the day you came to my apartment. You need to laugh more."

After the short visit with Billie, Sheldon felt so good that when he went to bed, he fell asleep immediately.

~~~~~~~~~~

Saturday afternoon and evening turned out to be just what Sheldon needed. Before dinner, he and Billie watched *The Glass Bottom Boat* with Doris Day, and he thoroughly enjoyed it.

Dinner at the club turned out well. The family all enjoyed it. Even Henry was on his best behavior, making only one off-beat comment—"Sheldon doesn't seem to be the uppity country club type," making everyone laugh, especially Sheldon.

Soon after dinner they went home. Sheldon suggested that the whole family join them in watching the second movie, *Bringing Up Baby* with Cary Grant and Kathryn Hepburn. He found himself laughing with the family until his sides actually hurt. And what's more, the leading man's total confusion, caused mostly by the heroine, felt very familiar. In fact he could relate very well!

Sheldon went home, feeling more relaxed and happier than he had in a long time. Bliss was right, he thought, he needed to laugh more. Also, Bliss, without knowing it, gave him another idea that could buy him more time. She told him that her favorite book, *Pride and Prejudice,* had been made into a television movie and suggested they rent it sometime and watch it. He remembered seeing it for sale in the video store. He decided to buy it for her next week instead of renting it.

~~~~~~~~~

Monday morning, Dr. Ackerman was in unusually good spirits as he waited for his class to settle themselves. This was the result of several things: The class, on the whole, was less tardy; they took less time to settle, and he seemed to be reaching students he never thought he could, namely Miss Josie Sorenson. She had admitted to him just the other day that she'd only taken the class to fill credit hours, but now she was fascinated with business and was considering making it her major. Thinking about it, he realized it had all started turning around when Miss Billie Bliss pointed out to him, after some confusing dialogue, that he came over as pompous and demeaning. Yes, he owed her a great deal.

~~~~~~~~~

Sheldon parked, turned off the motor and looked around the parking lot of the video store. So far as he could see, there was no one around he knew. He certainly wasn't going to venture into this place again unaware! Striding quickly over to the edge of the window, he peered in and studied all the occupants. Not seeing anyone he knew, he entered and began browsing, feeling less of a novice since he was a little more knowledgeable this time. Finding the aisle that displayed romances, he began looking for *Pride and Prejudice.* After some time, he realized that they were in alphabetical order.

Lora Lemmon was determined not to get caught again. Parking her car on the side of the building far away from Dr. Ackerman's Buick, she sidled around the building to the door. Opening it slightly, she looked around until she saw where he was, then stepped in quickly. Walking over to an aisle close to his, she hunkered down slightly. Sure enough, he was looking at the romances again, which validated her suspicions. She was sure now. Renting these romances did have something to do with Billie Bliss.

Sheldon searched the shelf, but couldn't find it. Concerned that they might have sold out of them, he walked over to the counter and inquired.

Lora peeked her head up just above the video shelf to watch him.

The clerk confirmed that they had the movie and explained to Sheldon where he could find it. He walked rapidly toward the area, wanting to get this errand over with as quickly as possible.

Lora saw Dr. Ackerman heading in her general direction. She crouched down on the floor, hoping fervently he wasn't coming down this particular corridor.

Just as Sheldon turned down another aisle, he stumbled over a large obstacle in the path and dived headlong onto the floor.

"Ouch!" the obstacle yelped.

Dazed and shocked, Sheldon sat up and looked at what he'd stumbled over. Stupefied, he found himself staring directly into the eyes of Miss Lora Lemmon! Mortified, Lora could only stare back, her face turning red as a poppy.

Her professor's mouth moved, trying to say something, but nothing came—finally he managed to blurt out, "Miss Lemmon!"

"H...hello, Dr. Ackerman."

The whites of his eyes had grown pronounced. He glared at her, wondering if he was going mad! "What...what were you doing on the floor?!"

"Well...I...uh..." Lora, not used to lying, was having a difficult time. "I was looking for a video for my mother," which was partially true.

Sheldon's dark brows knit together menacingly as he scrutinized the only videos she could be looking at down that low. Lora followed his gaze and saw a shelf full of videos on breast feeding and caring for infants!

Turning even redder, she looked at him and muttered, "I...guess I have the wrong aisle."

"Miss Lemmon," he began slowly, ominously, "why...are we...always...bumping into each other?"

"My my," said an austere and disapproving voice above them.

They both looked up to see a well dressed, silver haired lady glaring down at them. "Why are you two sprawled out on the floor like this? One could stumble over you! And you…" she said, glaring at Sheldon and shaking a finger at him, "you, at your age, should know better." She clicked her tongue disapprovingly and stalked off, shaking her head.

Flushing furiously, Sheldon shot to his feet. "I'm sorry, ma'am," he called to her retreating back. When he turned to further interrogate Miss Lemmon, she was up and walking rapidly for the door. His brows hovered over his suspicious, narrowed eyes, "Something is fishy here," he muttered under his breath as he watched her leave. "Surely this can't just be coincidence." He was so rattled, he forgot for a moment what he'd come in for, but after taking a couple of big breaths, he managed to get hold of himself. Finding the set of videos, he picked them up and went to the counter to pay for them.

Lora's old Volkswagon almost left a layer of rubber on the asphalt as she sped out of the parking lot. "Darn! I've done it again," she wailed, "What am I going to do? I guess I'm just not PI material." After driving a while, she calmed down and reasoned with herself rather vociferously, "Well, I have as much right to be in that video store as Dr. Ackerman! What can he do? How can he even ask questions about it?" Then, remembering that her suspicions had almost been proven today, she decided to stick to her detective work. Just a little more proof and—she wasn't quite sure what came after the 'and,' but—surely there was something…

Chapter Twenty-Three

Tuesday afternoon, Billie, filled with excitement, was helping her mother and Aunt Tilly prepare dinner. Sheldon had called Monday night and asked if he could bring the movie, *Pride and Prejudice* over the next night for them to watch together. Since her family had been wanting him to dine with them again, she invited him to an early dinner. He accepted only if she would allow him to bring the dessert, a specialty dessert from the country club.

Her mother was humming softly while Aunt Tilly was chattering about this and that. Billie had noticed how content and happy her family was of late—probably because she was. Having Dodds' concern and support had helped her even more than she would let herself admit—until lately. She dreaded the end of the project.

Uncle Henry walked in and growled, "It's about time you invited Sheldon to dinner again, Billie."

"Yes, it is," her mother agreed. "He's really gone out of his way to help you."

"He's such a pleasant man to be around, isn't he, Billie?" Aunt Tilly asked, probing.

"I'm glad you all like my professor," she said, smiling. "When will Papa be home?"

"He'll be home about 4:00. You wanted to eat right at 5:00 so you could watch that long movie."

"Good. I think I'll go visit with grandpa now that everything is done."

She found him in the library, sitting on the couch reading the evening paper. Billie plunked herself down beside him, leaned her head on his shoulder and sighed. Bill Bliss put his paper down and smiled. "And what was that big sigh for, Snooks?"

"Oh...nothing."

"Come on, ever since you were a little girl, when you wanted to talk, you did just what you're doing now."

"What do you think of Dodds?"

"I think he's a fine young man."

"But he isn't so young, Grandpa."

"By my standards, he is," he replied chuckling.

"You know what, Grandpa? I find myself wishing he were at least five years younger and not my professor."

"I know."

"You do?" she sat up and looked at him in surprise. "How do you know? Oh never mind," she said, smiling affectionately, "like you've told me before, you listen and watch instead of talking all the time."

"Exactly."

"What do you think about me wishing that?"

"Hey, there's my girl," her father interrupted poking his head in and smiling.

"Hey, there's my papa," Billie announced, running over and hugging him. "Thanks for coming home early tonight."

~~~~~~~~~

"Have a seat, Sheldon," Neal Atwood said. "Before I get to the reason I called you in, tell me how *Project Success* is going?"

"Even better than I expected, Neal. The young women are responding in a way that has made me realize even more, that this is a worthwhile project. It appears it may have a long reaching affect on their lives."

"Excellent, excellent! Now, Sheldon, I would like to ask you a favor. I have a nephew who is a CPA and owns his own accounting firm in Springfield. He wants to put more responsibility for his business in the hands of his accountants for a semester so he can commute back and forth and take a few business courses from you here at Fairfield. After the semester he'll return full time to his business. But I'm concerned. He's thirty-five and not married. He tells me that the reason he isn't married is because there aren't any more old-fashioned girls around. Now, that brings me to you. I'm wondering if you know of a lovely, old-fashioned girl you could introduce him to who could show him around the university. If you do, I would be most appreciative."

Sheldon couldn't believe his ears. Maybe what he was needing had just fallen into his lap. But, of course, he had to meet the young man before he could even consider it.

Neal seemed to read his mind. "Paul, my nephew, should be walking in any moment so you can meet him."

"What makes you think I would know a girl like this, Neal?" Sheldon asked, curious.

"Well, Sheldon, you seem to be a straight arrow. And since you're teaching a class full of young women. I just thought you might have come across a young woman like that."

"I would like to meet him first and then I'll give it some thought and get back to you." No sooner had he said this than a tall dark-haired, young man, opened the door to the dean's office.

"Oh, Paul, I'm glad you're here. I would like you to meet the professor I was telling you about, Dr. Sheldon Ackerman."

The young man's handsome face broke into a big smile and his hand shot out. "It's great to meet you, Dr. Ackerman, my uncle has been singing your praises, and he's given me both your books to read."

Sheldon shook Paul's hand firmly. "Thank you, Paul, it's nice to meet you," he said smiling while intently sizing him up.

"Both of you have a seat," Neal said.

Sheldon was impressed with Paul's clean-cut appearance, so proceeded to question him about his business, his goals and ambitions. Twenty minutes later, they parted company and Sheldon headed for the country club to pick up the dessert for dinner tonight.

All the way home and while getting ready, his mind went over the conversation with Paul Atwood, dissecting it, analyzing it. Overall, he was impressed with what he'd learned about him. However, something bothered him. He couldn't pin down whether it was something about the young man or whether it was something else.

By the time Sheldon drove into the Bliss driveway, he had reached a tentative decision. He picked up the dessert and videos and got out. After he rang the door bell, a glowing Billie answered the door. She was dressed in an off-white and lemon-yellow-pinstripe cotton shirt, tucked into plain white pants, belted with a lemon colored belt. What Sheldon noticed was that the jacket, which usually hid her figure, was missing, revealing alluring curves and a trimming waistline. Her long, slightly-curled, auburn hair hung loose in shiny folds over her shoulders. As he stepped in, a flower-like perfume wafted up to his nose. He stared at her, unable to speak for a moment.

"Dodds, you look handsome in that maroon shirt."

He flushed. Her frankness, still caught him off guard at times. "Uh, thank you. I guess you noticed me giving you...uh, as they say...the once over." He grinned sheepishly.

Her eyes sparkled as she smiled up at him. "Yes. The inches have been just disappearing. How do I look?" she asked, turning herself around slowly.

His breath caught. She was truly a beautiful girl, and in his mind, it was a sure thing that Paul Atwood would be smitten the minute he laid eyes on her.

"You look very nice," he replied stiffly. "I'm proud of what you've been able to accomplish."

"I didn't do it. Oh, I helped of course, but it was you, Dodds and your support and understanding."

He shook his head slightly, trying to dismiss what she'd said, but the expression in her eyes unsettled him the most. "Here," he said, a little too abruptly, handing her the sack of videos that made up the one movie. I bought *Pride and Prejudice* for you."

Her eyes lit up. "You bought it for me? Oh, thank you, thank you! I didn't get to see it when it was first shown on television. And now I can see it over and over."

"You mean we will be watching one we both haven't seen?"

"Yes, isn't it wonderful?"

Her childlike joy was infectious, making him feel like a school boy again. He carried the dessert to the kitchen.

Dinner with the family was enjoyable. Everyone was relaxed, feeling like old friends by now. The meal consisted of vegetables out of Bill's garden: snap beans, sliced tomatoes, corn on the cob and fresh homemade bread. Every one agreed that the dessert, the Club's specialty of milk cake covered with fresh red-ripe strawberries, was the perfect choice for a vegetable meal.

The family declined the invitation to watch the movie with them, so Sheldon and Billie were seated alone on the couch in the television room. Billie slipped off her sandals and curled up as she turned on the movie.

It turned out to be a long, but unforgettable evening for Sheldon. The story, the acting and the scenery were superb and he, like Billie got thoroughly caught up with the emotion and 'romance' of the movie, glancing at each other often in their enjoyment.

It was 11:00 when they walked to the door and out onto the porch together. "I can't remember when I've enjoyed an evening so much, Bliss," Sheldon said smiling down at her, noticing that the moonlight had turned her beauty into something ethereal.

"I can't either," she responded quietly.

"Let's sit here on the porch swing a minute, Bliss, I need to ask a favor of you."

"All right." They both sat down. The late evening August air was fragrant, still and humid. Frogs belched out their songs from a neighboring pond, blending harmoniously with the crickets. The pair on the swing were silent for a while, enjoying the sounds of summer.

"Dean Atwood," Sheldon began, "called me into his office this afternoon and asked me if I could get someone to show his nephew around the university, and I'm wondering if you would have time to do that for me?"

"Why would he ask you, Dodds? Can't he do it himself?" she asked, puzzled.

"Uh...well," he had to think fast, "the young man wants to take a couple of classes from me next semester so I guess he thought it a good idea that I introduce him to someone."

"Oh. That makes sense, I guess. I would be glad to do that for you, Dodds."

"Thank you, Bliss." Why did he feel guilty conniving like this? It was for her own good wasn't it? he reasoned with himself. It was so pleasant here in the swing with her, he hesitated getting up and leaving. Finally, he stood up to go. They thanked each other and said goodnight.

Billie sat back down on the swing and watched Sheldon walk to his car and drive away. She couldn't make herself go inside. The outdoors was soothing to the unsettling emotions that she'd been feeling lately when she was with Dodds.

The screen door squeaked open. She turned, startled. "Grandpa! What are you doing up this late?"

"I couldn't sleep. We didn't get to finish our conversation so I thought maybe we could finish it now. Are you too tired, Snooks?" he asked, sitting beside her.

"Not at all tired, Grandpa. I'm so glad you're here right now. I don't know what's the matter with me, but I kind of feel confused and..."

"Confused because you wish Sheldon were five years younger?"

"Yes."

"He's a very kind and handsome young man. It's understandable that you might get a crush on him. That happens now and then with student and teacher, doctor and patient and so on."

Billie looked over at him in surprise. "A crush? I don't have a crush on him, Grandpa, I just wish that there were younger men out there like him."

"Oh."

The hinges of the old porch swing rasped as the two moved back and forth, each deep in thought.

Billie broke the silence, speaking softly into the balmy air. "Ten years older is too much older, Grandpa."

"You think so?"

"Yes. I want lots of children."

"Oh. You think you couldn't have lots with someone ten years older?"

"I don't know, it depends."

"I take it, Sheldon is a confirmed bachelor."

Billie sighed. "It seems so, Grandpa. It's such a waste. I've been trying to think of some one I could introduce him to—some one he might want to marry. He's had such a lonely life, and it's just going to get lonelier. I mentioned it to him, and he ran out of my apartment so fast, that he, like Uncle Henry said, almost left his tall skinny shadow behind." She couldn't help smiling.

Bill Bliss smiled, too, but his was mainly caused by visualizing Billie broaching the subject to Sheldon of finding him a wife. "I suspect, Snooks, that Mr. Sheldon Dodds Ackerman just hasn't placed himself in situations where he could meet someone. But, I can guarantee—if he ever found anyone he was really interested in, he would be very vulnerable. His bachelorhood would fly right out the window.

Chapter Twenty-Four

Wednesday morning at 8:00, the phone rang at the Atwood residence. Neal Atwood picked it up.

"Hello?"

"Good morning, Neal, this is Sheldon. I think I've found the kind of girl you were describing to me yesterday. She's a young woman from my 280 class."

"Good!"

"If you'll tell Paul to be outside the door of my classroom this morning at 11:00, I'll introduce him to her. She has graciously agreed to show him around the campus."

"I can't tell you how much I appreciate this, Sheldon."

"Neal, you know it probably won't work out, don't you?"

"I know, I know. But at least I will have tried."

~~~~~~~~~~

Sheldon motioned for Billie to come over to his desk the minute she walked into class.

"Miss Bliss," he whispered, "Dean Atwood's nephew, who needs to be shown around the campus, will be outside the door right after class. I'll take you both into my office and introduce you, and the two of you can arrange a convenient time for the tour."

"All right, Dr. Ackerman." she said, her voice and manner both subdued.

"Is everything all right, Miss Bliss? You don't seem yourself this morning?"

"I'm fine, Dr. Ackerman," she said, giving him a brief smile, then turned abruptly, walking quickly to her seat.

Something is wrong, he thought to himself, the sparkle he'd seen in her eyes lately was missing. It was there last night when he left her. What could it be?

Because of his concern he had a difficult time getting into his lecture. Finally, he managed to put it aside momentarily.

After class, Billie waited in her seat until everyone left the room, then she and Sheldon found the young man waiting for them just outside the classroom. Sheldon noticed Paul's expression when he saw Billie and knew he was instantly captivated. Ushering them into his office, he invited both to have a seat, then introduced them. After visiting a few minutes, the two decided to tour part of the campus for an hour right then. Paul shook Sheldon's hand and thanked him, then he and Billie left together.

Sheldon sat at his desk thinking. He'd also watched Billie's reaction to Paul, but her face conveyed nothing. Though still quiet and subdued, she was very gracious to Paul. Feeling restless and vaguely disturbed about the two going off together, Sheldon frowned, wondering why.

~~~~~~~~~

Sheldon paced the floor in his condo. He'd been trying to reach Billie by phone off and on all evening, and here it was ten o'clock! Where could she be? He stopped by the phone and re-dialed.

This time Billie's dulcet tones came over the line. "Hello?"

"Hello, Bliss, where have you been?"

"You've been trying to reach me?" she asked, sounding surprised.

"Yes. I feel responsible about asking you to show Paul Atwood around, and I was concerned."

"There's no need for concern, Dodds. Paul and I went touring the campus again after my afternoon class, and then he wanted to take me out to dinner to thank me."

"Oh. How did it go?"

"It went very well. He likes the campus and all the facilities. He is particularly interested in taking classes from you. He thinks it will help him in his accounting firm and will help him make wise investments."

"Good. What do you think of Dean Atwood's nephew?" he asked trying to sound off-handed.

"He's very nice. I can't imagine why he's still unmarried."

"Are you through showing him around?"

"Yes, but…" her voice trailed off, becoming silent.

"What is it, Bliss?"

"He's going to be here until Sunday, and he wants me to go out with him every afternoon and every evening until he leaves."

The man works fast, Sheldon thought, disgruntled. He chastised himself; this was just what he hoped would happen wasn't it? So why did this news rankle him? "Did you accept?"

"I told him I would think about it."

"Do you want to go out with him?"

"I don't know. I should want to, he's handsome as well as nice. Do you want me to go out with him, Dodds? I will, if you think it would be a favor to Dean Atwood and therefore a favor to you."

"Don't go out with him as a favor to either one of us, Bliss. Only go out with him if you want to. Do you?" he asked again.

"I guess I owe it to myself to get to know him because he seems to have values," she stated, sounding tired.

"If you accept his invitations, will you do me a favor?"

"You want me to show someone else around the campus?" she teased.

"Not hardly. Just call me and let me know where you are going and when—and then call me when you get home?"

She laughed. "Just? You sound like an overly protective father, Dodds."

He flushed. What right did he have to ask all that? "Well…I uh, feel somewhat responsible."

"Don't. If I decide to go out with him, I will *not* call you."

"But…but, Bliss, we've been working together on your problem, I…I need to know how things are going," he pleaded.

The silence stretched out between them, each wondering about the other. "All right, Dodds," she agreed reluctantly, "I will call you as you asked, but only because you've done so much for me. I moved away from home to get away from this kind of over-protectiveness. But Dodds…" another long silence followed.

"What?"

"I really do not appreciate you acting like a father."

He heard a tone in her voice he hadn't heard before. He was silent for a moment thinking, then he spoke softly, "I promise you, Bliss—I don't mean to act like a father because I do not, I reiterate, I do not *feel* fatherly toward you."

~~~~~~~~~~

Lora was confused. She had waited around in the hall after class, only to see Dr. Ackerman usher Billie and a good-looking guy into his office. Then a short time later, she saw Billie and the guy leave together. She followed them for a while then realized that Billie was just showing him around the campus.

Later that evening Lora drove over to Billie's apartment around nine-thiry to see if anything was going on. Finding her place dark, she parked in a discreet place up the street and waited. A half hour later, a black Corvette turned into Billie's driveway. In the driver's seat was that cute guy with Billie beside him. Had they been out on a date? If so, she thought, all her suspicions and conjectures about Billie and Dr. Ackerman were false. Though feeling a little deflated driving home, she decided that a good PI would check it out further.

~~~~~~~~~~

The next three pleasureless and harrowing days dragged on interminably for Sheldon. The calls came from Billie as he had requested, but they were less than satisfying. He had found out in consecutive order that: Thursday afternoon Paul Atwood took Billie on an extravagant picnic outside of town; Thursday evening, they went out to dinner and afterward, attended a symphony; Friday, after the meeting, they went dancing. During the meeting Friday, Sheldon had tried to 'read' Billie since her calls revealed nothing but the briefest of facts. When he questioned her how she felt about Paul Atwood or about how he was treating her or about what his values were, she cut him off with a hurried, "I've got to go." She was still quiet and withdrawn as well as a little distant during the meeting, even though the other three girls and the committee were openly impressed with her success at losing inches.

When the girls had gone, Nettie, Hal and Robert asked him about Billie's change of demeanor, and all he could do was just shrug his shoulders. He felt miserable.

Saturday afternoon, Billie called Sheldon at home and informed him that she and Paul were going to watch videos at her parents home and have dinner with the family. He had hung up the phone feeling betrayed—that was *his* territory! Soon, he realized what he was doing; he was feeling possessive of Bliss and what they had done together. He reprimanded himself, smiling grimly, wondering why was he feeling this way? He certainly shouldn't be feeling this way! Bliss was only a student to whom he'd committed his support and help so she could become productive and successful in a business career. Disturbed that he hadn't totally convinced himself, he got up and stared out of the window.

Glancing at his watch, he decided that the Bliss family and their guest were probably eating dinner about now. Feeling restless, he decided to go for a walk. By the time he'd walked a couple of blocks, he found it much too warm and sultry. He turned around and decided to go for a drive instead. There was no need to stay home in case of a call; Bliss was perfectly safe.

~~~~~~~~~~

Sweat was dripping down Lora's nose as she sat in the car trying to study. All the windows were rolled down but there wasn't even a hint of breeze! She had driven by the home of Billie's parents and saw the Corvette in the driveway. After driving by the house over and over, she decided that the man was going to stay awhile. What would an astute PI do? she asked herself. Wait for them near Billie's apartment, she decided. So here she was, parked about a block away where she could see any car enter Billie's driveway.

Lora was also sweating it out over Billie and that man. They had been pretty thick the past several days, and she was now beginning to wonder if she'd been wasting her time. She got out of the car hoping to cool off, feeling more than a little unnerved and unsure over her suspicions about Billie and Dr. Ackerman. She paced up and down beside the car, mumbling to herself. "Since I've worked this long, I'll stick it out one more night—just to make sure."

~~~~~~~~~~

Sheldon found himself driving by the Bliss home around eighty-thirty, feeling chagrined with himself for pulling, what he considered, a high school tactic. However, he told himself once more, he was responsible for Bliss since he had introduced her to Paul Atwood, so he continued his surveillance. Seeing the black Corvette still in the driveway, he drove back toward Billie's apartment and on past up the hill. Noticing a blue Volkswagon parked less than a block from the apartment, he wondered—no, surely that can't be Miss Lemmon's car. I must be getting paranoid!

Dr. Ackerman's approaching car had sent Lora scuttling behind a bush where she watched as his car went by. "That was close!" she muttered. She stepped out quickly and got back into her car, feeling as skittish as a cat around a toddler.

What was Dr. Ackerman doing in this area anyway? Was it just coincidence? What if he drove by again? She simply couldn't afford to be caught one more time! This thought galvanized her into action. Immediately, she was out of the car and walking rapidly toward Billie's apartment. It was nearly nine o'clock and still light out, so she was hopeful she could find a place to hide where she could watch and not be seen by Dr. Ackerman—or anyone.

Scouting around behind the apartment, she tried to find a place directly across from Billie's front window. To her dismay, she discovered the bushes which offered the best hiding place, also shielded the offensive ant pile. "Maybe the ants are asleep," she mumbled to herself, "I don't remember ants coming out at night." She peeked into the bushes. No ants were in sight. Dare she try to step over the pile? Would it disturb them? she wondered. She had just decided not to chance it when all of a sudden, she heard a car enter the driveway. Ants or no ants, she dove into the bushes, desperately trying to straddle the potential danger.

Paul Atwood parked his Corvette, went around the car, opened the door for Billie and together they went into her apartment. Though just getting dusk, Billie turned on the lights. Lora was delighted, for they were in plain view from where she was standing, legs akimbo.

Lora watched them as they stood facing each other. From what she could see, it looked like they were having a problem. The man seemed to be trying to convince her of something, but Billie kept shaking her head looking very determined. Neither one looked happy. All of a sudden, the young man opened the door and stormed out of the apartment, looking angry and upset. He slammed the car door shut and backed out, screeching the tires all the way.

Well, thought Lora, I guess that's it, I might as well go home. Warily, she checked the window and saw that Billie's back was to it. She slid one foot tentatively out onto the grass just as Dr. Ackerman came pelting up the driveway. Jerking it back in panic, her heel dug a furrow across the top of the ant bed. Horrified, she looked down expecting hoards of the fiery little insects to come charging out to avenge this indignity. Holding her breath, she waited. Scanning the darkening area, she saw no movement. She exhaled a slow sigh of relief and again straddled the ant hill. By the time she looked up, Dr. Ackerman was knocking on Billie's door.

"Yes!" she whispered triumphantly, feeling pleased with herself for sticking it out. This just may be what she'd been waiting for. Her legs, tired from the effort of straddling the pile were beginning to quiver. Since she hadn't disturbed the ants with her heel, she reasoned, maybe she could carefully lower herself to a sitting position on top of the small mound. And if she sat very still, they would probably remain tucked in for the night.

"Dodds! What are you doing here?" Billie exclaimed, opening the door to Sheldon's knock and standing aside to let him enter.

"I was driving down the hill, and saw Paul Atwood backing out of the driveway so violently, I had to swerve to keep from running into him. What happened?"

"I don't want to talk about it," she said turning her back to him.

Sheldon was surprised. This wasn't like Bliss. "Wait a minute, Bliss, remember me, your support counselor?"

She didn't answer, remaining as she was, her back to him. "Bliss?" he questioned, stepping around to face her.

She quickly wheeled around again, but not so quickly that he didn't see the tears. Beside himself with concern, he pleaded, "Bliss, what is it?"

"Just the same old thing," she blubbered, edging around him to the refrigerator. She had just grasped the handle when Sheldon's hand covered hers, holding the door shut.

"Dodds! Don't do that, I want something to eat."

"No, you don't, Bliss, you just had a nice dinner."

She looked up at him with those liquid maple syrup eyes, a drop of which rolled delicately down her cheek. "Please don't tell me what I don't want. You don't even know what I want or don't want!" She pulled the refrigerator open. Sheldon slammed it shut. Billie became fierce in her struggle to open it. He grabbed her with both arms and held her tightly against him. Nevertheless, she continued struggling, but to no avail. Finally she gave up and began to sob against his shoulder. Sheldon loosened his grip enough to stroke her hair tenderly until the sobs subsided.

"Will you sit down and tell me about it, Bliss?"

"In a minute," she mumbled against his chest, not telling him that it felt so good in his arms, she didn't want to move. After some time, she reluctantly said, "All right, I'll tell you."

They both sat down at the small table. Sheldon reached for a tissue from the counter and handed it to her, waiting while she wiped away the remaining tears. Then unconsciously taking her hands in both his, he said, "Go on, Bliss."

"Paul Atwood asked me to marry him."

"So soon?"

"Yes," she whispered, looking like she might cry again.

"Why did that make you unhappy?"

"It didn't."

"Then why…"

"It's a long story."

"Please, don't start that again, Bliss."

A small impish smile twitched around her lips, "How many weeks do you have?"

Sheldon fought back a smile, "I warn you, Bliss, I'm in no mood to be teased."

"He's a very nice man, Dodds."

He waited for her to continue, but she didn't. His patience stretched, he spoke through clenched teeth, "Bliss, I…did you know there were times I've wanted to shake you?"

"You have?" She gave him a small wistful smile, "Why didn't you?"

Sheldon tilted his head, puzzled as to why she seemed amenable to the idea. "Would that have been proper?"

She smiled and nodded her head.

In spite of himself, he laughed. "Females have always been an enigma to me, Bliss, but you take the cake." Making an effort to become serious, he said, "Now—will you please tell me why you are unhappy over Paul Atwood's proposal?"

"All right, Dodds. After the dance on Friday, he took me to the park and we sat on a bench and talked, and then he asked me to marry him. He didn't even try to kiss me. I was very impressed with that. He assured me that all he wanted at the moment was permission to date me until I knew him better, and that I didn't need to give him an answer yet." She looked down and sighed.

"Go on. What did you say?" Sheldon asked, feeling anxious over what her answer might be.

"I had no reason not to give him permission to date me...but...." She stopped, hesitant to go on.

"So what happened?"

A sadness, that he hadn't seen for awhile, came over her face. Again he thought, she's as changeable as a child.

Another sigh escaped her lips. "On Saturday, he was very charming with my family. After dinner, when we were watching videos, he asked if we could talk instead. I was glad. I felt obligated to get to know him better—and besides I could tell he was bored with the video," she added, sounding disappointed.

"I asked him all about his family. I asked him why he hadn't married yet, and he said it was because he hadn't been able to find an old-fashioned girl until now. Then I asked him how many children he wanted and—that's what happened." She gave no other explanation, looking at him as if she expected him to understand.

Carrying on a normal conversation with this girl was about to be his undoing. "Are you going to explain?"

"Well," tears pooled up in her eyes, "he said he didn't want any children."

Sheldon was shocked. "Why in the world not?"

"Oh, I'm glad you're shocked too, Dodds. That makes me feel better." She managed a pathetic little smile. "He said that he was too old to start having children at his age. I said that any old-fashioned girl would want children and didn't he think of that? He said yes, but if she was the right girl for him, she would realize that it would be for the best, after all, the world was getting to be a pretty bad place in which to raise children."

Sheldon felt thoroughly depressed. If Paul Atwood was too old to have children then what about himself? Now, why was he thinking that? he wondered. "Go on, Bliss."

"I told him that I wanted as many children as I could have. So he had better look for another old-fashioned girl. Well, he spent the rest of the evening trying to convince me otherwise, but he'd already—killed the romance."

"Wanting children is part of romance?" Sheldon asked, wondering if he would ever learn what romance was.

"Of course, Dodds."

He thought about that a moment, then spoke slowly, "That makes sense to me."

"I'm so glad you feel like that, Dodds."

"What did you do or say to make him so angry?"

"I told him he was selfish for not wanting children. You see, Dodds...ROMANCE IS DEAD!" The tears started to flow again. Sheldon stood and pulled her up into his arms, holding her tightly, comforting her—telling himself that this was necessary so she wouldn't want food for comfort. But she felt so good in his arms, as she had a moment ago, he wondered which one of them was getting the comfort. They stood so long like this, Sheldon could no longer delude himself. It was time to go.

Reluctantly letting her go, he looked down into her face and smiled. "Are you all right now, Bliss?"

She smiled one of those Bliss smiles. "Yes, Dodds, I don't need to eat for comfort, you have given me enough."

Lora had been so delighted and engrossed in the sight of Dr. Ackerman and Billie hugging, she had bounced with excitement, totally forgetting her resolve to sit still. All of a sudden, she felt ants crawling up her legs and her arms! Squelching a scream, she stood up, straddling the mound. Clapping her hand over her mouth, she knew she had to get out—and now! Just as she started to emerge, Dr. Ackerman opened the door and came out onto the porch. It seemed to Lora that he was walking in slow motion down the steps and out onto the driveway. She panted, almost hyperventilating while lifting first one leg off the ground and then the other.

When she was sure he had time to walk down the driveway and on toward his car, she crawled through the shrubbery past Billie's window and almost fell through the bushes, trying to get out. Getting up, she ran down the driveway, stopping only long enough to make sure Dr. Ackerman was driving off. Crossing the street, she ran up the walk a short ways and stopped. Jumping up and down, Lora gasped, shuddered and clawed frantically at the ants which were now inside her cutoffs and up under her T shirt! She ran on to her car, got in and turned the key before the door was even closed. The faithful old motor came to life. Shoving it into gear, she made a U turn and headed toward the corner just as another car was turning the same corner. Brakes squealed, but Lora, half blinded by tears, ignored the frightened driver, turned right and sped toward home, weaving as she wiggled, gasped, and bawled.

A police siren screamed behind her. Looking into the rear view mirror, the blue and red lights whirled in a watery blur. "Oh no! I hope it isn't Officer Bates...Oh no!" she wailed as she pulled the car over to the side.

Arly Bates, couldn't believe his eyes. Surely, this wasn't Miss Lora Lemmon again! Getting out of his car, he walked up to the open window and peered in and saw a woman, her hands covering her face, peeking through her fingers. "Not you! Oh darn!" came the muffled cry behind them.

"Is that you, Miss Lemmon?"

"It is!" she wailed, removing her hands, "and I have ants inside my clothes," she gasped, "I gotta get home fast!"

"Miss Lemmon, I almost ran into you broadside as I turned the corner! he exclaimed, angrily.

"That...that was you?"

"That was me. Don't tell me you sat on another ant pile?"

"No, it...it was the same one," she wailed.

The flustered young officer didn't know what else to do, but what he did last time. "Follow me, I'll lead you home again. But we're going to have to have a talk, Miss Lemmon."

"Th..thank you, Officer Bates."

Ella Lemmon was feeling out of sorts with her daughter. She hardly saw her. Lately she was in and out of the house acting quite mysterious, and here it was after ten and she wasn't home yet.

The siren she heard off in the distance was getting closer and louder. She stepped out onto the porch and saw a police car speeding down the road. Her eyes widened in disbelief. It looked like Lora following!

"Not again! Stupid girl."

Chapter Twenty-Five

Sunday afternoon, Lora stood before the bathroom mirror, sniffling and talking to herself as she examined all the new ant bites which stood out glaringly on her face and neck. She had already dabbed medicine on as many as she could reach on her arms, legs and other places.

"I should get something out of this! First, I nearly die of ant bites, and then I nearly die from embarrassment when Officer Bates stopped me again. Ohooo," she wailed. "Yes, I should get something out of this." What she'd seen last night through Billie's window suddenly brought her to a decision—or at least a beginning of one. She smiled at her pathetic reflection, as she thought about it. "Yes! I'm going to go see Billie Bliss tonight. Tonight is the night."

She waited until eight o'clock and told her mother she would be back in about an hour.

"Are you going out in public looking like that?" her mother asked, aghast.

"Yes, Ma. See you later."

Lora drove into Billie's backyard and parked. No more hiding in the bushes! She sat there a moment, feeling her bravado ebb away— but one look in the mirror immediately brought it back.

She knocked confidently on Billie's door. When Billie opened it and saw Lora's condition, her sympathy was so sincere, Lora felt a wave of guilt.

"Oh my, Lora, did you get stung by ants again?"

"Yes."

"Come in and tell me about it."

"Thank you," Lora mumbled.

"Please have a seat. Can I get you a cold drink of juice?"

Lora sat down like a lump of clay. "No thanks," she mumbled again.

Billie sat down at the table across from her. "How did it happen? Did it happen as funny as last time?"

"Funny? I almost died of humiliation!"

Billie's eyes were wide with curiosity. "Tell me about it."

Lora told her the whole story, except *where* she got the bites. Billie reacted to every part of the story in a most satisfying way, Oohing and gasping in the appropriate places. Lora found great relish in the telling of it.

"Oh no, not Officer Bates again!" Billie exclaimed, her hands over her mouth in horror. When the story was all over, Billie said, "Tell it again."

Lora was glad to oblige, so caught up with it, she forgot why she'd come. As she told it again, Billie started giggling, then Lora joined in and by the time she had finished telling it the second time, they were both laughing so hard tears were running down their faces. When they gained control, Lora remembered something.

"I forgot to tell you. Officer Bates gave me a good talking to— telling me that he should give me a ticket for the reckless U-turn, but since I was suffering still with ants inside my clothes, he would let it go this time. He then told me that if he ever caught me getting bitten again, he'd throw me in jail just to protect me."

Billie's mouth dropped open, then they both burst out laughing again.

When they finally settled down, Billie said, "Officer Bates sounds like such a nice man."

"Yes," she sighed "and he's so-o-o good looking."

"But you left something out, Lora. Where did you get stung—and why did you let it happen twice?"

Lora's heart sank—could she go through with this? Billie was turning out to be a friend.

"What is the matter, Lora?"

"Uh...uh you're going to hate me, Billie...but I...I just have to after all I've gone through. I...I got stung by the ants in the bushes— right across from your window."

Billie looked blank. "In the bushes outside...in my backyard?"

"Yes. I sat on an ant pile in the bushes while...while watching you and Dr. Ackerman hug each other Saturday night."

Billie was so dumbfounded, she just stared at Lora.

"And what's more, I've...been following you and Dr. Ackerman," she blurted out.

"Wh…why?"

"Because I was in the video store when he was renting some steamy videos and I just put two and two together."

Billie was horrified. "Oh no, Lora, that was a mistake. He doesn't know anything about the movies today."

"Well, is a professor supposed to be hugging his student like I saw Dr. Ackerman hugging you Saturday night?"

"It…it wasn't what it looked like, Lora."

"Uh…what…what do you think Dean Atwood would do if I told him?"

"Lora! You wouldn't."

"I might…unless…"

"Lora are you…blackmailing me?"

"No. Well…I think so—sort of."

"What do you want from me?"

"I…don't know exactly," she said, her face puckering up, on the verge of tears. "I just…just want to get out of my situation and you, Billie, have so much."

"And you think this is the right way to get what you want?"

"No…but…"

"Lora, I want you to leave right now. I have to think about this. I'll talk to you another time—and don't you dare do anything until I talk to you again. Do you understand, Lora?"

"Yes," she said in a small, dismal voice. She got up, walked to the door and went out, feeling totally despondent. This wasn't the way she expected to feel—but then, she wasn't used to being a criminal.

Billie walked back and forth, seething with anger toward Lora, while at the same time not quite believing she could really do this kind of thing. Stopping abruptly, she ran outside across the small lawn to the bushes and looked in. Sure enough there was what was left of the ant pile and ants were swarming around, trying to rebuild their home. The evidence was there, but she wondered—would Lora really do what she had hinted? She walked slowly back to the porch and sat down on the steps. For some reason, Billie didn't believe she really would, but could she take a chance? What was she going to do?

The evening was turning into a soft, muted twilight, casting golden hues upon the bushes—Lora's hiding place. Breathing in deeply several times, the sweet-smelling air acted to calm her frazzled emotions momentarily, but soon she covered her face and muttered, "What shall I do?! What shall I do? I need Dodds." She needed his strong protecting arms around her as they had been last night.

How she had needed those embraces—and the hope that came with them, the hope that he might feel about her the way she felt about him.

It took going out with Paul Atwood to help her focus on and understand all the strange emotions she'd been feeling lately when she was with Dodds. All she could do those four days with Paul, was compare him to Dodds and as nice as Paul was, he always fell short. For the first time she acknowledged, to herself, the true depths of her need for him.

And what Mr. Sheldon Dodds Ackerman didn't know, she thought ruefully, was—her tears last night were more over the fear that he might not feel as she did. When he held her again, her hopes had soared.

She sat on the steps until long after dark, thinking. At last, she realized what she needed to do, what she *had* to do. Now, any hopes she had of something growing between her and Dodds, were gone, dashed by Lora Lemmon!

Chapter Twenty-Six

At 9:00 AM, Monday morning, Billie walked into the enrollment office of Fairfield University and formally dropped out of school.

She entered the 280 class at nine-fifty to attend for the last time. Noticing a group of girls gathering around Lora, she stopped by the group momentarily and peered in. Lora, who had begun telling the story of the second set of ant bites, became tongue-tied when she glimpsed Billie's face. Billie glared at her a moment, then turned and walked to her seat.

"Go on, go on!" begged the girls.

Lora's muteness soon passed. Caught up in all the attention, she told the story in dramatic detail, creating in her audience the gamut of emotions from horror to laughter.

This is how Dr. Ackerman found his class, all huddled around Lora Lemmon, but with Billie off by herself. This caused him a moment of reflection.

"Will you please all take your seats? It's time for class to start," he said in a voice loud enough to be heard above the commotion.

As the group dispersed, he saw Miss Lemmon, looking flushed and excited, her face and arms covered with a new set of red bumps.

"Miss Lemmon, will you please come up to my desk?"

"Y..yes Dr. Ackerman."

He studied her a moment and lowered his voice. "Don't tell me that those are more ant bites."

"They…they are, Dr. Ackerman."

"Don't tell me you sat in another ant pile?"

"No, Dr. Ackerman, not another one—the same one."

"The same one! Good grief girl, how come?"

Lora Lemmon, stuttered, shrugged her shoulders and turned as red as a pie cherry.

He studied her trying to fathom this ridiculous girl and her actions. Still smoldering over the incident in the video store, his jaw tightened. Through clenched teeth he said, "Please return to your seat."

Turning his attention to the class, he saw Bliss gazing at him intently. Their eyes locked. Something was wrong. He cleared his throat and began his lecture.

The minute class was over, Billie got up immediately, the first to leave the room. Stepping quickly over to Dr. Ackerman's office, she shoved an envelope under the door, walked rapidly out of the building, got into her car and headed toward her parent's home.

Sheldon felt great consternation over Bliss leaving so quickly, not even glancing in his direction. He'd wanted to talk to her.

When he unlocked his office door, he noticed the envelope. He picked it up and saw his name printed on the front. Puzzled, he walked around and sat down at his desk, opened it and looked at the signature. It was from Bliss! He began reading:

"Dear Dr. Ackerman," he frowned. Why the formality? he wondered. She was the one who wanted to drop the formality between them.

"It would be too difficult to explain this in person, so I'm writing it. First of all, circumstances have come up that make it impossible for me to remain in school and thus in Project Success. This is not of my own choosing, nevertheless, it is the way it has to be.

I have moved back home because of these circumstances, and I am asking you to please not contact me. It will be of no use—and it will be for the best.

There is absolutely no fault on your part. You are not to blame in any way. Be assured of that.

You have been so kind to me and as I have said, you have helped me greatly.

> Thank you for everything.
> Sincerely
> Billie Bliss"

Sheldon was stunned—unable to believe it, not wanting to. Why? He read and reread it. The first thought that came to his mind was he'd offended her with his embraces Saturday night—but then, as he read it several more times, two things stood out. "This is not of my own choosing" and "There is absolutely no fault on your part." These two sentences gave him comfort.

~~~~~~~~~

Lora hung around the halls a while, feeling despondent. All the excitement over, her life was back to what it was before she began her titillating detective work, drab and uninteresting. Also, her conscience was pricking her unmercifully—so much so, she was about to go to Billie, apologize and tell her to forget it. But not quite. She had to hang on to her plan a while longer. She needed to think about it. Besides, she had to get home and get ready for work. She'd missed so much lately, they had threatened to fire her.

The old tired feeling was back; she plodded out of the building to her car.

~~~~~~~~~

Sheldon stood on the Bliss porch at 4:00 PM ringing the door bell. Margaret answered it, and stepped out onto the porch, closing the door behind her.

"Hello, Sheldon," she said, a look of concern on her face. "How are you?"

"Not very well, Margaret. I guess you know about the letter Bliss wrote me?"

"Yes."

"May I see her?"

"She has asked us to tell you that she cannot see you."

"Why, Margaret, why? This comes as a great shock to me."

"I'm sorry, Sheldon, but I can't tell you why. She has asked us not to."

"You know what is behind all this then?"

"Yes."

"And you can't tell me?" he asked, distress in his voice.

"No, Sheldon, I'm sorry."

"But it's not of her own choosing as she said?"

"It is something Billie would never choose."

"And," he continued, "as she said, I'm not at fault?"

"That is absolutely correct."

"Please Margaret, tell me what is going on."

"I wish I could, Sheldon."

He looked down, his hands in his pockets, silent for a moment, then looked up, "Well...then I guess I'll be going," he said, his shoulders slumped in defeat. "Goodnight, Margaret."

Billie, heavyhearted, watched Sheldon walk slowly to his car and drive off. She wanted to run out to him and tell him everything was all right. But—she had to protect him—and his reputation at the university. She turned from the window to find her mother standing beside her.

"I wish you would change your mind, Billie. He was so unhappy."

"He was?" Her heart begged to know why he was unhappy, but she just said, "I'm going to drive out to Lora Lemmon's house now and talk to her, hoping I can find out what is in her mind—if I can."

Billie looked up the address, went outside and got into her car. While driving to Lora's house, her mind was filled with questions. What was she was going to do now that her life was so cruelly and abruptly changed? Acute loneliness gripped her. Never in all her adult life had she fallen in love with anyone or even come close—until now. And she was in love with a man ten years older who probably wouldn't even entertain the idea of marriage, let alone marriage to some one ten years younger! She blinked back the tears that blurred the road.

She drove into Lora Lemmon's graveled driveway, turned off the motor and studied the house and yard. The statement that Lora made, "you have so much," came to her mind. I do, she thought, have so much more than Lora. Billie dreaded the encounter with her, so much so she could hardly make herself get out of the car. However, it wasn't long before she found herself on the small porch ringing the door bell.

The door opened and a large, pasty-faced woman peered out. "Yes?"

"Hello, I'm Billie Bliss, a classmate of Lora's."

"Oh yes, she's mentioned you. Come in."

Billie stepped into the darkened room, trying to adjust her eyesight.

"I'm Ella Lemmon, Lora's mother. Please have a seat. Excuse the room, my health isn't good."

"Thank you," Billie sat down on a chair next to the couch, now able to see better—but what she saw depressed her. Ella Lemmon, in a pull-over shift and dirty house slippers, went over to the television, turned it down, pushed uncombed hair from her face, and shuffled over to the couch. She noticed the number of bottles of medicine on the lamp table, the drawn blinds, the clutter.

Ella saw Billie eyeing the medicine. "You see, I have migraines. I haven't even been able to work lately. And Lora has skipped work so much, they're about to fire her. I don't know what has gotten into her."

"Is Lora here, Mrs. Lemmon?"

"No, she finally went to work. Oh, she did say she was going over to see you first, though. Didn't she?"

"Oh, no. I've moved out of my apartment. She probably went there. I've moved to my parent's home at 303 Maple Ave. Would you tell her this, Mrs. Lemmon?" she asked, standing up to go.

While driving home, Billie's brows crinkled in concern. No wonder Lora wants to get out of her situation! Nevertheless, she reminded herself, that is absolutely no excuse for her behaving in such a wicked and devious manner!

~~~~~~~~~

Sheldon walked into his condominium shaking his head. For some reason he found himself thinking about the movie, *Pride and Prejudice,* and in particular, Darcy's gut wrenching agony over Elizabeth. In a startling flash of insight, he realized that it was an agony that *he* could now fully understand. Caught up in the welter of conflicting emotions, one thought struck him like the cold blast of a January wind—the thought of not being able to enjoy Bliss' company. It was more than he could bear.

The old habit of avoiding personal relationships asserted itself. Billie Bliss was just his student and a student who was ten years younger than himself! Besides, what ever made him think that a beautiful girl like her would even consider someone like him? It was obvious she could have her pick.

After two hours of pacing, agonizing, going over everything and analyzing his emotions, there was only one conclusion he could possibly make—he was completely and unalterably in love with Billie Bliss. He now recognized he had been for some time. As he compared his feeling for Bliss with what he felt for the young woman he'd fallen for years ago, he found that there was no comparison. The other was like a high-school crush compared to the love he felt for Bliss. And with Bliss, there was no vestige of the painful shyness he'd battled for years when in the presence of women.

A most wonderful fact flashed into his mind. Since Bliss was no longer a student at Fairfield University, he could take her out! He could take her to nice places as Paul Atwood had done. Recognizing, now, that the misery he felt while Paul was pursuing her—was just plain ol' harrowing jealousy!

The next logical step was to find out if Bliss would even consider him—but how could he? She wouldn't even see him! Somehow—he'd find a way.

After fixing himself a frozen dinner, Sheldon sat down at the table with pen and paper, determined to come up with some clues which would explain why Bliss dropped out of school, and out of the Project. The most haunting question was why did Bliss pull away from *him*? She had to have a good reason for her actions and there had to be some signals, signs or clues. It couldn't have come out of the blue, without a warning somewhere along the line.

He thought back over the past several weeks. Did Bliss say or do anything different, seem different? One thing came to mind; she seemed subdued for a while—not herself. He wrote it down. But—it seemed to be over with Saturday night. Remembering how it felt to hold her in his arms was both joy and torture!

He needed to calm down and think rationally—not feel. What was different, what was new, what was jarring of late? Getting up, he paced the floor thinking...thinking. Lora Lemmon, that's what. Everywhere he turned, she was there—bumping into him! But how could she figure in this? He couldn't see how.

And this morning before class, there was definitely another jarring note. All the girls were gathered around Miss Lemmon—all, but Bliss. She wasn't participating, nor in the middle of it as she was last time Miss Lemmon got herself into a pickle. No matter how he looked at it, there was one common denominator—Lora Lemmon. She had to be the problem. But how? Tomorrow he was definitely going to go see Miss Lemmon and question her.

Grateful that at least he had something to work on, Sheldon got ready for bed, feeling totally exhausted.

~~~~~~~~~~

Lora Lemmon stood on the Bliss porch at 9:00 PM, shaking like a poodle in a grooming parlor. When she got home from work, her mother informed her that Billie had come to the house to see her. It was hard to go over to Billie's apartment this afternoon, but coming here was worse. Who knows, her parents might even call the police! But— no matter—she had to get this over with. She pushed the doorbell and almost started hyperventilating.

The door was opened by a kind-faced, elderly man. "Hello, may I help you?"

"I…I came to see Billie. Is she home?"

"She is," he stated enthusiastically, smiling. "Come in."

"Oh no…th..thank you, I'll just wait out here."

"All right, miss, you wait right there and I'll get her."

The man's kindness made her feel a little calmer. She went over to the porch swing and sat down to wait.

"Hello, Lora," Billie said walking out the door and over to the swing.

"Hello, Billie."

"Your mother told me you came to see me today at my apartment."

"Yes, I did."

Billie sat down beside her on the swing. "What's on your mind, Lora?"

"I came to tell you…" a sob escaped. "I came to tell you that…I'm sorry!" She covered her face and cried.

Billie waited until Lora's crying let up, then asked, "And what does that mean, Lora, when you say you're sorry?"

She looked at Billie. "It means that I'm not going to…to blackmail you. I…I don't know why I started it all…I…I think it began when I was feeling discouraged and I began to feel jealous of you. I've never felt jealous of anyone before. And when I saw Dr. Ackerman in the video store, I was ready to think the worst—then I guess I began kind of pretending I was a private investigator. It seemed exciting at the time…and then…getting stung by ants and all, it just seemed like I needed to go through with it." Another sob escaped. "I'm so sorry for feeling jealous of you. I've promised myself I won't ever feel like that again."

Billie was silent, thinking. Lora looked at her anxiously. "Are you going to forgive me?"

"Blackmail is against the law, Lora."

"I know," she wailed. "Go ahead and call the police—but please make sure it isn't Officer Bates who comes to get me."

Billie found herself smiling. "I'm not going to call the police, Lora. And…I forgive you."

"You do?" Her tear-laden eyes opened wide in amazement. "Oh, thank you, Billie, thank you! I have been so miserable since last night, I could hardly sleep, and I could hardly do my job at work today."

"Will you do me a favor, Lora?"

"Oh yes, yes…anything!"

"Do you have a class tomorrow morning?"

"No, I don't have any classes on Tuesday and Thursday."

"Could you meet me at my apartment tomorrow morning at 9:00?"

"Is that the favor?"

"No, I'll tell you tomorrow."

"Okay and thanks again, Billie," she said standing up. "I…I can't believe you have forgiven me so soon. See you tomorrow."

Billie sat on the porch swing and watched Lora go to her car and drive off, feeling grateful for Lora's complete remorse. She could now put into operation a plan she'd conceived to help Lora. It was predicated upon her apologizing and backing down on her threat. She hadn't expected it so soon.

She remained in the swing, thinking about her life now that the threat to Dodds was over. What should she do? She knew she couldn't go back to school and continue as before; every thing was different now that she was hopelessly in love with him.

Chapter Twenty-Seven

Lora was waiting on the steps of Billie's apartment when Billie drove up.

"Good morning, Lora," Billie said smiling.

Lora looked down, sheepish and dejected. "Good morning, Billie."

Billie sat down on the steps beside her. "It's a beautiful morning isn't it?"

"Better morning than yesterday, that's for sure," Lora mumbled, her head bowed.

"I would think so," Billie said, studying her. "Now, for the favor. Would you consider moving into my apartment for a few months—at least for three? I've paid the rent that far ahead."

Lora's head jerked up. She stared at Billie, not believing her ears. "Move into your apartment? Why?"

"I'm making other plans which may mean moving out of Claytonville, but in case I want to move back, I want to leave my furniture here. I need someone to live here whom I can trust to take good care of everything while I'm gone."

"You...you trust me?"

"Yes, I do, Lora."

"How can you trust me after..."

"I don't know, Lora, but I do."

"But...but I should pay you rent."

"Oh no, not while my furniture is here. If I took it out so you could put your own in, then I would expect rent."

"Are you sure you want to do this, Billie?"

"I'm sure."

Lora shook her head, not believing her good fortune—good fortune she didn't deserve!

"Come on inside, Lora, I want you to look at some clothes."

They both got up and went inside and Billie said, "Can you see that I've lost weight?"

"Oh, yes! You are so lucky to have been chosen for the Project."

Billie opened her closet and pulled out all of the clothes that she had been wearing when she was overweight and laid them over the couch. "These are all too big for me now. I was wondering—you and I are about the same height and you seem to be the weight I was. I wondered if you could use them?"

Lora could hardly believe it. These were all the beautiful clothes she'd been envying. "Oh...yes! Yes I could."

"Try them on and see."

Lora tried on each one and they all seemed to fit, perhaps a tad snugly, but she was determined to lose weight, now! Her green eyes were sparkling with happiness. "Oh thank you, Billie. Thank you! I don't deserve all this from you." The tears started rolling down her cheeks.

Billie hugged her. "Yes, you do. Hey, I have an idea, why don't I style your hair? I have kind of a knack for it."

"You do? Oh, let's do!"

Billie studied Lora's face and asked, "Do you like Josie's windblown hair style, Lora?"

"I do. She's such a pretty girl."

"Well, I think that style would look very nice on you. I've seen golden highlights in your hair right after you've washed it. I have a special shampoo that will bring out those highlights even more, and make your hair more glossy besides."

"You do? I've wondered how you kept your hair looking so shiny, Billie."

Billie studied her face some more. "You know, I've never seen such beautiful, large green eyes as you have, Lora. And your high cheek bones and petite mouth make you look like someone an artist would want to paint. You are much prettier than Josie."

Lora listened, wide-eyed, trying to internalize this amazing assessment of her looks.

An hour later, Lora looked into the mirror at herself. Her hair, shiny and blow-dried into the stylish, loose, windblown look, was no longer stringy and dull. The light green cotton pant set did wonders for her, too.

"Lora, that green makes your eyes look even greener and your complexion looks like peaches and cream—even with the ant bites. You are so pretty."

"I am? You really think so?"

"I know so. Now, Lora, will you move into my apartment?"

"I will. But I'll have to sneak a few things over at first and move in gradually until I can break the news to my mother. I'll start preparing her. She has become very dependent on me."

"Your mother needs to find a way to get back to work and quit using you as a crutch."

Lora's eyes widened. "You think so, too? I've been feeling guilty for thinking that very thing—and Ma is good at making me feel guilty."

"Here are the keys to the apartment, Lora. I've got to go now. There is food in the cupboards, the refrigerator and freezer, please use it. I'm going around the front and tell Mrs. Griffen, the landlady that you'll be living here for awhile."

Lora watched her go, thrilled and excited, feeling like a modern-day Cinderella.

Billie rang the doorbell and Mrs. Griffen appeared, opening the screen door. "Come in, Billie."

"Here's the check, Mrs. Griffen, for September, October and November that I said I would probably bring to you. My friend, who will be living here and taking care of the apartment, is Lora Lemmon."

Driving home, Billie smiled. She felt so pleased at the make over she'd done on Lora. As she'd suspected, Lora had basic good looks and all she needed was a new hairstyle, flattering clothes, a little makeup and—a happy expression to bring out her beauty. She found it rather exhilarating to play *Pygmalion.*

~~~~~~~~~~

Sheldon impatiently attended to his duties all morning until 11:30, then looked up Lora Lemmon's class schedule and address. Taking the chance that she might be home for lunch, he decided to try to see her there.

Pulling up into the Lemmon driveway, he sat in the car a moment, contemplating the neglected house and yard, feeling hesitant to go in.

Nevertheless, he got out of the car, walked up to the house, and rang the door bell. He heard a television blaring loudly. He rang again.

Presently, the door opened a crack. "Yes?"

"Hello, I'm Dr. Ackerman, Lora's teacher at school."

The door opened wide. "Oh, do come in Dr. Ackerman, Lora has spoken of you."

He stepped inside, adjusting his sight to the darkened room.

"I'm Ella Lemmon, Lora's mother." Please excuse me, but I'm suffering from a beastly migraine. But do have a seat, Dr. Ackerman."

"Thank you, Mrs. Lemmon," he said, trying to see the chair to which she pointed. When he sat down, he saw that Mrs. Lemmon appeared to have just awakened. Her hair was frazzled and her robe revealed a night gown underneath.

Ella Lemmon sat down and reached over to the lamp table, opened a prescription bottle and took out a couple of pills. "Now, what can I do for you, Dr. Ackerman? I do hope Lora is doing all right in your class."

"That isn't what I came to talk to Lora about, I just need to ask her a few questions about something else. Is she here?"

"No, she isn't. I'm sorry. She told me she was going over to the apartment of a classmate—Billie Bliss. Those two must be getting thick, Billie Bliss was here to see Lora yesterday morning."

Sheldon's brows rose. "Is that right?" He stood up abruptly. "Well then, I'll run over there and see her. Thank you, Mrs. Lemmon."

On the way over, Sheldon was sure now that Lora Lemmon had some answers. His spirits rose at the thought of seeing Bliss. Surely, she would be there if she had company. In his excitement, he parked behind Lora's Volkswagon not even noticing that Billie's car was missing. He ran to the porch and rang the doorbell, his heart pounding.

The door opened and a young woman stood there, her eyes wide with shock and concern. She looked familiar. They stared at each other for a moment.

"Dr. Ackerman!"

"Miss...Miss Lemmon?" he asked in amazement.

"Yes."

"What are you doing in Miss Bliss' clothes?"

"She gave them to me."

"She what?" He pushed his way in and looked around. "Where is she?" he asked, glowering at her.

"I...I guess she's at home."

"Well, what are *you* doing here, if *she's* at home?"

"I live here. She asked me to stay here and take care of the apartment because she is going to move from Claytonville as soon as she finds a job."

Sheldon fell into a chair—trying to absorb what he'd just heard. "Why is she going to move from Claytonville?" he asked in a barely audible voice.

Lora shook her head. "I don't know, she didn't tell me."

Maybe I'm wrong about Miss Lemmon, he thought, but reaching into his coat pocket, he pulled out the letter anyway. "She wrote me this letter. I was wondering if you would mind reading it."

Lora reached for it and began reading, while Sheldon studied her closely. Her hand started to shake, and she dissolved into tears.

"Oh, no! She's quit college and moving out of town because of me."

Sheldon stood up and pulled the letter from her hands, asking in an ominous voice, "And why is that, Miss Lemmon?"

She plopped herself down on the couch and bawled loudly. With no compassion in his demeanor whatsoever, Sheldon stood waiting for her to gain some control—which didn't seem to be forthcoming.

"Miss Lemmon!" he yelled to be heard above the hysterics. She looked up into his scowling face, and only wailed louder. He sat down and waited, tapping his fingers together impatiently.

Finally, Lora got up and went over to the counter, picked up a box of tissues, pulled out a couple and blew her nose thoroughly.

"You...you want to know why I sat on an ant hill twice, Dr. Ackerman?"

"Not particularly, Miss Lemmon. That, I'm afraid, is way down on the list of things I would like to know."

"I spied on you and Billie," she blurted out in a defiant voice.

Sheldon's mouth dropped open and it remained so as he tried to internalize her statement. "Spied? Where?"

"Out on top of the ant pile."

"Miss Lemmon…" his voice turned ominous again. "Don't play games with me. Explain."

"I'm not playing games, Dr. Ackerman, I spied on you both while sitting on top of an ant pile. I didn't know it was an ant bed the first time, but the second time I spied, I knew."

Sheldon's patience had reached its limit. "Miss Lemmon, I don't care whether you knew it was an ant hill or not," he roared, "just tell me where in the blazes the ant hill is!"

"Out in back," she said in a plaintive voice.

"Show me," he ordered.

Lora led him outside and over to the bushes and pointed. "Inside there."

Sheldon looked in and saw ants swarming all over a large mound of dirt. Pulling his face out, he looked over at Billie's window directly across from the bushes and then over at Lora, his face revealing total shock, as well as dawning understanding. "You were spying on us!"

"That's what I said."

"Whatever possessed you to do such a thing?" he asked, barely able to hold in his mounting anger.

"So…so I could find out some juicy information."

"Miss Lemmon, I don't want to choke you right out here on the lawn, let's go inside," he threatened, leading the way.

When they were both inside, he closed the door. "Let's both sit down and discuss this calmly," he said slowly, "what do you mean by—juicy information?"

"You didn't see me, but I was in the video store when you first went in to rent some movies. I watched what kind you were renting and became curious."

Sheldon flushed. "Go on."

"I began to suspect that they had something to do with Billie Bliss so I began following you."

His jaw dropped. "I knew it. I knew it!" he jumped up and leaned over her, shaking his fist at her in a menacing manner. "I began to suspect. It couldn't have been mere coincidence bumping into each other all the time. But why…why would you want to know anything? What could you possibly gain by it?"

"I...I don't know why," she said, cowering under his shadow. "At first, it just seemed exciting, and I told myself I was doing it for the good of Fairfield University."

"What were you going to do if you found out something 'juicy,' Miss Lemmon?" he asked, his voice hoarse with anger.

Lora sat up straight and looked him in the eye. "I did find out something juicy."

"On who?" A sliver of fear penetrated his anger. He sat down again and asked hesitantly, "Surely, not on Miss Bliss and that young man?"

"You mean that cool guy she just dated?"

"I guess that's a description you young women might use. Yes."

"No."

He was visibly relieved. "Then...who?"

"You and Billie Bliss," she stated triumphantly.

He stood up abruptly. "You couldn't have!"

"But I did. I saw you hugging her twice last Saturday night."

"You...you were out in the bushes that night?"

"Yes, I was and I had a new set of ant bites on Monday morning to prove it."

"Good grief, girl, you...you are a peeping Tom...or something like that." Sheldon paced around the small room, scowling and muttering under his breath. He stopped abruptly. "Wait a minute here," he said, suspicion clouding his face, "what does all this have to do with Billie Bliss dropping out of school and moving away?"

Lora began to wail again. Frustrated, Sheldon sat down and once more waited her out.

Pulling out another tissue, Lora blew her nose and confessed. "I kind of blackmailed her, I asked her what Dean Atwood would do if I told him what I saw."

Sheldon was stunned. "Good Grief!" Thoughts were swirling around in his mind as he tried to piece it all together—then he realized—Bliss quit school and *Project Success* to...to...protect him!

Lora, who had been watching her professor's face intently, was surprised to see an expression of total relief replace the one of shock. She waited, curious...then his gaze turned upon her.

"Miss Lemmon, your confession has just saved me from a life of misery."

"It has?" she asked with wide-eyed astonishment. "If...if I have, I'm very happy about that...and Dr. Ackerman...if there's anything I can do for you, just let me know. I would like to make it up to you."

"Yes, yes," he muttered, her remark only penetrating the surface of his mind, which was now at 303 Maple Ave. Suddenly, it got through and an idea began to form. He jumped up, excited. "Miss Lemmon, I just might take you up on your offer. I may be contacting you soon."

He was out the door so fast, Lora couldn't reply. She watched him get in his car and back out.

Sheldon screeched to a stop as he came to the end of the driveway. What was he thinking about? Miss Lora Lemmon, like all females, had so confused him, he'd forgotten to ask her a very important question. He returned his car to its former position and got out.

Lora, surprised to see him come back, opened the door before he even had time to ring the bell. "What is it, Dr. Ackerman?"

"May I come in, Miss Lemmon? I forgot to ask you something."

"Of course, come in. What is it you want to ask me?"

His eyes narrowed suspiciously, "You're wearing Billie Bliss' clothes, living in her apartment, is this because you are blackmailing her?"

"Oh no, Dr. Ackerman. I talked to her Sunday night about maybe telling Dean Atwood what I saw—but I felt bad when I got home, so bad I could hardly sleep all night and I could hardly concentrate in school all day and at work. I went to see Billie that night and apologized and asked her to forgive me."

Sheldon was puzzled. "Then why did she give you her clothes and let you live here?"

"I don't know, Dr. Ackerman. She just asked if I could meet her here this morning and I said yes. I was shocked at her kindness. I told her that I didn't deserve it all, but she insisted that I did."

Sheldon frowned and shook his head. "Well, I just don't know what to say. Good day, Miss Lemmon." He turned on his heel and left.

On the way home, Sheldon tried to sort it all out. What were Bliss' plans now that his being disgraced was no longer an issue. His mind, however, soon turned to the idea that came to him when Miss Lemmon offered her help. Trying not to let his excitement carry him away, he knew what he needed to do before he could pursue it any further. And it had to be done—tonight.

Chapter Twenty-Eight

All during the meal, Nettie and Don Newman, Sharon and Hal Ozog and Molly and Robert Bittle had watched Sheldon seesaw between excitement and nervousness. They were more than curious, they were on the edge of their seats. When Sheldon called this afternoon and invited them to dinner at the country club because he had to have their help on something, they knew it was serious. Sheldon's social habits were usually predictable, so asking them to get together on a Tuesday night was very much out of the ordinary.

They were finishing up their dessert and small talk, when Nettie asked, "Sheldon, when are you going to tell us the reason for inviting us here tonight?"

"It's very private. Let's have coffee in the lounge, and I'll tell you."

As they all settled themselves in the private room, Nettie, Sharon and Molly gave each other knowing, yet questioning glances. The waiter came in with the coffee, placing the cups, sugar and cream on the table between them, and left.

Everyone, but Sheldon, picked up their coffee. He fidgeted, feeling more than a little foolish, and very nervous.

Finally, Robert blurted out, "Come on, Sheldon, out with it."

"I...uh," He cleared his throat, "I find that I'm...I'm in love."

Molly Bittle squealed. "I knew it! I just knew it."

"You did?" asked Sheldon astonished.

"We all did," Nettie said, beaming with delight.

Sheldon looked around at each of them. They were all smiling. "How did you know?"

Hal chuckled. "It was obvious, Sheldon. At the meetings lately you broadcast it every time you looked at the lovely Miss Billie Bliss."

"You might have realized it before I did then. I'm afraid it snuck up on me. I need your advice and counsel. As you well know, I'm ten years older than Bliss and I want each of you to tell me how you feel about this. Can it work with that many years between us?"

"How does she feel about you, Sheldon?" Robert asked.

"I don't know," he answered, his dark brows furrowing in concern. "But...she did do something just recently which showed me that she cares for me in some way—whether it's the way I would like, I don't know. I can't even begin to find out, unless all of you give me your feelings about the discrepancy in our ages."

"As for me," Robert said, "I can't say. With some couples, it definitely wouldn't work, with others it wouldn't matter."

"It does seem, Sheldon," Hal began, "that Billie Bliss is a very mature young woman."

"You have my go ahead, Shel," Nettie said smiling. "I think it might work with you two; I've watched you both closely. I think you should at least pursue it and find out for yourself if she minds the difference in your ages."

Nettie's husband, Don, grinned. "I go along with Nettie, I trust her feelings."

Molly and Sharon both enthusiastically agreed with Nettie. Robert, the psychologist and counselor was the only hold-out, refusing to commit himself either way.

Sheldon beamed with happiness. "I can't tell you how much I appreciate all of your input. At least, I can now go ahead and pursue it with more confidence. Thank you. But I do need to tell you that Bliss has dropped out of school, and therefore out of *Project Success*."

Everyone registered shock. Nettie spoke up, "Why, for goodness sake, when she was doing so well?"

"For now, I can't reveal that until I talk to Bliss and maybe not even then."

"How do you know she's dropped out, Sheldon, if you haven't talked to her?" asked Hal.

"She wrote me a letter and shoved it under my office door."

"Why didn't she tell you in person?" Robert asked.

"I think because she knew I would try to talk her out of it."

"Well, then," Robert said, echoing Sheldon's own thoughts, "you're free to date her now that you're no longer teacher and student."

Twenty-seven year old Officer Arly Bates had graduated from the Police Academy only two years ago and was the youngest officer on the Claytonville Police force. He was still considered a "greeny" by the guys down at the station, and they found any excuse to razz him. The latest razzing came over the two episodes he had with that silly girl who had the unfortunate habit of sitting on ant hills.

Since he'd just finished taking care of a police call in the vicinity of the Lemmon home and was due for a break, he decided to check on Miss Lemmon and see how she was feeling.

It was 8:00 PM and the first time he'd seen the Lemmon house while it was still light. He frowned at the sight, wondering if the man of the house was lazy or if there was a man of the house.

He got out of the car, and walked slowly up to the porch and rang the bell. Ella Lemmon, peeking out between the blinds, wondered what kind of trouble Lora was in now! She muttered to herself, "All of a sudden, it seems, everyone wants to see Lora. Can't have any peace at all." She padded to the door and opened it.

"Hello, Officer Bates. Anything wrong?"

"Hello, Mrs. Lemmon. No, nothing's wrong. I was in the area and decided to check on your daughter. How is she after that second round of ant bites?"

Ella Lemmon looked relieved. "She seems to be fine, thank you."

"Is she here, Mrs. Lemmon?"

"No, she isn't. She's visiting a friend at her apartment, but I can give you the address. Just a minute." Ella disappeared into the dark interior. After a few minutes, she returned and handed him a piece of paper.

"Thank you, Mrs. Lemmon, I think I'll run over there and check on her."

While driving to the address on the paper, Officer Bates knew that this trip wasn't necessary, especially since he was off duty for a while. Entering the driveway, he saw Miss Lemmon's blue Volkswagon. He parked a few yards behind the Volks, deciding that the apartment must be at the back of the house. Getting out and walking to the porch, he noted that it was the correct number, so rang the bell.

A pretty young woman answered it. She looked familiar and as he stared at her, she turned pale, revealing a few red bumps on her face.

"Miss uh...Lemmon?"

"Y...yes, Officer Bates," she answered fearfully, barely audible.

"I hardly recognized you."

"I hardly recognize myself. I had a make over."

"You did?" he questioned, smiling at her candidness.

"You're here to arrest me, aren't you?" Lora asked, on the verge of tears. "But...but how did you know? Who told you?"

Officer Bates was confused, "Who lives here, Miss Lemmon?"

"I do."

"I thought you lived with your mother."

"I do. I haven't told her yet that I'm going to be living here soon."

"May I come in, Miss Lemmon."

"Oh, yes...excuse me, come in," she said, her face crinkling into tears.

"Miss Lemmon, what is it? Why did you think I came to arrest you?"

"Because...I'm a...a Peeping Tom and a...blackmailer." She folded up onto the couch, covered her face and sobbed.

Officer Bates could only stare at her in an attitude of disbelief. Now what had he gotten himself into? Surely...he hadn't heard right! "Miss Lemmon, will you please stop crying. I don't know what you're talking about."

She looked up, her cheeks wet with tears. "You don't? No one sent you here to arrest me?"

"No. I just dropped by your house to see how you were doing after the last set of ant bites. Your mother gave me this address."

"Then you didn't know?" she asked, about to cry again.

"I don't know anything."

"Then...then I'll have to confess" she wailed. "It's true what I said."

"I don't believe you, Miss Lemmon. You're just...just a little hysterical. Get hold of yourself," he demanded.

Lora stood up abruptly and held out her wrists. "Go ahead. Handcuff me and take me to the station. I want to get it over with."

"Stop this, Miss Lemmon! I think the ant bites have affected your mind."

"Come with me if you don't believe it, and I'll show you." She led the way outside and over to the bushes. "Just look in there, Officer Bates and you'll see an ant pile."

Arly Bates stuck his head inside the bushes and sure enough—he saw an ant pile. Pulling his head out, he looked at Lora. "So what does this prove?"

"That's where I sat...twice! A girl named Billie Bliss lived here, and I was spying on her and Dr. Ackerman. Then I came back and told Billie Bliss that I might tell Dean Atwood what I saw if..." Her voice trailed off.

"This is clear as mud...but...if what?"

"If nothing..."

"Then you didn't blackmail this Billie Bliss?"

"Officer Bates, Dr. Ackerman is our professor and I saw them hugging and I threatened to go tell Dean Atwood that I saw them...if..." Again, she stopped.

Officer Bates feeling thoroughly frustrated asked again, "If what, Miss Lemmon?"

"I don't know."

Arly Bates wished fervently that he hadn't followed his impulse to check on this ridiculous girl. He sucked in a deep breath and began, slowly and articulately, "Let me get this straight, Miss Lemmon, you purposely sat on this ant pile to peek into the window across from here. Is that right?"

"No, I didn't *purposely* sit on the ant pile, "she replied, incensed. "It was dark and I didn't know it was there. I got tired of standing so I sat down, but it wasn't long before I found out what I was sitting on. However, I couldn't move or they would see me as he was leaving."

Totally confused, Arly waited for the rest of the story, but all he saw was more hysterics about to erupt. "Stop. Please, calm yourself, Miss Lemmon. May I ask you then, why did you sit on the ant pile a *second* time when you knew it was there?"

"My legs got tired, and I thought if I sat down very carefully and didn't move, the ants wouldn't come out. Then I became so intrigued at what I was seeing, I forgot it was there and wiggled."

"What did you say you saw?"

"I saw them hugging."

"Is that all?"

"But…but Dr. Ackerman is a professor and Billie was his student."

Arly Bates heaved a sigh, shaking his head. "Now uh…what did you do with this information?"

"I…I blackmailed Billie," she wailed, holding out her wrists again. "Handcuff me and take me down to the station!"

Officer Arly Bates, flustered and confused, pulled the cuffs from his belt and snapped them on her wrists. They walked over to the Claytonville police car. She waited until he opened the door for her on the passenger side. She sat down in the front seat, bawling. The rattled young officer, got in the car, backed out and began to drive, bewildered as to why he had this hysterical young woman handcuffed and in his car in the first place! He was now desperately trying to figure out what in all billy-heck he was going to do with her!

Mrs. Griffen, the landlady, hearing all the commotion, looked out her window just in time to see a policeman carry off Lora Lemmon. Running to the phone, she called Billie.

"Billie, come quick, a policeman just drove off with your friend, Lora Lemmon."

Billie gasped. "Oh no! I'll be right there." Telling her mother she'd be back soon, she grabbed her purse and ran out of the kitchen to her car. This has to be a mistake, she told herself.

At the apartment, she saw that Lora's car was still there. She got out just as Mrs. Griffen came running down the driveway to her.

"Oh, I'm glad you're here, Billie."

"Maybe the policeman was a friend of Lora's, Mrs. Griffen."

She shook her head. "I don't think so, Lora was blubbering at the top of her lungs as he drove out."

"Oh dear. What in the world could be the problem?" No sooner had she asked this question, than the policeman, with Lora in the front seat, drove back into the driveway. "Excuse me, Mrs. Griffen, I'll find out what's wrong then come and talk to you later."

"All right, Billie, but I need to know what is going on." Reluctantly, Mrs. Griffen went back into the house.

The policeman got out of the car looking nervous and very upset.

"What is the matter, officer?" Billie asked, walking up to him.

He just shook his head while walking around and opening the door for Lora—who promptly refused to budge. "Come on, Miss Lemmon, get out of the car—now!"

"No. I want you to take me to the station and book me."

Billie, who had followed the officer, said, "Lora, do as the officer says."

"Tell him, Billie. Tell him that I'm a blackmailer and a Peeping Tom!"

"Yes, tell me Miss," he said, looking at her imploringly, "I would certainly like to hear your version of the story."

"I will. But first, Lora, you need to get out of car."

"All right," Lora muttered.

"Let's all go into your apartment and have a talk," suggested Billie.

Bates was totally relieved that someone with a level head had taken charge.

When they were all inside, Lora said, "Billie, this…this is Officer Bates, and this is Billie Bliss, officer."

"You, then, are the one Miss Lemmon thinks she blackmailed?"

"Officer Bates, does Lora need to be handcuffed?"

"Oh no..no," the flustered officer mumbled, quickly unlocking the cuffs, "she insisted on it and I only did it to keep her quiet—I think," he added under his breath.

Billie smiled. "Now, let's all sit down and try to understand one another."

"Thank you, Miss Bliss, I would like that very much."

"First of all, Lora Lemmon did *not* blackmail me."

"B…but I did."

"Correct me officer if I'm wrong, but when someone thinks they have something on another person, in order to call it blackmail, that someone has to extort something from the person, is that right?"

"That is certainly the way the law defines it."

"What did you ask me for, Lora, in order to keep you from telling Dean Atwood?"

"Well, I…I don't know."

"Think hard, Lora, what did you want from me?"

Lora shook her head, a blank expression on her face, "I must have wanted something or I wouldn't have told you what I saw."

"All right, Lora," Billie said patiently, "think, what was it?"

"I...I guess I didn't get that far in my plans," she said, her voice quivering.

"All right, then, think about it now, pretend you're planning it out thoroughly."

Lora thought about it, frowning. The minutes ticked by. All of sudden, she gazed at Billie, a look of surprise on her face. "I didn't want *anything*!"

"Then why did you spy on Miss Bliss and Dr. Ackerman?" Officer Bates demanded.

Tears threatened again. "Because I saw Dr. Ackerman rent some videos that weren't proper and..."

Billie quickly took over, "And you were trying to be a loyal student of Fairfield, I think. May I tell the story, Officer Bates?"

He let out a breath of relief. "You certainly may."

Billie told him, as briefly as possible, about *Project Success* and how she had a special problem that Dr. Ackerman had been trying to help her with. She explained that Dr. Ackerman had never indulged in television entertainment or movies, just symphonies and such, so therefore was a complete novice about the movies and videos of today. Because of this, when he rented the videos to prove something to her, he mistakenly rented some improper ones.

"Lora was in the video store the day he rented them, and since she is also in Dr. Ackerman's class, she knew about the Project. She was shocked that Dr. Ackerman would rent those kind of videos and deduced correctly that maybe they had something to do with me and felt something was going on that wasn't right. I think, Officer Bates, Lora is a frustrated detective and she did only what she thought would prove that things weren't right. She saw us in what looked like a compromising situation. It, of course, was innocent as Dr. Ackerman was just holding me to keep me from doing something that wouldn't have been good for me."

"Is that all it was?" Lora asked.

"Yes."

"I'm sorry, Billie," she wailed.

"You've already told me you were sorry, Lora, remember?"

"Then tell me, Miss Bliss," requested Officer Bates.

Billie finished the story, telling him how Lora approached her Sunday night, how miserable she felt all night and all the next day, then how she came to her Monday night.

"She apologized and asked my forgiveness, Officer Bates. I assure you, she was very remorseful."

Lora was beginning to feel quite noble as she heard the story from Billie's lips.

Thoughtfully digesting the information that Miss Bliss had presented, the officer turned and gazed at Lora for some moments. "Can you see, Miss Lemmon, that it was not your business to find out what was going on with Miss Bliss and her professor?"

"Oh, I can, Officer Bates. I'll never do that again."

"And, Miss Lemmon, I suggest that if you want to play detective again, you need go to the Police Academy and get some legitimate training."

Lora shook her head. "I've changed my mind, Officer Bates. I've decided that I'm definitely not PI material. And even if I were, I would never...never want to be one. I'm through with detective work forever."

Chapter Twenty-Nine

Sheldon was feeling so keyed up and excited over his idea to pursue Bliss and the plans he'd been making for implementing it, he was surprised to see that it was 3:00 AM. He decided he'd better get to bed so he'd be clear-headed enough to put the idea into action immediately after the 280 class this morning.

~~~~~~~~~~~

Just after Dr. Ackerman closed his lecture, he requested that Miss Lora Lemmon see him after class. He could see the surprise on her face and then the concern.

"What is it, Dr. Ackerman?" Lora asked nervously, standing on one foot then the other.

He noted that she was wearing another outfit that had belonged to Bliss. Lora Lemmon looked nice in it, he thought, but not nearly as nice as the previous owner.

"Could I see you in my office for a few minutes, Miss Lemmon?"

She nodded solemnly and followed him to his office. He closed the door and walked behind his desk.

"Please have a seat, Miss Lemmon."

"Th..thank you."

His eyes aglow with excitement, he proceeded immediately. "Miss Lemmon, do you remember you said that if there was something you could do for me, you would be glad to?"

"I do, Dr. Ackerman, and I meant it."

"Since you're used to slinking around in order to avoid detection, I need you to do that very thing for me."

"Oh, but Dr. Ackerman, I've sworn off slinking around."

He smiled. "I'm very glad to hear that, Miss Lemmon, but this is for a very different purpose and I think you'll be quite happy to do it." He then explained it to her.

~~~~~~~~~~

Billie woke up feeling depressed. Last night, she felt happier than she had in a couple of days while helping Lora out. She was glad to meet the officer who had been so kind as to lead Lora home in both of her self-created emergencies. But this morning, she realized the happiness for Lora had not sustained her through the night. She missed Dodds terribly, but what was really bothering her was that he hadn't tried to contact her since that one time. This told her more than she wanted it to. He must feel relieved to not have to deal with her and her problems any more. Certain, now, that he had no feelings for her, except affection of a dedicated professor for a student, she wondered what she was going to do. Try as she would, she'd found it almost impossible to make plans for the future. Making herself get up, she was determined to get on with her life.

~~~~~~~~~~

Wednesday night, Lora asked to get off work a little earlier so she could accomplish the task for Dr. Ackerman. As she entered the driveway of Billie's apartment, which was now hers, she saw that Dr. Ackerman was already there waiting for her.

"Thank you, Miss Lemmon, I certainly do appreciate this," he said handing her a red rose in a beautiful single-stem, crystal vase and an envelope which she was supposed to deliver to the porch of the Bliss home.

"Your welcome, Dr. Ackerman. This is so exciting!"

"Good luck. As I said, it's very important that you aren't seen. If you were to be caught, you couldn't explain it very well since you aren't a very good liar, Miss Lemmon," he said, smiling. "I'll see you tomorrow night here at the same time?"

"I'll be here, Dr. Ackerman."

Lora decided that this kind of detective work was much more rewarding. To prepare for it, she checked out the clothes Billie had given her. She chose a navy blue, cotton pant suit. "This will be perfect," she said out loud, "It won't be so easily seen at night." It was getting dark a little earlier now, so she was able to park closer to Billie's house than she had anticipated. She parked a block above on the opposite side of the street.

Warily she approached the house at an angle so that those inside couldn't see her. She stood near the front porch checking it out carefully, deciding upon the best place to hide.

Stealthily walking up the steps to the front door, she placed the vase and envelope on the porch directly in front of the door, and rang the doorbell. She turned and scrambled down the steps and into the bushes in front of the house, glad for her recent practice at squeezing into such places. Moments later, she heard the door open, then silence. Her heart pounded furiously as she heard someone coming down the steps. It was Billie! She looked around, waited a moment and then went back up the steps and into the house. Lora let out the breath she'd been holding—waited a while, then snuck off across the lawn and ran up the block to her car.

Billie, walked into the house holding the rose and envelope, frowning. Turning the envelope over, she saw in typed letters, 'Miss Billie Bliss'.

"What have you got there, snooks?" Grandpa asked, coming out of the library.

"I don't know, Grandpa."

Matilda, who had scurried out of the kitchen to see who rang the bell, gasped in delight. "Oh how lovely, and how romantic, Billie. They're probably from your professor."

Billie looked askance at her aunt as she walked into the kitchen, placing the crystal vase and rose upon the table. "Aunt Tilly, Dr. Ackerman calls me Bliss, not Billie—and besides, this wouldn't be his style. He tried hard but he's totally clueless about romance, let alone doing something romantic like this."

Her grandfather who also had followed her into the kitchen, asked, "Are you going to open the envelope and read it?"

Billie sighed, feeling bored with it all. "I guess, Grandpa." She opened it and read:

"She walks in beauty, like the night
Of cloudless climes and starry skies;
And all that's best of dark and bright
Meet in her aspect and her eyes...."
(Lord Byron)

"How beautiful, Billie. Who is it from?" asked Matilda eagerly.

"There's no signature," Billie said in exasperation. "Someone thinks he's being very clever by remaining anonymous." She promptly went over to the waste basket under the sink and threw the poetry in.

"Oh no!" Aunt Tilly exclaimed. "Don't throw it away. You never know, you might wish you'd saved it."

Billie just silently shook her head and walked out of the kitchen and up the back stairs to her bedroom.

"Our girl is certainly having a hard time of it," Bill stated to Matilda.

"Well," she said, getting into the waste basket under the sink, "I'm going to save it for her whether she likes it or not."

Bill smiled. "Good girl, Matilda."

Upstairs, Billie got ready for bed, turned out the lights and lay there thinking. No way was she going to allow herself to be harassed by some would-be Romeo.

The next night, around the same time, Lora, with three red roses wrapped in green paper and an envelope in her hands, ran across the Bliss lawn to the bushes. She waited...then ran up the porch steps. Setting the items down as before, she rang the bell and again retreated quickly into the bushes. Feeling even more nervous than before, she felt that this time someone would look more carefully for the courier. Hearing the door open, then soon close again, she was relieved, but puzzled. Waiting longer this time before venturing out of the bushes, Lora dashed across the lawn to the welcoming darkness of the over-hanging limbs of the trees that edged the lot.

Matilda, who had opened the door, quickly and delightedly retrieved the treasure off the door step, hurried into the kitchen calling Billie. Removing the crystal vase, with its single rose, she replaced it with the three roses and envelope, then went in search for Billie. She found her in the library looking at a map with her father.

"Billie, go into the kitchen and see what you got tonight."

"Not now, Aunt Tilly, later."

Billie and her father were going over her options job-wise and conferring together on where to look for this job.

"I wish you would reconsider getting another job here in Claytonville, Billie."

"I wish I could, Papa, I hate leaving you and the family, but right now it's best for me to get away."

It wasn't 'till 10:00 PM when Billie entered the kitchen to get a glass of milk, that she remembered she told Aunt Tilly she would look at the latest gift from the anonymous Romeo.

She poured herself a glass of milk, reflecting on how her family was now concerned over her lack of appetite and loss of weight.

She picked up the new arrivals and breathed in deeply the rich, aromatic fragrance. She sat down and sipped her milk, debating whether to even open the envelope—but curiosity got the best of her. She opened it and read:

> "I ne'r was struck before that hour
> With love so sudden and so sweet,
> Her face it bloomed like a sweet flower
> And stole my heart away complete...
>
> I never saw so sweet a face
> As that I stood before.
> My heart has left its dwelling place
> And can return no more."
> *(John Clare)*

Billie read the poem several times. "How beautiful," she whispered. "Who could have sent this?" She sighed. All the poem managed to do was oppress her with loneliness for her true love. Leaving it on the table for Aunt Tilly and the rest of the family to read, she went upstairs to bed.

~~~~~~~~~~

Sheldon had never felt such sweet misery as that which filled his soul while typing the next poem for his beloved Bliss. When he was through, anxiousness tormented him. He agonized—wondering how Bliss was reacting to his gifts of love. Could she have possibly guessed who sent them? If so, how did she feel about him? Could such a beautiful, kind and wonderful girl as Billie Bliss learn to care for a man like him?

Nettie, Sharon and Molly each had called him to see how he was, and each had asked what he was doing to win the girl he loved. He assured them that he was working on it and thanked them for their moral support. And how he did appreciate it. He longed to visit with his mother and ask her advice. At least she had left him a legacy of poetry books. Not only did he find them soul satisfying—but very useful.

~~~~~~~~~~

Thursday evening, in the driveway of her apartment, Lora was delighted to take the long white box Dr. Ackerman handed her.

"Is it a dozen red roses?"

Sheldon smiled. "It is. And the card is inside."

"Oh, Dr. Ackerman," she sighed, "this is all so romantic."

"You really thinks so, Miss Lemmon?" he asked, feeling pleased over her reaction.

"I do."

"Good. Well, good luck tonight. I commend you for not getting caught," he said, smiling at the memory of her bumbled sleuthing while trying to follow him.

~~~~~~~~~~

Lora drove up to her usual parking place against the curb a block away. She waited a while, hoping it would become dark enough that the white box wouldn't be so apparent as she walked toward the Bliss home. Her heart beating wildly against her chest, she ran across the lawn to the corner of the house. Once there, she waited, watched, listened, then ran to the steps and up. Quickly placing the box in front of the door, she rang the bell. She almost stumbled as she ran back down but managed to squeeze into the bushes in record time. The door opened abruptly and she heard a male voice, "Who's there? I know you're there, show your face before I call the police."

Lora almost choked, she was so scared. She heard him come down the steps muttering under his breath. He proceeded out onto the walk and looked around.

"All right, you coward, if you don't show your face, I'll dump the box into the garbage can and my niece will never see it."

Lora almost audibly gasped at this, but managed to restrain herself. However, she did notice a little smile on the face of the grumpy ol' man as he walked back up the steps. Hoping desperately that this was an indication he was just teasing, she waited with bated breath.

After the man entered the house with the box, Lora waited even longer before exiting for fear he was waiting to pounce on her the minute she stepped out of the bushes.

Arly Bates cruised slowly down Maple Avenue. There had been a burglary in the area and his assignment was to be on watch tonight. His eyes caught sight of a familiar old blue Volkswagon parked in an odd place on Maple Avenue between houses. He stopped, got out of his car and crossed the street to look at the license plate. Sure enough, it belonged to Lora Lemmon! He looked around, shining his flashlight in several directions but couldn't see her anywhere. Getting back into his car, he drove very slowly down the block, looking on both sides, hoping she was all right. The foolish girl. She had a penchant for getting into scrapes.

A movement caught his eye. A dark figure was running across a lawn. He pulled over to the side, turned off his lights and watched. The figure turned right, walking rapidly up the sidewalk. Making a U-turn he slowly followed. The figure crossed the street and stopped at Lora Lemmon's car. Driving past and making another U-turn he parked behind the Volks and turned on his headlights startling the person. It was Miss Lemmon! He got out and walked toward her glowering.

"So why are you sneaking across someone's lawn, Miss Lemmon?" he growled.

Her hand covered the gasp and her eyes stared wide with shock. "O-Officer Bates?"

"Yes Ma'am, it's me. What have you got to say for yourself?"

"Ohoo..." she wailed. "I can't tell you."

Arly Bate's heart sank. Surely, this girl, foolhardy as she was, couldn't be the burglar.

"Miss Lemmon, there have been burglaries in this neighborhood and you were acting mighty suspicious, so it's very important that you tell me what you were doing."

"I can't...not until I talk to Dr. Ackerman."

"Dr. Ackerman? *The* Dr. Ackerman, the one you saw hugging Billie Bliss?"

"Yes."

"Why, for Pete's sake?"

She whimpered. "I told you I have to talk to Dr. Ackerman. Can you follow me to my apartment, and I'll call him?"

Arly looked at his watch and saw that it was only ten minutes before he was off duty so agreed to follow her.

"I promise I won't make a break for it."

Arly chuckled. "You do overwork the drama, Miss Lemmon."

On the way, Arly just shook his head, wondering why *he* was the one who seemed destined to always get tangled up with this emotional and melodramatic girl!

Arriving at the apartment, they got out of their respective vehicles and Lora waved him inside as she ran ahead into the apartment. She suggested that he have a seat while she dialed Dr. Ackerman's number.

"Hello, Dr. Ackerman? This is Lora Lemmon. I need you to come down to my apartment immediately. I'm in trouble."

Officer Bates rolled his eyes.

"No, I didn't get caught, but the grumpiest man came out and picked it up....He's Billie's uncle?....I don't know what kind of trouble I'm in. Officer Bates didn't tell me. He wants me to tell him....Yes, a policeman is right here waiting for you to come down....All right, thank you, Dr. Ackerman."

Officer Bates couldn't help chuckling at the swivet this Dr. Ackerman must be in at the moment. Miss Lora Lemmon was a master at putting a guy in one.

"Can I get you a cold glass of juice, Officer Bates?"

"No. Thank you."

"Lora's voice quivering slightly, she said, "I was almost scared out of my wits twice tonight."

"Oh? By whom?"

"By you, for one."

"You scared *me*, Miss Lemmon."

"I did? How?"

"I saw your car parked in a strange place, between houses, and you were nowhere in sight. For all I knew, someone with harmful intent might have grabbed you."

"You worried about me?" she asked, a wistful smile on her face.

"I did, Miss Lemmon—and I'm wondering why *I* always have to be the one to pull you out of your scrapes or be around when you are about to get into one."

Lora thought about this. "I don't know either. It does seem rather unusual doesn't it?"

"Yeah! Wait 'till the guys down at the station hear your latest escapade tonight."

"Oh dear!"

A few minutes passed in uneasy silence before a loud knock startled Lora. "That must be Dr. Ackerman." Opening the door, she invited him in.

Sheldon, worried and frowning, turned to the policeman. "What is it, officer?"

"That's what I would like to know. I was on duty watching a neighborhood this evening where a burglary had taken place. I was driving down Maple Avenue and saw this figure sneaking across a lawn. I followed it, and it turned out to be Miss Lemmon here. When I asked her what she was doing sneaking around, she said she couldn't tell me without talking to you first."

Sheldon blew out a breath of relief, then turned to Lora. "Being that loyal is beyond the call of duty, Miss Lemmon. You should have told the officer."

"My name is Officer Bates," he said standing up. Yours is Dr. Ackerman, right?" Sheldon nodded.

"Well, Dr. Ackerman maybe you'd better tell me what Miss Lemmon was doing."

Sheldon flushed. "It was perfectly innocent. I asked her to deliver some roses and a card several nights in a row to a young woman, and

I…uh didn't want the young lady to know they were from me—just yet, that is."

"And what is this young lady's name?"

"Miss Billie Bliss."

A slow smile spread across the officer's face and his gaze turned to Lora. "The Billie Bliss that Dr. Ackerman was hugging?"

Sheldon's head jerked back, shocked. "How…how did you know about that?"

Officer Bates' smile gradually turned into a belly laugh. Sheldon stared at him, shocked and puzzled. When the officer was able to suppress his amusement, he said, "I'm sorry, Dr. Ackerman, but I just couldn't help it. You wouldn't believe how I found that out and the way I found it out."

Before Sheldon could pursue the subject any further, Lora volunteered some of the pertinent information. "Dr. Ackerman, it was Officer Bates who rescued me both times when I was being devoured by the ants."

Understanding began to dawn on Sheldon. "I have a feeling, Officer Bates," he said, chuckling now himself, "that you and I could share some Miss Lemmon stories, and have more than one good laugh."

"I don't think I like that," Lora spluttered.

"Like it or not, Miss Lemmon," Office Bates retorted, "It's a fact. Well, I'll be leaving you two to your business. It has been nice to meet you, Dr. Ackerman."

Sheldon smiled. "It's nice to meet a fellow who can commiserate with me, Officer Bates."

Arly turned to Lora and grinned. "And—I'm certainly glad I didn't have to arrest you on burglary charges, Miss Lemmon. Good night."

Lora giggled. "Me too. Goodnight, Officer Bates."

Sheldon sat down and let out an explosive breath of air. "You really had me worried, Miss Lemmon."

"I was worried, too. But everything's all right now, Dr. Ackerman. My mission was successful," she stated proudly, relating what happened when Billie's uncle found the box.

"I'm sure that was a little frightening, Miss Lemmon. I thank you, but you're through delivering for me. I'm planning to make the delivery, myself, tomorrow night."

~~~~~~

Henry entered the library where Billie and her parents were discussing her plans. "I thought I could scare the rascal out of his hiding place tonight by telling him if he didn't show himself, I'd throw this in the garbage can," he said grinning as he handed her the box.

Billie shook her head in consternation. "If he was out there, Uncle Henry, he probably took you seriously."

"I was serious—almost. Open it and let's see."

Billie, feeling now more curious about her secret admirer, opened the box. Upon seeing a *dozen* red roses, she gasped in delight. She inhaled their fragrance, then opened the card and started reading silently.

"Billie, do read it out loud," requested her mother.

"Uncle Henry doesn't want to hear this romantic folderol, as he calls it," she teased.

"Well," he cleared his throat, "I'll listen, go on."

Billie began to read:

> "The fountains mingle with the river,
>   And the rivers with the ocean;
> The winds of heaven mix forever,
>   With a sweet emotion;
> Nothing in the world is single;
>   All things by a law divine
> In one another's being mingle:
>   Why not I with thine?
>
> See! the mountains kiss high heaven
>   And the waves clasp one another;
> No sister flower would be forgiven
>   If it disdained its brother;
> And the sunlight clasps the earth,

> And the moonbeams kiss the sea:
> What are all these kissings worth,
> If thou kiss not me?"
> *(Shelley)*

Billie found herself profoundly moved. All in the room were silent, wondering. Even Henry was at a loss for words. For some reason Billie thought it sounded like—could it be?

"Excuse me everyone, I'm going to find a vase for these." She walked to the door, then turned to her family. "Oh, by the way, tomorrow night, *if* there are more flowers on our doorstep, *I* want to answer the door."

Chapter Thirty

The trip to rescue Miss Lemmon from the grip of the policeman had taken up valuable time—time he needed to prepare for tomorrow night.

For a moment Sheldon stood by the window gazing down at the lights of Claytonville, this time without the feeling of desperate loneliness he'd felt before, but with a burning desire to successfully win Billie Bliss for his wife. Ah…how good that sounded! His bachelorhood, he hoped, was about to end.

He sat down at the kitchen table, pen and pad in front of him, and a pile of poetry books. For some time he thought, he meditated, he prayed. Thoughts and inspiration came—encouraged by the intensity of his desire.

Pondering on his shyness—how it had narrowed the world in which he'd lived for so many years, he marveled at how Bliss had broadened it. Discovering the depths of his soul was a poignant experience. Loving and living, which he had denied himself for so long, was wonderful, but painful. He knew he was taking a chance—but life itself was a chance—a glorious chance to live, love and endure life's trials with courage.

He had been selfish by closing himself off from life, realizing it was the coward's way. Tears dropped onto the paper. It was then and there he made a vow to himself and to God that no matter the outcome of his present course, he would never again run away from life. He would, after this, give of himself, his heart to all with whom he associated.

Also, he marveled at what he'd learned about himself. Always aware he had inherited his father's painful shyness, his practicality and love of hard work, he was unaware of the legacy from his mother—the sensitive and poetic side of his nature—until now.

~~~~~~~~~~

That night, Lora slept in the new apartment for the first time. She woke up to the new surroundings at first feeling a little disoriented.

Suddenly, the realization that she could now have more control over both her environment and her life flooded her with happiness.

Lora thought of her mother still in that dark environment she had created for herself. The familiar pall of anxiety and guilt began to settle over her. Immediately, she suppressed it, remembering something she'd read in a self improvement book: "We make the choice how we live." Her mother chose to live as she did. She decided, however, that she would still look after her—but it had to be in a different way than she had before. She would figure it out later.

Smiling, Lora allowed herself to remain in bed a little longer, thinking about last night and the statement Officer Bates made about his worry over her. To a certain extent it was his duty as a policeman, but she hoped it was more than duty this time.

She jumped out of bed, pulled the sheets and blanket up and folded the bed under, making it into a couch once more. Looking around, she noticed with great satisfaction that the little apartment was still neat. She hoped that neatness really was part of her nature. If not, she'd make it so. Billie Bliss was her idol and she was determined to become more like her.

After selecting something from her new wardrobe, she noticed, with excitement, that the clothes did not feel quite as tight as they had. She brushed her hair, noting that after washing and styling it herself yesterday, it still looked fairly nice, and the ant bites were almost gone. Deciding to ask Billie about what makeup to buy, she proceeded to prepare herself some breakfast.

Today was the day she planned to break the news to her mother that she was moving out. As far as her mother knew, she had stayed the night with Billie Bliss. Even though she'd been preparing her all week for this event, her mother wasn't accepting it well at all—whining, crying and trying to work on her sympathy. He didn't know it, but Officer Bates had given her the impetus and courage to make the break.

~~~~~~~~~

Sheldon waited for the class to assemble. He nodded at Miss Lemmon, giving her a knowing smile. She looked positively radiant this morning. What a different demeanor she has now, he mused. The sour expression she had just a few short weeks ago, was gone. Yes, Bliss certainly had a positive influence on others besides himself.

He managed to get through the lecture, even though both happiness and nervousness alternately kept pressing in upon his consciousness. In spite of this difficulty, a strange phenomenon occurred. Many of the class members, including Miss Lemmon, came up and told him how much they enjoyed his lecture, smiling and thanking him. Since his lecture was not as organized as usual, it left him wondering. What was different about it that the class members would take the time to compliment him?

~~~~~~~~~~

Officer Bates was experiencing a different kind of phenomenon. Friday afternoon he'd been called to handle a problem in the vicinity of Ella Lemmon's home. As it often did, the domestic dispute was solved by his appearance—not because he did anything, but because the couple ganged up together against him. Climbing back into his car, he shook his head as he reflected on how contradictory human nature was at times.

Since the area was near the Lemmon home, he wondered at his own contradictory nature. Since the last episode with Miss Lemmon, his thoughts kept returning to and focusing on her—as they had after all the other episodes with her. Why? he asked himself. She had proven to be nothing but trouble, and he didn't have any guarantee that it would be any different in the future. He shook his head in frustration. The girl was so childlike, so vulnerable, she needed looking after. But—he was sure of one thing, it wouldn't be him!

As he was thinking about her, he found that he'd automatically turned onto Lora Lemmon's street. After a couple of blocks, he was about to turn around when he noticed her blue Volkswagon parked in the Lemmon driveway with a door open and the trunk lid up. Presently, he saw Lora carrying a load of things to the car. He drove on, pulled into her driveway, parked behind her car and got out.

"Good afternoon, Miss Lemmon," he said as her head came out of the trunk.

Her mouth dropped open in surprise and then she blushed. A pleased smile crossed her pink face. "Officer Bates! What are you doing here?"

"I had a call in this vicinity, and I saw your car so I dropped by to say hello."

"You did?" she questioned in wide-eyed amazement. "Thank you...hello."

"What are you doing?"

"I'm moving out, but I'm afraid my mother isn't taking it too well."

"I have about ten minutes before I need to get back to the station. Need some help?"

"Why...thank you," she said. The sparkle in her large green eyes was duly noted by the young officer. "I have two more loads. If you take one, I can leave a little sooner."

They walked together to the front porch. He waited outside, but could hear Ella Lemmon wailing, carrying on, spewing out accusations. Lora, looking distressed, appeared at the door and handed him a box which he promptly carried and placed in the trunk, then walked back to the porch. Lora handed him the second load. Taking it from her, he carried it to the car, shoved and pushed things aside, fitting it into the crowded trunk.

"Is that all?"

"Yes," she replied breathlessly.

"It sounds like your mother is pulling some histrionics."

Raising her brows, she asked, "Is that what they are?"

"You didn't know?"

She shook her head, still contemplating the thought.

"Like mother like daughter."

Lora, incensed, replied, "Officer Bates, I...I don't pull histrionics."

Arly Bates laughed. "Then what would you call all the dramatics when you insisted I handcuff you, and take you down to the station?"

She thought about this a moment as she looked into his warm blue eyes. A little smile on her lips, she said, "Well...maybe I was a little over emotional. But...you must be a brain," she said, "using words like histrionics."

Arly flushed with pleasure. Though said in a lighthearted manner, he could see that she was sincerely impressed, and he knew from experience she was too honest to play games. Painfully honest, in fact. "Just because I'm a policeman, doesn't mean I haven't had a college education," he stated.

"You have?" her eyes revealed unadulterated admiration, pleasing him further.

He grinned. "You must be a brain, too. You know the meaning of histrionics."

"I do, but only because I'm an English major. And I'm truly grateful to you, Officer Bates, for pointing out the histrionics in my mother. Now, I won't feel so guilty over her tears."

"Good," he said smiling. "Well, Miss Lemmon, I must be going. It's been nice talking with you in a normal manner about fairly normal things—no ant bites, no sneaking over lawns and so on."

~~~~~~~~

It had occurred to Sheldon earlier that if he were going to make the delivery himself tonight, he couldn't make the Friday night *Project Success* meeting. Hastily calling Nettie, he requested that she conduct the meeting and excuse his absence.

At last—the moment had arrived. He was personally taking this last offering of love to his beloved Bliss.

Parking his car a block away, he pulled out the long white box and headed for the Bliss home. His heart clubbed against his chest as he moved warily across the lawn. At the corner of the porch, he stopped a moment, listening, checking to see if it was safe. Deciding it was, he stealthily walked up the steps. Placing the box down in front of the door, he rang the bell, ran back down and around the porch, crouching low. He held his breath, waiting. The door opened and closed very quickly. Presently he heard the squeak of the porch swing. Whoever came to the door, had remained outside! His heart thumped as he listened intently. Soon, he heard an audible gasp.

Billie had dropped the lid of the box onto the porch as she counted the roses. Three dozen red roses! She picked up the envelope and carefully laid the box of roses down on the porch. Her heart raced with excitement as she opened the envelope. Was she foolish to hope? The moment she began to read, her eyes blurred with tears. It was! It was from Dodds! It was Dodds who had been sending the mysterious notes and roses! Her heart bursting with joy, she blinked away the tears and read:

TO BLISS

WHAT IS ROMANCE?

Romance is the ethereal essence of life
Between man and a woman
When they meet
When they listen and learn the other's heart
They unravel their values and beliefs.

Romance is the mystery of a woman
Discovering facets of her femininity
As she smiles at his bumbling efforts,
As she admires his obscure talents,
She makes him feel like a hero.

Romance is tender and fragile,
So often, so easily destroyed
By a look of lust,
By a kiss…suggesting more,
Selfish desires and passions.

Romance is the protection of virtue
While the relationship grows
By a look of tenderness,
By lips touching, suggesting later,
Unselfish desires and passions.

Romance, the essence of life that gives life,
Wanting to give to each other
As they bear and nurture children,
As they teach them values and love
Always nurturing each other.

Romance is what keeps marriage alive,
Sparkling with freshness of new love
By each one giving all,
By unselfish acts of love,
With guidance of God above.

THE QUESTION

Romance is dead, she whispered in saddened tones.
It is? I questioned. Please explain,
I can't, in this I feel alone,
Her expressive face revealed much pain.

I want to help if I but may,
She said, I'll show you if you wish.
Proving it she did day by day,
From the movies, was that a kiss?

A kiss? tears glistening in soft brown eyes,
It stole my emotions, upon them it tread,
What is Romance? I ask. She only sighs.
I will prove Romance is alive, I said.

I search for answers on my Quest,
For Love and Romance I must find
I found them, and they filled my breast
Will she accept, our hearts to bind?

Romance is yet alive and well
In my heart and yours my lovely Bliss!
I adore you, I love you, I must tell
Am I worthy of your tender kiss?
                    (Dodds)

Sheldon, nervously waiting and listening, thought he heard a sob.
He jumped up, stepped around the porch—and there she was—on the

walk! Was she looking for him? Before he could truly formulate the question, she was running towards him.

"Dodds, it *was* you who sent the flowers and poems!" Reaching him, she gazed up into his face and repeated the phrase, her voice soft as velvet, her smile radiant as the early morning sun, "It was you. It was *you* who wrote these last poems."

Sheldon stood looking down at her, all of a sudden feeling awkward and shy. "Yes...I did." He breathed in her presence—the old feelings, which used to plague him and momentarily surfaced, left, leaving only a smile of joy on his face. With gentle fingers, he wiped the tears from her cheeks. Slipping his forefinger under her chin, he held her face up as he gazed into her brown eyes, glistening with the mixture of moonlight and tears.

"I love you, too, Dodds," she whispered.

"You do?" he asked, incredulous. Did I hear correctly, he wondered? Did she really say...? Instead of questioning such joy, he slowly bent down, burning with anticipation he touched her lips tenderly with his. A searing emotion propelled his arms around her, pulling her close, pressing his lips onto the softness of hers, telling her more than words could tell. They clung, arms enfolding each other, enthralled in a glorious rapture that each felt life had denied them. Some moments later, they reluctantly parted, gazing into each other's eyes.

"Did I hear you whisper something, my darling Bliss?" he asked, wanting to hear it again, to make sure he'd really heard correctly.

"You did, my wonderful Dodds. I said...I love you."

"Are...are you sure?"

"Can you doubt it after my kiss?"

He smiled and pulled her into his arms, holding her tightly, trying to capture forever what still felt like a dream. "No, I guess I can't. Never in my wildest imaginings, did I think I would ever be kissed like that by the most beautiful girl in the world."

They remained wrapped in each others arms, feeling unspeakable joy for many moments, then Sheldon whispered into her ear, "May I come over next Tuesday night around seven thirty?"

She pulled away, frowning in distress. "Why that long? That's three nights and four days away?"

Her distress over their being parted for a few days enveloped him with happiness. "I know, Bliss, but I have to go out of town in the morning, and I won't be back until late Sunday night. Then, I have some important things to do Monday and Tuesday before I see you again."

Finally, reluctantly, she agreed. "All right. If I must wait that long, I'll see you Tuesday night."

He lifted her hands and kissed them both. "Goodnight, beautiful Bliss."

"Goodnight, my dear Dodds."

He turned and ran across the lawn to the sidewalk and on up the block. Billie watched him go, feeling bereft—yet, gloriously happy.

Running up the front steps, she picked up the box of roses and the poems and went into the house. As she closed the door, her family seemed to appear from all directions, anxious to hear the latest from her secret admirer.

She smiled at them. "Come into the library, I have something to tell you."

They followed her in and stood, looking at her expectantly. "Sit down everyone."

When they were all seated, she sat down, opened the box and showed them the roses. Her mother gasped. "How many roses this time?"

Billie sighed, "Three dozen."

"My goodness, my goodness!" exclaimed Matilda, clasping her hands together.

"Did he dare show his face tonight or was still he hiding like a scared Tom cat?" Henry blurted out, trying to sound his usual caustic self.

"Uncle Henry, do you want to hear the poems or do you want to just grouse? Do all of you want to hear?" she asked.

"How can you ask that, Billie? Of course we do," answered her mother.

Her father and grandfather were both silent, but smiling. Billie began, purposely omitting the salutaion. Looking up now and then to see if any one of them was beginning to guess the author, but saw only eager attention. When she was through, she looked at each one.

"Do any of you know who wrote them?"

Grandfather smiled, nodding yes. Her father said, still a little puzzled, "I think I do, but I can't imagine *him* writing a poem."

"Is it...is it Sheldon Ackerman?" her mother asked, her eyes wide with hope.

"It is," Billie said, smiling. "It is, mother."

"How do you know, did he finally show his face?" asked Henry.

"He did, Uncle Henry. He waited for me to read the poems, and then he appeared."

Matilda almost bounced up and down in the chair, "So what happened?"

Billie, hesitant to reveal those gloriously private moments, looked down. Bill Bliss spoke for the first time, "And what would you expect would happen? He gave her a resounding kiss on the lips."

Matilda squealed, "Is that true, Billie?"

Billie blushed a delicate pink. "Yes...and I returned his kiss with...with great feeling...you see, I told him...that I loved him."

Bill Bliss clapped his hands. "Good for you, snooks!"

"Oh Billie," her mother said, tears in her eyes, "I'm so happy for you, we all like Sheldon so much."

Will Bliss got up, pulled his daughter, his only child, to her feet and put his arms around her. "My baby girl, I, too, am happy for you."

Henry, who had been sitting there with his mouth open, taking it all in, slapped his knee and laughed. "By jigger! You didn't scare him away after all."

Chapter Thirty-One

Friday night, Lora stretched and yawned. Looking at her watch she saw that it was 9:45. Putting away her studies, she was just about to get ready for bed when the phone rang, jarring the silence. She sighed in exasperation. Since she'd moved in, the phone had rung incessantly, and all the calls were from boys wanting to talk to Billie! She thought she'd informed the last of them of Billie's move.

"Hello?"

"Hello, Lora?" a male voice said. So surprised that it was for her, she didn't answer.

"Lora?" the voice repeated.

"Yes, this is Lora."

"This is Roy Fawkes."

"Oh, hello, Roy."

"I know it's late, but I was wondering if I could come over and take you out for an ice cream cone?"

"I was just going to get ready for bed."

"But it's Friday night, Lora."

"I get sleepy on Friday nights, just like I get sleepy on other nights, Roy. I don't want an ice cream cone tonight."

"Well then, can I come over for just a few minutes and visit. I won't stay long."

"Why?"

He laughed. "Because I like you, and I want to get to know you better."

Lora hesitated. She didn't know Roy very well, and didn't feel inclined to know him any better.

"Ah, Lora, just for a few minutes."

"Oh, all right, but just for a few minutes." She hung up the phone feeling vaguely uneasy.

She met Roy in one of her classes a while back and last week he walked her to her car. The next day, he asked her out, but she turned him down, telling him she was too busy trying to move to her new apartment. He'd asked her where and she told him. Now she was sorry she had. She dated a lot in high school and a few times in college. It only took a few times to become disillusioned with the college boys and she didn't expect to feel any different about Roy Fawkes.

Ten minutes later, the door bell rang, and Lora invited Roy in. He looked around approvingly.

"Nice apartment you have here."

"Thank you. Have a seat, Roy."

He grinned. "Thanks, Lora," he said sitting in the chair.

Lora sat down on the couch. They visited about the class they had together, the campus activities and then Roy turned the conversation on himself, bragging about his grades, how he was going to law school next year and how a law firm was already begging him to join them when he was through.

Finally, Lora yawned. "Well, Roy, you said you were only going to stay a few minutes and it has already been a half hour. I want to go to bed now."

He stood up and sat down beside her on the couch. "Go ahead. How about my staying the night?" he said, slipping his arm around her waist.

Lora stood up, incensed. "You leave right now, Roy Fawkes!"

"Ah come on, baby," he said pulling her back down, "just one little night?"

"No! Take your hands off me!" she exclaimed, frantically trying to fend him off.

"Just a kiss or two then."

"No!"

"Come on, Lora," he demanded, his hands holding her tighter. The phone rang.

"I have to answer that, Roy," she stated, grateful for the reprieve.

"Let it ring."

"No, it might be my mother, and she'll worry."

"So? Let her worry."

"She...she'll come right over if I don't answer, Roy," Lora said, beginning to feel frightened.

"All right, I'll let you go long enough for you to tell her good-night...but make it quick."

She jumped up and grabbed the phone. "Hello?"

"Lora," her mother whined, "I've been waiting for your call all day. Why haven't you called?"

"Oh, hello, Officer Bates."

"Officer Bates? What are you talking about, Lora, this is your mother."

"You want to come over and ask me some more questions? Now? All right, Good bye."

Roy gaped at her. "That was a cop?"

"Yes."

"He's coming over to ask you some questions?"

She nodded.

"Why?"

"I don't know for sure. I...uh was involved in an incident. He may have more questions about it. I think it would be best if you waited outside in the bushes until he leaves."

Roy stared at her. "Are you nuts?"

"No, but Officer Bates might go nuts if he sees you here this late. He's investigating something..."

"I better leave then."

Trying to hide her uneasiness, she put on a seductive look and said, "Oh no, don't leave, Roy, he won't stay long and then you can come back. I really would like to get to know you better, if you agree to take things...a little slower."

"All right, where did you say?"

Lora pointed out the location, carefully explaining that he needed to hide in the bushes directly across so he could watch the policeman come and go. He ran out the door and scrambled into the bushes.

~~~~~~~~~~~

"Hey Arly!" Sergeant Olsen hollered, "wait up. There was a hysterical woman on the phone wanting to talk to you."

Arly was tired. He was just getting ready to go home, but walked over to Doug Olsen's desk. "Did you get her name?"

The Sergeant grinned. "Her name is Ella Lemmon. Any relation to that girl you rescued from the ants?" He noted that Arly's face came alive at the mention of the name, a far cry from the exhaustion and irritation he'd seen there a moment ago.

"What did she say, Doug?"

"As far as I could make out, it sounded like she wanted you to go over to her daughter's apartment, that something was wrong."

"Am I off duty?"

"Not any more, Arly, get your butt over there," he ordered through his grin.

~~~~~~~~~~

Lora watched the bushes nervously, hoping that her plan worked. "Hang on, Roy, he should be here any minute," she yelled from the doorway.

"Okay, but it better be soon, I'm getting tired of this."

"Were the ants still there? she wondered, more nervous now.

The phone rang. "Hello?"

"Lora! Are you all right?" screeched her mother. "I called the police station and asked someone to send Officer Bates over there immediately."

"Oh, thank you, officer!" she said loudly. She hung up the phone and ran back to the open door. "That was the police station, Roy. They said Officer Bates would be here any moment."

"Well, I'm getting darn tired in here. You better make it worth my time!" he yelled.

Lora cringed inside at all the lies she had told tonight, but cringed even more over Roy Fawke's threat.

"OW! What the hell...there are ants in here!" He started out of the bushes just as the headlights of a car drove up and parked behind his car. He jumped back in, swearing under his breath.

Arly quickly got out of the car and ran up to the door, which was now closed. He banged and it opened immediately. "What is..."

He stopped short when he saw Lora back away from the open door, with her finger to her mouth. He stepped in quickly and closed the door. "What is the matter, Miss Lemmon?"

"There's a man in the bushes standing in the ant pile."

"Why, for Pete's sake?"

"Because I told him to go there. He'll try to get out, open the door quick and look," she said hurriedly.

Arly did as she said. He saw a pant leg quickly disappear back into the bushes. Leaving the door open, he turned his back, mouthing, "What do you want me to do?"

Lora went over to the desk and wrote. "Let him stay in there awhile longer. He deserves it!"

Arly grinned and so stood in the doorway pretending to talk to Lora. "What did he do?" he whispered.

She whispered back, "He was forcing his attentions on me." She noticed, with great satisfaction, that Officer Bates' face turned grim with anger.

Arly formulated a plan in his head, allowing enough time for the ants to do a thorough job. Presently, he heard profanity come from the bushes. "Good bye, Miss Lemmon," he said loudly, then whispered. "Lock your door." He ran down the steps and over to his car. Arly backed out quickly. Parking across the street a few doors away, he turned off his lights.

"Let me in, Lora! I'm being eaten alive by ants!" yelled Roy Fawkes. When the door didn't open, he tried to open the door himself and when he discover it was locked, he swore. "Lora, I have ants inside my clothes! I need to take them off...quick! It's your fault, Lora, so let me in!" The door remained closed. Roy couldn't wait a second longer, he had to get home. He ran to his car, jumping up and down, cursing loudly, then got in and started the car. Backing out of the driveway like a maniac, he turned, burning rubber as he drove up the street.

Making a U-turn, Arly followed him. Presently, Roy began weaving just as Lora had. He was going to enjoy this, he thought, a grim smile on his face. The car ahead turned right and Arly followed, turning on his lights and siren. Startled, and stinging from a score of bites, Roy almost lost control. His car swerved to the left, then to the right. Finally managing to pull his car over, he jumped out, squirming, brushing and jumping up and down, muttering under his breath.

Arly walked up to him slowly. "May I see your license, sir?"

Roy pulled out his wallet as quickly as he could and handed it to the officer who took his time studying it.

"I need to give you a breath test. You're driving was very erratic."

"No officer! I'm not drunk. I have ants all over me and even inside my clothes," he stated frantically, squirming and digging at himself. "I have to get home and take off my clothes!"

"Well...that's a new one. And..." Arly slowly drawled, "I thought I'd heard them all."

"Please, officer! I'm being eaten alive!"

"Where were these ants that you didn't see them?" he asked, sounding suspicious.

"Uh...in...uh a yard."

"A likely story, Mr. Fawkes. Ants are dormant at night."

"But...but officer, I...uh disturbed their hill. Please officer," he whined, still pulling at his clothes.

"No matter, you were speeding and weaving all over the road. I'm going to give you a ticket."

"Okay...okay, but hurry, officer."

Arly took his time writing out the ticket, all the while Roy Fawkes cussed under his breath.

"Watch your language, Mr. Fawkes, or I'll take you in for being disrespectful to an officer of the law. Oh, by the way, what were you doing in that yard?"

"I was visiting my girl friend."

"May I have her name?"

"W...why?"

"Answer the question."

"Lora Lemmon."

"Oh? Miss Lemmon is a friend of mine."

"Are you...the officer who was just over there?"

"Why yes...where were you?"

"I was in...uh the bushes."

"What were you doing, spying on Miss Lemmon?"

"No...no! Please, officer, let me go..."

"If I ever catch you over there again, I'll find a reason to arrest you, Mr. Fawkes. The whole thing sounds very suspicious."

"I promise, I won't, officer, just let me go home."

"Are you sure?"

"Yes, yes!"

"You promise to not have anything to do with her anytime, anywhere?"

"I promise!"

"All right, but you better keep that promise."

"I will, I will!"

"I think I'll follow you home so you won't attempt to speed like you were before."

~~~~~~~~~

Immediately after Officer Bates left, Lora called her mother. "Hello, Ma."

"Lora! Are you all right?"

"I'm fine, Ma, thanks to you for being so sharp and calling Officer Bates."

"He got there then? Good! What happened, Lora?"

Lora related the whole story except the incident of the ants. She hadn't told her mother where the ants were, and she'd made the decision not to. How could she make her mother comprehend why she did what she did when she herself didn't fully understand?

"Oh, Lora, it isn't safe to live on your own, you need to come home."

"One of these days, I'll bring you over here and show you how safe it is. I promise I won't ever let a boy come over here again unless I know him really well. I've got to go now, Ma, I'm really tired. Thanks again for being so astute at getting my message."

Ella Lemmon was pleased that she had done so well for her daughter. "You're welcome, Lora. Now be sure to call me tomorrow won't you?"

"I will, Ma, for sure, goodnight." Lora hung up the phone and went over to the couch and plopped down exhausted, but still feeling angry at Roy Fawkes. She smiled, savoring the punishment she'd inflicted on him. It wasn't long, however, before her thoughts turned to Officer Bates. He'd caught on so quickly, and handled the whole situation so well! She sighed, wishing the college boys were as nice and on the ball as he was.

A knock at the door startled her. "Who is it?" she asked anxiously.

"Officer Bates."

Quickly opening the door, she smiled, relieved and happy to see him. "Officer Bates, what are you doing back? Please come in."

"Thanks. I came to report and ask you some questions," he stated abruptly.

"Oh? Then please have a seat. May I get you something to drink?"

"No thank you. Where did you meet that creep you sent into the bushes?"

"I met him in one of my classes at school. He called tonight and asked to come over."

"How well did you know him?" he interrogated.

"Not well."

"Then why did you let him come over?"

"W..well, that's why he did come over because he said he wanted to get to know me."

"Inviting him into your apartment wasn't very smart, Miss Lemmon."

"I know, but he wanted to take me out for an ice cream cone and I said no, that I wanted to go to bed."

"So, why did he come over?" the officer asked, his eyes boring into her unmercifully.

Lora tried to blink back tears. "I...he kept insisting...and he said he would stay just a few minutes."

Arly Bates saw the tears and realized what he was doing. He got up and began pacing. The objectivity a policeman should have was long gone. He was working now on an emotional level. He cared too much about this...naive, imprudent, oblivious girl! He stopped and glared at her.

"Do you know that all the guys at the station are ribbing the life out of me?"

Lora blinked in confusion at the abrupt change of subject. "What for?"

"They could see it before I did."

Her eyes wide with concern, filled with tears again. "W...What did they see?"

"When I told everyone down at the station about the first time you were stung by the ants and I led you home, they could see it then."

"Oh no, I am in trouble," she cried, covering her face.

"Yes, you are Miss Lemmon." He spoke more gently now, "you're going to have to put up with me."

She looked up at him, tears dripping from her chin,"What d..do you mean?"

"What I mean is," he said, handing her a tissue from the kitchen counter, smiling at the tears and at her whole reaction, "that I have come to care for you—against my better judgement."

The tears stopped instantly. She wiped the residue up with the tissue and blew her nose. "Wh…what did you say, Officer Bates?"

"My first name is Arly, Lora. If you heard that I've come to care for you, you heard right." He smiled.

She stared at him with wide, unbelieving eyes. "I can't believe it," she said standing up in order to examine his grinning face and wonderful blue eyes.

Arly took her hands in his, "Believe it, Miss Lora Lemmon, believe it." He exhaled a heavy breath. "*I* finally do."

"But…but what did you mean about the guys at the station?" she asked fearfully.

"They saw that I was interested in you the very first night I reported your foolish shenanigans."

A look of astonishment replaced the fear."You…you were interested in me before…even before my makeover?"

Arly Bates laughed.

Lora was puzzled. "Why are you laughing?"

"Because you are so delightfuly funny—and so painfully honest. Please, Lora Lemmon, don't ever change."

Smiling with tentative joy, she replied, "But getting to know me under such circumstances—how could you like me—I just don't understand?"

"Because, under those crazy circumstances, I discovered wonderful qualities in you, unlike any girl I've ever known or dated. The guys at the station are right. Without realizing it, I think I was taken with you the moment I watched you jump up and down in front of that old Volks, and you told me you'd sat right on top of an ant pile."

"Really?" She gazed at him, then smiled shyly. "You know what?"

"What?"

"I have a confession to make to you, Officer...I mean, Arly, I...I've had a crush on you since the moment I first saw you."

"You have?" Arly's heart accelerated with excitement. "I can't believe it. I thought I'd have to work like crazy to get you to like me. Does that mean that now...I can come and see you in a normal fashion?"

"Yes," she sighed, smiling.

"You mean I can take you out on a date?"

"Oh yes...Officer Bates...I mean, Arly."

"I'm off early tomorrow night. If you aren't busy could I have a date then around six?"

"I'm off work early tomorrow night, too. Yes!"

"All right! I would like to take you out to dinner, is that all right?" Beaming, she nodded.

"And what are you doing Sunday afternoon?" he asked.

"Not anything in particular."

"How about a Sunday afternoon picnic?"

She clapped her hands. "Oh yes! I love picnics. "I'll make the food."

"Great!" Arly said with relief, "and I'll bring a watermelon."

He walked to the door, turned and smiled at her, noticing that her happiness had changed her face from a pixie-like prettiness—to beautiful. "Goodnight, Lora," he said softly.

She sighed. "Goodnight, Arly Bates. I like your name."

Chapter Thirty-Two

For Billie Bliss, the weekend was almost unbearable, it seemed so long. She was sustained only by the miracle that had brought such abundant happiness into her life.

Matilda surprised her niece by handing Billie the first verse she had thrown into the waste basket and also the second one that was left carelessly lying about.

"Oh, Aunt Tilly, thank you!" Billie said hugging her. "You were so much wiser than I. You sensed right away that they were important."

Matilda smiled, feeling great satisfaction. She and Margaret, each on separate occasions, had requested the privilege of reading all the poems again. Now that they knew who had left them on the doorstep, they saw them in a totally different light. When Matilda reread them, she had squealed with delight. Margaret, in the privacy of her bedroom, shed a few tears as she read and reread them, feeling more gratitude than she could contain. That there was a man of Sheldon Ackerman's caliber in the world today, was something she herself found unbelievable. And that he would come into Billie's life and appreciate her, in spite of her off-putting actions and attitudes concerning romance...and then prove that he, too, a seasoned man in the world of business, did indeed have the same high values—and understood romance! It was more than she had dared pray for. She smiled through her tears, wishing that all women could have a Sheldon Ackerman or a Will Bliss in their lives, especially her sister Matilda.

The atmosphere in the Bliss home had changed considerably since Sheldon Ackerman had declared his love for their daughter/granddaughter/niece. A quiescence permeated the household resulting from the serenity which emanated from all within it. Particularly Will Bliss, who knew that he was safe in giving his cherished and only daughter to Dr. Sheldon Dodds Ackerman, a man of integrity and kindness, a man who would love and support his daughter.

Bill Bliss went around with a smile on his face, his eyes twinkling more than usual, reminding everyone, "See, I told all of you everything would work out well for our girl."

Even Henry smiled more and groused less as he thought of the good luck that had befallen his silly, idealist niece—nothing of her own doing, he felt sure.

Billie studied the poems more than either her mother or aunt, especially the ones Sheldon had composed himself. She was in awe that this special man had come into her life. Not only had Dodds made the effort to *learn* what romance is, but he had turned out to be the most romantic man she'd ever known!

At times it seemed unreal, especially the all too brief encounter with Sheldon Friday night when he kissed her—once only. But what a wonderful kiss! She would remember it always. All weekend she had lived in a state of reverie. In all the romantic movies she'd seen, in the few romantic novels she'd read, no kiss could equal it. In her mind, because of her acute awareness, she had become an *expert* on whether a kiss was the kind which elicited emotion—all the right kind of emotion! And she was certain she was being totally objective.

Here it was only Monday, would tomorrow night ever come? she wondered with a sigh.

~~~~~~~~~~

After his class, Monday, Sheldon retired to his office to make an important phone call. He called Bliss Hardware and Feed and visited for a moment with Will Bliss, then made an appointment with him. He didn't know how they did it today, but he wanted to show respect for Billie's father and ask for her hand, and he wanted it to be at Will's office.

The appointment made, he locked up his office and left to attend to other important things, his heart almost bursting with happiness. His class had noticed his state, especially Lora, who smiled knowingly, feeling privileged that she was the only one in class who knew why.

If it weren't for what he had to do, Sheldon was sure he wouldn't make it until tomorrow night to see Bliss.

Monday evening, Lora sat on the porch of her apartment enjoying the late August evening, going over in her mind the crazy circumstances which brought her and Arly together. How strange that it always turned out to be Arly who was around to rescue her instead of another policeman. And how lucky she was.

Saturday night, he took her to one of the nicest restaurants in town. She wore one of the dresses that Billie had given her, an emerald green, and she fixed her hair as Billie had shown her. Arly told her she was beautiful! No boy had ever told her that before.

It was heavenly just talking and getting acquainted with him, as he said, "in a normal fashion." During dinner, she asked him many questions, finding out that he came from a family of six including his parents and that he was the oldest of the siblings. He said that his parents and three sisters lived in Springfield and that he wanted to take her to meet them as soon as they both could get time off work. She could hardly believe it all.

She hadn't yet told her mother about Arly. Still cringing at the thought of taking him over to see her, which meant taking him inside the house, she remembered how Arly had reacted to her reluctance.

"But, Arly, I...I'm afraid you won't want to date me any more if you really see the kind of person my mother has become and the way she keeps her house. She didn't used to be like this."

He smiled. "I know what kind of a person you are, Lora, and I've seen your little apartment when you haven't been expecting me and it was neat as a pin, so don't worry a minute about that. It's important that we go see her sometime."

Nevertheless, she knew she would continue to worry until the visit was over. She decided to think about something more pleasant—the picnic yesterday. Arly raved about her cooking. She'd made fried chicken, potato salad and baked beans, all of which happened to be in Billie's cupboard and freezer. Lora knew she was a good cook. She certainly had had a lot of practice at it. Her father passed away when she was ten years old, making it necessary for her mother to go to work. From the time Lora turned twelve, she was expected to fix most of the meals. When Arly told her she was a good cook she felt grateful for all those years she was forced to prepare the meals.

She and Arly had so much to learn about each other, they didn't even play at the park; they just sat on the lawn and asked tons of questions. She smiled as she thought about it. Billie didn't even know about her exciting news. On impulse, she decided to run over to Billie's house and tell her. Stepping inside to get her purse, she went back outside, she locked the door and got into the car.

Driving up Maple Avenue, a half a block away from Billie's, Lora realized that it was late. Pulling over to the curb, she stopped the car and turned on the overhead light to look at her watch. It was ten fifteen, much too late to knock on someone's door. Turning off the overhead light, she was about to make a U-turn and go back, when she thought she saw a dark figure run across a lawn to the Bliss driveway. She turned off the motor and headlights. Arly said that there had been burglaries in this neighborhood. Maybe someone was going to rob Billie's house! Since her view was blocked by the neighbors bushes, she got out, walked up the sidewalk looking for something to protect herself with. Seeing only a small dry limb at the base of a tree, she picked it up and then walked stealthily up to the Bliss driveway.

The house was dark, but the moon was shining brightly. She couldn't see anyone around the front of the house so she decided to look in the back. Edging through the portico, she stopped. Sure enough, there he was...doing something to Billie's car! Her heart raced with fear. Grateful that she had on Billie's navy blue pant set, she tiptoed toward his back, her hand gripping the stick so hard it hurt.

Arly Bates was glad that it was the last night he had to cruise this neighborhood. Tomorrow he would be on the day shift. He was driving up Maple avenue when he saw a blue Volks parked against the curb. Surely, he thought, shaking his head, it can't be Lora's again! He pulled up behind it. It was!

He glowered. "For Pete's sake, what is that girl up to now?" Turning off the headlights and ignition, he got out. He walked quickly, looking around. When he arrived at the Bliss Driveway, he saw two dark figures through the portico. One was hunkered down by a car door. In the moonlight the other one looked like...like Lora! She was sneaking up behind him with something in her hand! His heart hammered against his chest. By the time he reached them, Lora was shoving the thing into the back of the mystery figure.

"Stick 'em up!" she shrieked.

The man was so startled, he almost fell over into a heap, but managed to stand up and turn around.

"What the hell…you holding me up with a stick, lady?"

"You bet she is!" Arly yelled, holding a gun on him. "And you better raise your hands for her."

"Arly?" she squeaked, "How…how did you get here?"

"How in the hell didja both get here?" snorted the shaken intruder.

"Shut your mouth," Arly barked, taking the handcuffs from his belt.

The lights of the back porch went on and Will Bliss came running down the steps. "What in the world is going on out here?" His jaw dropped as he immediately assessed the situation.

"Well sir, I think this man was trying to steal your car."

"What can I do to help, officer?"

"You can put the cuffs on this bum for me. I can do it myself, but it's a little easier if…" His voice trailed off. What Arly didn't want to say was: 'I was scared spitless for this girl and my hands are shaking.'

Before Arly could say another word, Will had the man handcuffed. By then, the whole family had come out and gathered around, staring in shock.

"Lora!" Billie exclaimed. "What are *you* doing here?"

"That's what I want to know," growled Arly.

All eyes turned on Lora who was now visibly shaking. "W…well…I was driving over to see Billie, when I realized how late it was. I was about to turn around and head for home, when I saw a d..dark figure run across a lawn and go into the Bliss driveway. Officer Bates said there had been some burglaries in this neighborhood and…no way was I going to let him rob the Bliss family."

The man snorted. " This dumb broad was trying to hold me up with a stick."

Arly grabbed the man by the collar so quickly, he about choked on his last words. "One more peep out of your mouth, and I'll stuff a gag down your throat so far, it'll choke you."

The small crowd watching this episode, was impressed with Officer Bates, except Will Bliss, and he was curious; why such a vehement reaction? The officer seemed to have more than a routine interest in the whole situation.

The Bliss family, with the exception of Billie, were stunned over this strange young lady who apparently tried, in a very foolhardy manner, to protect them. Will turned to his daughter. "Who is this young woman, Billie?"

"Excuse me," Arly interrupted. "Let's don't have any introductions until I get this man down to the station. I need you to come along, Lora."

"I'm..I'm shaking so bad, I can't drive, Arly."

"You aren't driving, you're riding with me in the front seat. We'll come back later and get your car."

The family, still dumbfounded, watched until the threesome were out of sight. Will Bliss turned to his daughter, a grim expression on his face.

"Billie, we are all going to gather at the kitchen table, and you're going to tell us who that foolish young lady is who risked life and limb in order to protect the Bliss family."

When they had seated themselves around the table, Billie told her family that this was *the* Lora Lemmon. She reminded them of the whole account—the saga of how Lora had misguidedly trespassed into their lives—but tonight had risked her own safety to protect them from a car thief.

~~~~~~~~~

An hour and a half later, Arly dropped Lora off at her car and proceeded to follow her to the apartment. "Well," he muttered to himself, "some of the guys down at the station have now met the impossible Miss Lora Lemmon, whose latest caper was holding up a thief with a stick!" He was sure that the minute he and Lora left, their hoots probably raised the roof. Arly was glad he wasn't there; he would be tempted to deck a few. There was nothing funny about it. Lora had risked her life for a car—and he was furious with her. The fear he felt when he saw Lora in danger, catapulted him into an awareness of what he really felt for her and precipitated a decision far ahead of its time.

Lora drove into her driveway and Arly drove in behind her. Turning off his engine, he got out and followed a very subdued Lora up the steps to her apartment.

"May I come in, I have something to talk to you about."

Lora studied Arly's glowering face. "You can come in if you won't bawl me out."

Arly, not promising anything, stepped in and sat down, feeling totally exhausted. Lora sat next to him on the couch. Looking over at her, he asked, "And why would I bawl you out, Miss Lemmon?"

"You know."

"I want to hear it from you."

"I don't want to say it, Arly Bates."

"Well, what do you have to say for yourself then?"

"I won't do anything like that again."

"I don't believe you."

A knock on the door startled them both. Who could be calling this late, they wondered? Lora got up and opened the door. It was her landlady.

"Mrs. Griffen! Uh…come in."

Mrs. Griffen nodded and walked in looking harried. She was dressed in her robe, her hair in disarray indicating she had once been in bed tonight. Arly stood up as she entered, and she looked at him nervously. "What is wrong, officer?"

"Why nothing, Mrs…"

"Arly this is my landlady, Mrs. Griffen. Mrs. Griffen this is Officer Bates."

Arly nodded at her. "How do you do, Mrs. Griffen. What can we do for you?"

"I am turning into a nervous wreck. All the shenanigans going on around here, police cars going in and out, tires screeching, yelling and banging on doors are driving me crazy. It seems you are in perpetual trouble, Miss Lemmon. I'm afraid you'll have to move."

Lora gazed at her in shock, but before she could say anything, Arly piped up, "She *will* be moving, Mrs. Griffen."

Lora whirled around to him, certain she hadn't heard correctly. "What?"

Arly ignored her. "Mrs. Griffen, I assure you there is nothing wrong. I promise that things are going to quiet down from now on. You see, I'm going to marry Miss Lemmon and see that she stays out of trouble."

Lora gaped at him, not believing her ears. Mrs. Griffen studied the young man, realizing that he was serious. Her face softened into a smile.

"Why, how nice. So that's why a police car has been here so often. Congratulations to both of you. Well, Miss Lemmon, I certainly won't worry about what is going on back here anymore; you're in good hands. Good night."

Lora closed the door and turned to Arly, her face one of incredulity. "You didn't have to say that to get me out of trouble with my landlady. I could have explained it all to her."

"You think I would lie like that to get you out of trouble?"

"Well, I lied to Roy Fawkes to get myself out of trouble."

"I didn't tell Mrs. Griffen a lie, Lora. I have to marry you to keep you out of trouble."

Her brows contorted. "You...you are serious?"

"I am very serious," he said, grimly.

Lora's eyes widened, then filled with angry tears. "Arly Bates, how dare you want to marry me for that reason."

"You give me no choice."

"Oh! You...you are an egotistical...presumptuous, uh...uh brute! You can't make me marry you, so leave right now, Arly."

Arly stared at her. He'd never seen her angry; in fact he wondered if she ever got that way. A smiled twitched at his lips, thinking how cute she was.

Lora opened the door and stamped her foot for emphasis. "Leave, Arly, right now!"

"I'm sorry, Lora. I have been a presumptuous...brute." The twinkle in his eyes said otherwise. "Can I stay and explain?"

With lips pressed together tightly, she held her ground, standing fixed by the open door.

"Please, Lora," he implored, his eyes pleading.

Her determination crumbled. Slowly she closed the door. "All right, you can stay for a few minutes, but..."

"Lora," he said, taking her hands in his, "when I saw you in danger tonight, I thought my world was going to fall apart."

"You did?" she asked, amazed.

"I knew that I cared for you, but when I thought I might lose you, I knew that I loved you. I love you, Lora."

"Y...you do?" she asked, her green eyes widening in awe.

"I do. And when I thought I might lose you, I panicked. I have no way of controlling you and your actions unless I marry you."

Lora pulled her hands away, her eyes flashing with anger, "You are not only presumptuous, Arly Bates, but you are a...a ...dictator!"

He smiled. "I am? I mean, I sound that way don't I? I'm sorry again, Lora. What I meant, is that I would have more right to keep track of you if you were my wife. But that isn't the only reason I want to marry you...I love you and I want to take care of you and protect you from...yourself...and"

"The answer is...no!"

"What?"

"The answer is no, Arly."

Arly was now getting scared...she meant it. "Lora, please sit down."

"Why?"

"Please..." he pleaded.

"All right, but only for a minute. I'm not going to change my mind."

As soon as Lora sat down, Arly knelt down in front of her. "Will you marry me, beautiful Lora. I need you."

Lora's eyes softened. No man had ever called her beautiful or— said he needed her. Still, she remained silent.

"I know I've acted like a bumbling idiot tonight, Lora, but I feel desperate, I don't want to lose you. I've been looking for a girl like you and I began to think there wasn't one left in the world. Please, will you marry me?"

His words turned her gaze into a starry-eyed expression. Finally, she smiled. "M...maybe."

Arly sat beside her on the couch and reached for her hands. "Oh, thank you, Lora. At least that gives me some hope."

"I want to finish school, Arly."

"I want you to finish. You can finish even after we're married."

"I can?"

"You can, my lovely Lora." He stood up and pulled her to her feet, put his arms around her, bent down and kissed her with great tenderness.

Lora melted. Never had she been kissed like that. She looked into his earnest face and wonderful blue eyes. "I...I think I love you too, Arly."

A grin spread clear across his face. "You do?" He danced her around and around, 'till they were both so dizzy they laughed and fell into each other's arms for support.

He gazed down at her lovely, flushed face and smiled. "You don't have to give me a final answer yet, Lora, but I'll be waiting on pins and needles until you do." He held her close for a few moments, his breathing uneven, then bent down and kissed her forehead and then once more on her lips, but this time with the mixed emotions of the evening: fear, anger, protectiveness and—love. He pulled away abruptly and walked to the door. "Goodnight, Lora."

"Goodnight, Arly," she answered in a soft breathless voice.

Stepping out onto the porch, she watched him until he opened his car door, then she yelled, "Thank you for rescuing me tonight, Arly. You are my hero!"

Chapter Thirty-Three

Tuesday morning, Sheldon awoke earlier than usual, feeling an excitement that three months ago he would have thought impossible. If it weren't for the loose ends he had to tie up today and the class he had to teach, he was certain that the day would drag by unbearably.

By 5:00 PM, he was home trying to make a snack for himself, unable to eat a full meal because of excitement and nervousness. His life had already changed, but after tonight, he hoped and prayed that it would change even more. Since Bliss had declared *her* love, he was almost one hundred percent sure...but there was that small doubt. Could a beautiful young woman like Bliss...would she....?

~~~~~~~~~~

There was also excitement in the Bliss household. Margaret made homemade strawberry ice cream and Henry and Bill took turns cranking the non-electric ice cream freezer. Matilda made crisp sugar cookies to go with it.

Everyone tried to act nonchalant around Billie since no one, except Will really knew if or when Sheldon would propose. After all, Sheldon Ackerman had been a bachelor for so long, would he be amenable to a different kind of life? Nevertheless, the ice cream and cookies were a celebration.

Up in her bedroom at 6:50, Billie's excitement had unnerved her to the point, her hand was shaking, making it an ordeal to apply lipstick.

She stood back scrutinizing herself, hoping that she looked as nice as she wanted to. She'd bought a special dress for tonight, a filmy summer cotton that she found at one of the Fall sales. It was pale cream with tiny covered buttons starting at the v-neck and ending at the v-shaped line three inches below the waist. The skirt flared out in a circular fashion. She wore gold and pearl earrings and a small bracelet of the same. Her hair hung loose upon her shoulders. She shook it nervously. Taking a deep breath, she ran downstairs, wanting to be the one to answer the door.

Just as she reached the last step, the door bell rang. Her heart leaped up into her throat as she walked to the door. She opened it and there stood Dodds, looking so handsome, it nearly took her breath away. He wore a gray summer sport coat over a light casual shirt and dark gray pants. In his hands he held a crystal vase with one white rose. They gazed at each other in wonder, and finally, Billie invited him in.

Sheldon couldn't believe the vision before him. Bliss' lustrous auburn hair, hanging loose upon her shoulders, stood out gloriously against the pale cream of her dress. Her soft brown eyes sparkling with happiness, held his, then his eyes moved to the dress, noticing the lovely, slim curves of her body that were so distinctly revealed by the form fitting dress. He tried to say something, but his voice caught and the only thing that came out was a husky whisper.

"Bliss...beautiful Bliss. Are you just a vision or are you real?"

"I'm very real, my handsome Dodds."

He smiled, unable to speak for a couple of moments. Finally getting his voice back, he said, "May we go into the library?"

"Yes. I warned every one to stay out of sight because I didn't know where you wanted us to visit."

Billie closed the library doors and turned to Sheldon, looking at him expectantly. He explained that the library held a special place in his heart since it was the place where they had their first meeting for *Project Success.* Then he handed her the rose.

She searched his deep blue eyes and saw an expression in them that sent a thrill through her, knowing that the one white rose meant something very special. "Thank you, Dodds," she whispered.

"Let's sit down, Bliss." He led her to one of the couches then took the rose and set it on a table. He sat beside her, pulled out a paper from his inside coat pocket and handed it to her, his eyes twinkling with a mixture of excitement and mirth.

Tipping her head to one side, she wondered, expecting the usual poem that had accompanied all his flowers. She unfolded the paper and began reading,

THE KISS

Since first poor Adam fell from tranquil bliss,
Each man's downfall has been a woman's kiss.
Each skirmish won with lips in fair encounter,
Leaves man an offering on Diana's altar.
Oh muse from Mount Parnassus cast your glance,
And give some light to men who wish on chance;
Or on their ego feed a hero's pride,
And think that they have won the blushing bride?
    No battle plan can match the cunning miss
Who lets a man think he secured the kiss.
Take heed all men through each and every land,
A kiss is how the maiden gives her hand.
A woman's lips will make on bended knee,
A man become what ne'er he wills to be.
A kiss will cowards change 'till they be brave,
And even fools will cease to play the knave.
    Oh wretched fate that e'er to women gave,
Such power that dooms a man to worrier's grave.
On earth, of all that Cupid's powers be,
A woman's kiss will yet make senses flee.
Oh Adam since you fell from heavenly bliss,
Each man has been self-tortured by some miss.
But if the Fall by some is ever hissed,
Just pause and think what all men might have missed.
                    Dodds

Billie smiled and read the poem again. She looked up at him and laughed. "Surely, you didn't write this, Dodds, as indicated by your signature? It sounds like something from the collection of Alexander Pope."

He laughed, his eyes full of merriment. "Smart girl! I tried to mimic his style. Never in my wildest imagination, did I think I could ever turn into a poet. But... 'A woman's lips will make on bended knee, a man become what ne'er he wills to be.'" They laughed together, then suddenly, Sheldon's face became serious. He slid off the sofa kneeling on one knee before her, his eyes searching hers.

"My dearest Bliss, will you do me the honor of becoming my wife?"

Her warm brown eyes filled with tears of joy. Without the slightest hesitation, she replied, "I will!"

Tears of joy also blinded Sheldon momentarily as he fumbled in his coat pocket, bringing out a small velvet box. He opened it up and handed it to her. "This belonged to my mother, would you consider wearing it?"

Billie blinked away the tears and her hand shaking slightly, took the box from him and studied the beautiful old ring. She gasped in delight. On a gold band, large fire opals flanked each side of the very large pinkish diamond.

"It's the most beautiful ring I have ever seen."

A look of relief flooded his face. He took the box from her and pulled the ring from its housing. "It probably won't fit, but let's try it." He pushed it gently onto her left finger.

"It fits perfectly, Dodds," she exclaimed with excitement.

"It does, doesn't it?" he said, just as excited. He stood up and pulled her up and put his arms around her waist. "I love you, Bliss of my life."

"I love you, my wonderful poet."

"May I" he asked, "have another one of those magical kisses that turned me into one?"

Billie put her arms about his neck and he bent down, his lips gently touched hers, savoring the warm softness until he could stand it no longer. He pressed his lips into hers with the merciless ardor of pent up longing and passion of many lonely years. When reluctantly they pulled apart, he covered her face with kisses.

"Oh Dodds," she said breathlessly, "do you realize that you really did what you said you'd do? You proved to me that romance is not dead."

He smiled in happy triumph, "I did, didn't I?"

"And do you realize just how *romantic* our whole relationship has been?"

"Yes, starting from the beginning when you wrote that silly note, telling me that it was my fault." They both laughed. Sheldon turned serious. "Let's sit down, Bliss, we have some decisions to make—like when can we be married?"

They sat on the couch, holding hands, smiling, looking deep into each other's eyes. "When do you think we should be married, Dodds?"

"Next week. You see, my Bliss, if we are going to have a whole passel of children, we had better get started."

Feeling as though she might burst with happiness, she exclaimed, "You're right, Dodds, how about two weeks from now? I only want a simple wedding in the back yard. The weather in middle September will be wonderful, warm and balmy. Is that all right with you?"

"It's more than all right. I thought you would insist on a couple of months to prepare for it, so I decided to bargain for a week to start with." He was so excited, he picked her up and swung her around. When he set her down, she looked up at him, her eyes sparkling with happiness.

"Let's go tell the family that we're engaged. Dodds. We are *engaged*! I can hardly believe it."

He laughed. "I can't believe it either."

She looked at the ring on her left finger, still aware of the unfamiliar feel of it. "Let's go show them my beautiful ring. I wish I could have known your mother, Dodds, I feel privileged to wear it." She put her hands over her mouth and closed her eyes. "I'm dreaming, I know I am…but then, I feel my ring and I look into your eyes and see and feel your love and I know I'm not. It's real! And oh," she picked up the poem that had been left upon the couch, "may I read this wonderful poem to them?"

Sheldon flushed, "Well, I don't know…I"

"I've shared all the others, Dodds. In fact Mother and Aunt Tilly have read them over several times…and I have read them at least a hundred times."

He chuckled, "Oh…go ahead, apparently I'm an open book around here."

"And you know what, Dodds?"

"What?"

Mother and Aunt Tilly must have had a feeling you'd propose tonight. They made homemade ice cream and sugar cookies."

Sheldon's eyes lit up, realizing that his appetite had returned. "Great, let's go celebrate, my Bliss."

Chapter Thirty-Four

Wednesday morning early, Billie picked up the phone and called Lora. While the phone was ringing, she admired her ring and sighed.

A sleepy voice said, "Hello."

"Oh, Lora, did I wake you? This is Billie."

"No, my alarm just woke me."

"When can I come over, Lora, I have some wonderful news."

"You have?" she asked eagerly, the sleepiness gone. "Can you come over at 11:30 this morning?"

"I can. See you then, Lora."

At 11:40, Billie and Lora were seated at the small table, smiling at each other. "After you tell me yours, Billie, I have some news for you."

Billie's eyes lit up even more. "I can hardly wait to hear." Then she held out her left hand. "Dodds and I are engaged."

Lora squealed. "You are? I'm so happy for you! The ring, it's very unusual, but beautiful."

"It was Dodds' mother's"

"It was? Oh," she sighed, "how very special."

"Now, tell me your good news, Lora."

"Arly asked me to marry him."

"He...he did? I can't believe it. I have suspected he liked you, Lora...but marriage?"

"Well, he asked me for the wrong reason."

"Oh? Tell me about it. Tell me everything from the beginning."

"I will, if you'll tell me everything."

So the two girls, now feeling like old friends, exchanged their unusual stories, each giving to the other the interest and empathy that only friends can give.

As Billie stood up to leave, she asked, "So when do you think you will be able to give Arly an answer?"

"I don't know for sure. We need to date and get to know each other more. He wants to take me to Springfield to meet his family."

"Wonderful! Are you going?"

"Not until I get slim like you, Billie. The clothes you gave me are getting looser gradually, but not fast enough. I'm embarrassed to let his family see me overweight. I didn't used to be like this."

"He has fallen for you just like you are, Lora."

"Did Dodds fall for you when you were still overweight?"

"He says, as he looks back, that he fell for me almost from the start, but didn't realize it."

Lora smiled. "We both have wonderful men, that's for sure." Her face became serious. "But no way am I going to meet his folks until I'm slim like you, Billie."

~~~~~~~~~

Early Wednesday morning, Sheldon called all the DeePees and invited them to dinner at the club at 6:00 PM, informing each that he had an important announcement to make. The squeals from Molly Bittle almost deafened him, she was so excited, but he refused to tell her another word until they were all together. He'd told Bliss last night about the dinner, and had requested she wear the lovely dress she was wearing.

The phone lines between, Molly Bittle, Sharon Ozog and Nettie Newman were buzzing as they guessed and conjectured with excitement and curiosity what the announcement would be. They were sure they already knew.

When Sheldon and Billie walked into the country club dining room at 6:05 PM, everyone was already there. Sheldon grinned from ear to ear as he and Billie, hand in hand, walked over to them.

"I want you all to meet my fiancé, Billie Bliss."

Molly Bittle squealed again, Sharon and Nettie smiled and the men all clapped.

"Will wonders never cease!" exclaimed Robert.

"I know you are acquainted with three of these people, Bliss, but I would like you to meet Nettie's husband, Don, Dr. Ozog's wife, Sharon and Dr. Bittle's wife, Molly."

Billie smiled. "I'm so pleased to meet all of you."

They all encouraged Billie to call them by their first names now that she would soon become one of the DeePees. Then Billie held out her hand for all to see her ring, explaining who it had belonged to. They were effusive in their compliments.

The dinner was excellent and the conversation consisted mainly of general questions directed at Billie and Sheldon. After dinner, they all retired to the lounge for their after dinner coffee and conversation.

Sheldon knew it was coming, and Nettie was the first to ask. "Now that we're in a private room, it's time to divulge all, Sheldon. You've been close mouthed and mysterious long enough. You owe it to us."

Billie looked over at Sheldon, puzzled, and he explained, "Small bits and pieces of our relationship came out now and then and Nettie, Sharon and Molly tried to find out more, but I could only promise that one day, maybe you, Bliss, would tell them yourself. Now, if you don't mind, I would like us both to tell our story. Is that all right with you?"

She looked over at her fiancé adoringly. "I'd love to, Dodds. Where shall we begin?"

He grinned. "With the note you wrote me, of course."

Their audience was more than responsive as they heard the account. With both Billie and Sheldon explaining Billie's unique problem, their friends understood, particularly Nettie, Molly and Sharon. They all laughed, some teared up and other times just quietly listened with rapt interest. When Lora Lemmon came into the story, the laughter really began and Billie laughed the hardest, finding out things she hadn't known about Sheldon and Lora. The greatest fun was when Sheldon told of falling over Lora in the video store. Then came the strange tale of Lora and the ants, Lora and her 'almost threat' and everything that followed after.

The next surprise to Billie was finding out that Lora was Sheldon's courier with the roses, requiring her once more to hide in the bushes.

They all clapped when the fascinating story ended. "But," Nettie said, "we must hear the poems, especially that last one called—THE KISS.

Sheldon flushed. "That's carrying it too far, Nettie."

"Then at least," insisted Hal, "we need to meet this Miss Lora Lemmon."

"Interesting that you should say that, Hal," Billie said, "for I suggest that she replace me in *Project Success*."

~~~~~~~~~~

Sheldon drove into the underground parking of his condominium. "Where are you taking me, Dodds?"

They had said goodnight to their friends, and he had driven here without explaining. "Well, Bliss-of-my-life, I live on the top floor of this building. What I was wondering is…would you mind if we live in my place here until we can build us a house?"

She leaned over and kissed him. "I would love to. I would love to live anywhere with you."

"You see, Bliss, I own this building."

Billie's brow rose questioningly. "You mean you own the condominium?"

"No. I mean I own the whole building. I built it as an investment."

"This whole building is yours?" she asked incredulously.

"Yes."

"I knew you were a brilliant businessman, Dodds, but I didn't realize you were that well off."

Sheldon smiled, put his arm around her and drew her close, realizing that now was the time to tell her just how wealthy he was. "My grandfather left me a small inheritance and I made an investment. I was lucky, for it turned a nice profit for me. I invested the profits." He told her everything, and in the end, he named all he owned. When he was through, he waited for her reaction…and waited. "Bliss?"

"That means…you are very rich, Dodds!" she exclaimed in hushed tones.

"Yes, my Bliss, very."

"Oh! How exciting! We're rich, Dodds."

He laughed, happy at her reaction. "Your father was quite surprised, too."

"My father? How does he know?"

"I told him when I asked for your hand. He seemed quite pleased that I could support his daughter in a proper manner."

Billie sighed. "How romantic that you asked for my hand."

Sheldon laughed again. Wrapping her in his arms, he kissed her full delectable lips long and lingeringly. Her warm response left him a happy man. He got out of the car, opened her door and led her to the elevator. Billie was quiet, still trying to take it all in as they rode to the top.

As they stepped into Sheldon's condominium, Billie gasped in delight. "This is very attractive. Did you do the decorating, Dodds?"

"Yes, and I know it isn't what a woman would choose," he began apologetically.

"Oh, but, Dodds, I love it. It looks like you." She walked around the big room looking at everything. "The colors are strong and the furniture massive—all wonderfully decisive and masculine—like you." He flushed with pleasure. She walked over to the big picture above the fireplace. "And this watercolor on the wall is beautiful. It shows your sensitive and artistic side," she said, smiling knowingly. She examined the room further. "The decorative items, such as this large vase and the bronze statue of Lincoln definitely point out your strong aristocratic character. Everything is well placed, well organized—like you."

She walked over to him and smiled, her eyes filled with admiration, "Everything in here is of the finest quality, telling me that you have made money, and that suggests to me a number of things, including your ability to interact and work well with men."

Sheldon's chest swelled with that special feeling that only comes to a man who is sincerely admired by the woman he loves. This confidence, inspired by a woman, Sheldon knew instinctively, was the kind that made men want to climb the highest mountain, build the greatest empire, dig the best ditches, paint the finest pictures, hammer the straightest nail and while he's at it, leave the world a better place.

With moist eyes, he put his arms around his beloved and held her close, praying that he would someday be worthy of her love and admiration.

Chapter Thirty-Five

Two and a half weeks later, on a Saturday morning, William Bliss, in the presence of a small group of friends and relatives, gave his daughter, Billie, in marriage to Sheldon Dodds Ackerman. This special occasion was held in the backyard of the Bliss home while the last vestiges of summer lingered on, mingling with the coming of a new season.

The bride, with one significant white rose in her lovely auburn hair, wore a simple white gown. Her groom, dressed in a black tuxedo, stood beside her with one matching white rose tucked into the lapel of his coat.

The glow of happiness that radiated from the bride and groom renewed everyone's hope and faith in their own marriage or marriage to be.

Those in attendance were the immediate family, a few relatives from the Bliss side of the family, Henry's children and grandchildren, several close friends of Will and Margaret and a few business associates. The DeePees were all there smiling, relieved to see their friend finally lose his bachelorhood and join the ranks of the happily married.

Arly Bates and Lora Lemmon, special guests of the bride and groom and the bride's family, were present, holding hands and looking almost as happy as the bride and groom.. They had been issued an invitation with a special 'thank you note' enclosed for their part in protecting the Bliss family from the neighborhood car thief.

Margaret and Matilda had prepared a lovely buffet brunch, which they served out on the large back porch. Every one mingled and congratulated the bride and groom, who, as quickly as they possibly could, exited, anxious to leave on their honeymoon.

~~~~~~~

A week later, back from their honeymoon, Sheldon, under the guise of observing the social amenities, hosted an open house at the Maple

Hills Country Club for all his colleagues at the university, his business associates from several cities and for the rest of the friends of the Bliss family in Claytonville. Sheldon's real motive was to show off his lovely bride.

As the evening ended, the DeePees—Hal and Sharon, Don and Nettie, Robert and Mollie—cornered Sheldon and Billie for one purpose—to ask one last question.

"All right, Sheldon," Robert said, "we all want to know why you called Billie by her last name Bliss?"

"Yes, Shel," Nettie said, smiling, "tell us."

He looked at them, contemplating the answer. He gazed down at Bliss' lovely smiling face, now upturned to his. Her luminous brown eyes, were also curious and questioning.

A slow smile spread across Sheldon's face. His deep blue eyes glowing with happiness, he answered them while gazing at his bride.

"Because, my good friends, getting to know Billie Bliss and being married to her...has simply been—*pure bliss*."